PRAISE FOR THE MATER

"Diane Vallere has stitched u[...]
an intelligent, resourceful her[...]
a great supporting cast and a c[...]
of the fashion business adds an extra layer of authenticity.
Suede to Rest is a strong addition to the cozy mystery genre."
—Sofie Kelly, *New York Times* bestselling author
of the Magical Cats Mysteries

"Toile, taffeta, and trouble! . . . Diane Vallere skillfully blends
two mysteries in this smart and engaging tale that will keep
you guessing to the very end."
—Krista Davis, *New York Times* bestselling author
of the Domestic Diva Mysteries

"Vallere weaves a tapestry of finely knit characters, luxurious fabrics, and . . . murder."
—Janet Bolin, national bestselling author
of the Threadville Mysteries

"Diane Vallere has fashioned a terrific mystery, rich with
detail and texture. Polyester Monroe is a sassy protagonist
who will win your hearts with her seamless style and breezy
wit. The first in the series promises readers hours of deftly
woven whodunit enjoyment."
—Daryl Wood Gerber, Agatha Award–winning author
of the national bestselling Cookbook Nook Mysteries

"I highly recommend *Crushed Velvet* as well as the Material
Witness Mystery series. I especially recommend it to those
who like fabric stores, kittens, a touch of romance, and end-
less possibilities. With delightfully engaging characters and
riveting mystery, it is a series I am looking to see more of!"
—Open Book Society

Silk
Stalkings

DIANE VALLERE

BERKLEY PRIME CRIME, NEW YORK

An imprint of Penguin Random House LLC
375 Hudson Street, New York, New York 10014

SILK STALKINGS

A Berkley Prime Crime Book / published by arrangement with the author

BERKLEY® PRIME CRIME and the PRIME CRIME design are trademarks
of Penguin Random House LLC.
For more information, visit penguin.com.

ISBN: 9780425270592

PUBLISHING HISTORY
Berkley Prime Crime mass-market edition / August 2016

PRINTED IN THE UNITED STATES OF AMERICA

10 9 8 7 6 5 4 3 2 1

Cover illustration by Brandon Dorman.
Cover design by Sarah Oberrender.
Interior text design by Tiffany Estreicher.

Penguin
Random
House

*This book is dedicated to
the Hollywood Orchard.*

ACKNOWLEDGMENTS

Thank you to my mom, Mary Vallere, for sewing lessons, trips to Levine's, and a handed-down passion for fabric. You're at the heart of every Material Witness book. Special thanks to Richard Goodman for feedback, both positive and negative, and to Kendel Lynn, the best friend I could wish for. Thank you to my agent, Jessica Faust; editor, Katherine Pelz; and the team at Penguin Random House for turning my manuscript into a book (though I stand by my suggestion to call this one *Satin Worship*). And to Josh Hickman, who sits silently by while I try to get it all done but instinctively knows when to break out that magic phrase: "Would it help if we had pizza tonight?"

One

The clock would strike midnight in two minutes. This was important for a few reasons, not the least of which was that the crowd of couples who filled the interior and exterior grounds of Tea Totalers, my friend Genevieve Girard's tea-shop-turned-Parisian-nightclub, would filter down the sidewalk of Bonita Avenue and make their way toward the Waverly House for their annual stroll through the historic mansion's gardens.

The other reason midnight was important was that the coordinators of tonight's event had synced every clock in our small town of San Ladrón down to the second. They were set to chime, ring, buzz, and otherwise announce the arrival of twelve A.M. It was one thing to imagine the impact of that type of alarm coordination, but it might be quite another to experience it. If the several hundred guests who sipped champagne and nibbled at petit fours and hors d'oeuvres at Tea Totalers had followed suit of the city and set their cell phones to ring, too, we could be looking at the kind of noise level that might launch missiles over Cuba.

Genevieve approached me with a flute of champagne. "Poly, things turned out better than I had hoped! We've gone through almost seventeen pounds of Brie, and the crusty French bread disappears as fast as it comes out of the oven. I've served almost as much of my special blend of tea as I have champagne. And people are asking if I'll cater their parties. People who have lived in San Ladrón their whole lives are telling me they wish they'd come here earlier. This idea was genius. It's really putting me on the map." She handed me a glass of champagne and clinked it with hers. "It's putting you on the map, too," she added.

Genevieve had opened Tea Totalers a few years ago, with the help of her French husband. He was no longer in the picture, thanks to seedy business dealings with people who thought murder was an appropriate solution to a business dispute. Genevieve had been the number one suspect in her husband's murder, and I'd been instrumental in helping clear her name. In return, she'd been instrumental in helping me open Material Girl, the fabric shop I inherited from my great-uncle several months ago. Tonight we were both reaping the benefits of hard work and creative marketing.

Genevieve spun around her café's interior with her arms out. The champagne in her flute spilled from the glass, but she didn't seem to notice or care. "Can you believe it? It really does feel like we're in Paris at midnight."

I followed her gaze around the newly made-over café. I'd gotten the idea to use French fabrics from my shop to build on the theme Genevieve had wanted for the interior. Long toile curtains framed out sheer panels of voile that had almost gone into the Dumpster behind my fabric shop thanks to a wicked case of mildew, but an intensive treatment with vinegar and fresh air had cleared the fabric of its musty scent and brought it back to life. The chairs had been re-covered in gingham, provencal, linen, and even more toile, and napkins, place mats, and serving trays had been trimmed with the same fabrics. That was by day.

But tonight, for the Midnight in Paris party, I'd stepped things up a notch. Deep midnight-blue velvet covered the existing butter-yellow walls. I used a heat-set technique to create a fleur-de-lis pattern on the velvet that mirrored the pattern woven into the voile sheers, and I'd covered the chairs in luxurious velvet seat covers tied back with thick ivory grosgrain ribbon. Small tea light candles sat in clear glass votives on windowsills, tabletops, and counters inside the café.

The organizers of the city's part of the event—decorating the street between Tea Totalers and the Waverly House—had hung strands of tiny white twinkling lights around the exterior of the buildings and in an arch over the street, creating a blanket of stars under which people danced to the jazz quartet on the corner. The local high school had crafted a scale model of the Eiffel Tower that sat in the middle of the intersection of Bonita and San Ladrón Avenue. The roads had been closed for the night, so people could spill out into the street and enjoy the transformation of our small town.

"Are you heading over to the Waverly House when the bells chime? I bet Vaughn would love to see you in that dress," Genevieve asked.

I blushed. Since inheriting the fabric store and moving to San Ladrón, I'd spent enough time with Vaughn McMichael to get past the unfortunate first impression where I fell through a window and knocked him to the ground. We'd dined together, worked side by side, and even gone on a date. We'd also accused each other of having ulterior motives, resulting in alienation. And by *we*, I mean *me*, but I'd rather not get into that right now.

"I don't want to talk about Vaughn," I said.

"Didn't he have that dress made for you?" Genevieve asked pointedly.

"I don't want to talk about that, either," I said to her. Much like the interior of Genevieve's shop, I'd stepped up my own appearance for the night. I usually wore black all the time, but I'd traded it for a shimmering gold gown with a sweetheart neckline, embellished on the shoulders with spirals of matte gold and silver sequins. The gown was fitted around my waist and hips and cascaded to the floor in a pool of fabric.

"Poly, you had just as much to do with the garden stroll at the Waverly House as you did here at Tea Totalers," Genevieve said. "You have to go."

I didn't know how to explain to Genevieve that I was nervous about showing up at the Waverly House for more reasons than I could count.

The Waverly House was the most significant historical building in the town of San Ladrón. A Victorian mansion turned museum, it had become a certified landmark years back and now boasted a restaurant, a monthly murder mystery party, and the most exquisite gardens in the town. Adelaide Brooks, the most energetic and elegant seventy-year-old I'd ever met, managed the building and the day-to-day business.

The annual party had been the landmark's major fundraiser for years, and the money brought in from this singular party determined their operating budget for the following year. People flocked to San Ladrón for the night to consider the Waverly House for weddings and parties. All would have been fine, except that this year, the most powerful man in San Ladrón had raised questions about zoning and put a scare into the suppliers who donated food and drink. That halted any planning that could take place. It didn't help matters that the most powerful man in San Ladrón was Adelaide's ex-husband.

Or that he was Vaughn McMichael's father.

Only a few people knew that I'd been the one to come up with the idea of changing the location of the annual garden party to Genevieve's newly reopened shop. Food and drink distributors had been happy to make their regular donations, and Genevieve had been thrilled at the opportunity. After applying for her liquor license (ironic in a shop called Tea Totalers), she had been pleasantly surprised by the outpouring of support from suppliers who donated food and drink for the evening, and local restaurants who loaned out employees to help.

Ticket sales for the Midnight in Paris cocktail party still benefited the Waverly House, as did separate ticket sales to gain entrance to the exquisite gardens behind the Victorian manse at midnight. Adelaide had sidestepped the zoning regulations by leaving the restaurant and bar open for paying customers. Landscapers had been hard at work on the grounds surrounding the landmark, and whatever it was that they were planning to debut had been kept a well-guarded secret. All Adelaide would say was, "It's more magnificent than I ever could have expected." The perceived success of the night would be determined to be true or false tomorrow when she would tally the money pulled in by selling tickets and subtract out any unforeseen expenses. I didn't want credit for the idea. I wanted everyone to get what they wanted—or needed, in the case of the Waverly House—from the event.

Bong-Bong-Bong-Ding-Bong-Chime-Buzz-Clang-Ring-Bong

Midnight arrived, announced by a cacophony of sounds that originated from a distance of several miles. The chimes, bongs, dings, and dongs were slightly off from each other, resulting in a white noise that mixed with the various cell phone alarms that went off from the pockets of people around us. A couple of people put hands over their ears, and a few kissed like it was New Year's Eve. Conversation became impossible.

The drummer struck up a rhythm on the high hat, and the man playing the upright bass plucked out a note for each strike of the clock. Cheers erupted from the crowd.

When the noise died down, I heard a voice behind me. "Let me guess. That's your cue to turn into a pumpkin?" asked Charlie Brooks. Charlie was the resident tough girl and my closest friend in town. As a full-time mechanic with her own auto shop, Charlie favored work jeans, chambray shirts, and rock concert T-shirts, but tonight she wore a man's tuxedo over a white fitted T-shirt. The jacket was boxy, but the T-shirt hugged her fit body. The pants sat low on her hips and broke over red Chuck Taylors. "I heard you tell Frenchy you weren't going to the Waverly house. Good call. Wanna grab a beer at The Broadside?"

"The Broadside's closed. Duke and his bartenders are working for Genevieve tonight. Didn't you notice?"

"I just got here. This kind of thing isn't my scene."

"Which part don't you like? The free food or the free booze or the free ambiance?"

"The raising-money-for-rich-people part."

Rich people who gave her up for adoption, I thought to myself, but I didn't say out loud. Not many people knew Charlie was related to the wealthy McMichael family, and she wanted to keep it that way. I didn't judge her for her animosity toward Vic McMichael and Adelaide Brooks, but I wondered if there would be a day when she regretted not forging a relationship with her birth parents.

This wasn't the first time I'd thwarted a plan of Mr. McMichael's. When I first inherited my family's fabric store, he tried to buy it out from under me. We'd gone toe-to-toe a couple of times since then. My ex-boyfriend, Carson Cole, was a financial analyst in Los Angeles and maintained a fantasy about becoming Mr. McMichael's protégé, even after our breakup. When the businessman had threatened Genevieve's tea shop, I'd called Carson to step in and save the day. Considering Vaughn was on his father's payroll, he'd been more than a little hurt that I hadn't asked him for help. Yet another reason I wanted to keep a low profile tonight.

"You're a liar," I said.

She raised her pierced eyebrow.

"Not a lot of people get away with calling me names."

"If you didn't care about this thing, you wouldn't have bothered to dress up."

"I'm meeting up with someone I haven't seen for a while. Thought I'd make an effort. Besides, you're one to talk," she said, scanning my ensemble from top to bottom.

Again with the dress.

"So I'm not wearing black for one night. It's not like it's a religion or anything."

She held her hands up and backed away. "It's a nice dress. You wouldn't be hoping to run into anybody while wearing it, would you?"

Before I could answer, Genevieve reappeared. "Hi, Charlie, are you coming to the Waverly House? I want to go and Poly won't come with me."

Charlie crossed the interior of Tea Totalers and looked out the front door. People filled the street, laughing and carrying on. A few policemen stood on the corners, trying to remain serious but failing miserably. One lady walked up to the town's sheriff, took his hand, and twirled like a ballerina. He let go of her hand and adjusted his hat. Charlie went inside and we followed her. A few minutes later, the front door opened and Sheriff Clark walked in.

"Is this a closed party or can anybody join?" he asked.

"Well, hello there, Sheriff Clark," sang Genevieve, who might have possibly had too much champagne. She must have been thinking the same thing, because she handed her glass to him. "Help yourself to champagne. I can't stand it anymore. I want to go see the gardens!" She hiked her dress up so the hem wouldn't drag and ran out the front door. "Poly, lock up when you leave?"

"Sure," I said.

Clark took the proffered glass and drank half. He lowered the glass and scanned me. "Nice dress," he said. "You going to waste it by staying here in hiding?"

"You heard Genevieve, she asked me to lock up."

"It takes about four seconds to lock a door." He looked at Charlie.

"Yo, Frenchy, wait up," Charlie called. She ran past Sheriff Clark without an acknowledgment and went outside.

I looked at Clark and shrugged. He shook his head and walked out front. I found Genevieve's keys and grabbed my beaded handbag from behind the counter. Sheriff Clark waited while I locked up the doors, and I said good-bye before trailing after Charlie and Genevieve.

Sheriff Clark and Charlie had had a secret romance that fizzled over a miscommunication. It was probably just as well that they steered clear of each other. When I pictured them being a couple, I was reminded of what happened to the gingham dog and the calico cat.

Genevieve, Charlie, and I were among the last of the people to reach the Waverly House. Volunteers from the historical society stood in front of a ten-foot-tall version of the Arc de Triomphe, fabricated for the evening by the employees of Get Hammered, the local hardware store, out of chicken wire. Green ivy and colorful flowers had been threaded through the wire. Couples walked under the arch to the luscious lawns behind the Waverly House, pointing at the gazebo, the white iron benches, and the brick pavers that had been carved with the names of each person who had made a donation when the building was in need of repair. They were trying on the location with their eyes, wondering how it would feel to celebrate a major event in the middle of all of this Victorian majesty.

"Excuse me," said a woman to my left. "Are you Polyester Monroe? Of the fabric shop on Bonita?"

"Yes, but I go by Poly."

"What's your shop called? Fabric Woman?"

"Material Girl."

"That's right." She held out her hand and I shook it. "I'm Nolene Kelly. I've heard people say you were responsible for the transformation of the tea shop for tonight. Who knew you could transform a place with fabric," she said.

"I hope people will be inspired to try it themselves," I said.

"It's a nice idea but it'll be a hard sell. People around here aren't used to making their own clothes or slipcovers or curtains."

"I had a lot of help," I said modestly.

"But it was all her idea. Wasn't it amazing?" Genevieve chimed in.

"It was very impressive. And the fabric—that was from your store?" Nolene asked. She tipped her head as she posed her question, and her dangly earrings set off a faint tinkling sound.

"Yes."

"Before you moved here, you worked in a dress shop in Los Angeles, didn't you?" It was odd to hear my recent history told to me by a stranger. "I'm afraid I've read up on your background. I'm the coordinator of Miss Tangorli, San Ladrón's annual beauty pageant. Since you're new around here, you probably don't know much about it."

"You're right, I don't know much about the events of San Ladrón. This is my first time attending the Waverly House's annual party." I glanced around me. Genevieve and Charlie had migrated in separate directions: Genevieve toward the gardens, and Charlie toward a strange man who stood alone a few feet from the tea and juice station outside. He had a white ponytail and black leather blazer over a black T-shirt and black trousers.

"Rumor has it there wouldn't have been a party if it weren't for you." Nolene winked. "But I'm not here to spread rumors. I'm here to find judges. I've locked in two so far."

Immediately I felt awkward. "I don't think I'd be qualified to judge a beauty pageant."

"Don't worry about that. I have something else in mind for you."

Two

She looked over my shoulder. "How about we finish this conversation at your shop tomorrow morning?"

"Sure." We agreed on a time and she hurried away.

I looked around for my friends. Genevieve had been swept to the center of the crowd by people who wanted to congratulate her on her café's contribution to the magical evening. Charlie and the strange man were huddled together alongside the building. I started to approach them. She looked my way, said something to the man, and they turned and walked the other direction.

I closed my eyes, breathed in the night-blooming jasmine, and tried to place my great-aunt and great-uncle in the scene, as if a time-travel machine had been provided for the night. I felt a hand around my waist and heard a voice in my ear. "I was hoping to see you tonight," Vaughn said. I opened my eyes and turned to face him.

Vaughn was no stranger to black-tie functions. Tonight he wore a classic-cut black tuxedo with a white shirt and a gold silk bow tie that was slightly crooked. Without thinking, I reached up and straightened it. He put his hands on my hands and lowered them, then bent down and kissed me on the cheek.

"The dress suits you," he said.

"What, this old thing?"

He smiled and offered his arm. I threaded my hand through the crook of his elbow and he led me under the Arc de Triomphe to the gardens.

"Nolene didn't get to you, too, did she?" he asked.

"I don't know. She said she wants to come to the shop tomorrow to talk about a proposal. I'm kind of at a disadvantage. She knew a lot about me and I know nothing about her. What can you tell me about her?"

"She works for Halliwell Industries, the fruit conglomerate of San Ladrón."

"'Fruit conglomerate'?" I repeated. "You're making that up."

"Halliwell Industries is the closest thing to one, if you ask me. Harvey Halliwell is a self-made millionaire, thanks to fruit. He brought exotic citrus to San Ladrón from China, Trinidad, and Japan. His lab is world renowned, and they've done some incredible genetic splicing between seeds, producing fruits that were otherwise rare in the United States."

"And Nolene Kelly works there."

"She's the assistant to Harvey Halliwell, head fruit." He grinned. "She mostly handles his personal business, but the annual Miss Tangorli pageant is her baby. Harvey turned the reins over to her a few years ago and she turned it into a circus. I've been trying to stay busy helping out tonight, but she cornered me. Next thing I knew, I'd agreed to judge her pageant."

I stepped away and studied his face. "You, a beauty pageant judge?"

"I like to think I can recognize beauty when it's in front of me."

I blushed, thankful for the midnight darkness, and looked away.

"There's a lot that I don't know about San Ladrón," I said. "First garden parties, now beauty pageants. And let me guess, your family has a stake in the pageant."

"Nope. As luck would have it, we don't."

"Luck?"

"I'm not sure what else to call it. When my dad first started investing in San Ladrón, Harvey was his business partner."

"When was this?"

"In the seventies. They often didn't see eye to eye on business decisions, and one day they flipped a coin to see if they'd stay together or dissolve the partnership. My dad won the coin toss and Harvey was out." He flipped a coin from his own pocket into the air and caught it midflip. "Luck."

We walked along in the dark, studying the mix of orchids and hibiscus, breathing in the scent of the jasmine mingled with honeysuckle. The gardens had been tended to perfection, a gentle tangle of dark vines and long blossoms interspersed with low ground cover, and colorful patches of blossoms I couldn't identify. Each separate patch of garden was like a story. Pinks and purples in one corner, blue and white in another.

Most of the grass was trimmed low but interspersed with wide glass vases that had been countersunk into the ground and filled with water. Water lilies floated on them. Bright pink flowers appeared to float on the grass, and around the perimeter of the garden were tall cat-o-nine-tails, and tall purple flowers that waved in the gentle night breeze. A small white bridge had been constructed in the back of the historic mansion. It was a surreal impressionist experience, as if we were walking into a painting by Claude Monet. The gardeners who made this happen had achieved a floral wonderland I couldn't have imagined in my wildest dreams.

"So Harvey started the pageant?" I asked as we stepped from one lily pad paver to another.

"Yes. A couple of winners have gone on to be Miss California, and one won Miss America."

"We made pageant dresses at my old job," I said, "but it sounds like this is on a different scale."

"Things have been gradually getting out of control. Last year a few of the contestants dropped out because their families couldn't afford to keep up with the expectations."

"That's a little silly, isn't it?"

"Hard to say. The pageant brings a lot of business to San Ladrón, and it's one of the events, like the garden party tonight, that give us press outside our own bubble. Salons are booked to capacity and dress shops can barely keep up with the demand." For the second time that night, he glanced at my dress. "I would think a dress like that would be very popular," he said.

"It's not for sale." I smoothed my hand over the champagne silk.

"I'm glad I had a chance to see you tonight," Vaughn said. "The dress looks even better than I imagined it would. And before you ask, yes. I've imagined you in that dress."

He slipped his fingers down to my own fingertips and raised my arm. He twirled me like Sheriff Clark had twirled the woman on the street, then brought my arm down to my side. The couple in front of us moved and we stepped forward so as not to hold up the crowd.

"The pageant used to be called Miss Orange Blossom, but the city wanted to change the name because people kept confusing it with Pasadena and the Orange Bowl. The city planners wanted something that related to San Ladrón history, which meant citrus. Harvey made his first million when he brought Tangorli trees to San Ladrón, so it became the Miss Tangorli pageant."

"What *is* a Tangorli? I've never heard of it."

"It's a tangerine-orange-lime hybrid. Harvey first brought the tangor—a tangerine-orange hybrid—here from China in the early seventies. His lab spliced the seeds with a lime to create the Tangorli. It has the sweetness of a tangerine but a hint of sour from the lime. Surprisingly refreshing. This whole town was built on the citrus trade, but most of the fields were plowed under for development. Harvey bought twenty acres of land out by San Ladrón Canyon where the original citrus fields were, turned the soil, and planted the seedlings that his botanists grew in the greenhouse. He ended up with the first crop of Tangorlis in the country." Vaughn chuckled. "I've seen pictures of him from back then. He believed in his crop and wanted everybody to know him as the man who brought Tangorlis to town. He wore orange everywhere he went: his car was orange, his clothes were orange, he even dyed his hair bright orange. He made arrangements to underwrite the whole pageant if the city would rename it."

"And just like that, the city agreed?"

"No. They listened to proposals from everybody who had a suggestion. You know *Ladrón* means 'thief,' right? That's the only reason they didn't want to go with 'Miss San Ladrón.' Too much risk of negativity attached to our city. Unfortunately, after the pageant boosted the fruit, Harvey went from being a millionaire to a billionaire."

"Doesn't sound too unfortunate for Harvey," I said.

"In a way it was. Rumor started that he stole the tangor seeds from China and people referred to him as a thief anyway."

"And you said he was your father's first business partner?" I hadn't known Vaughn for long, but I knew anything that pertained to his father was a touchy subject.

He nodded. "Most people remember how my dad inherited a small sum of money and how he turned a string of good investments into his business. Some of those investments were him and Harvey."

"But you said they didn't see eye to eye. What did they disagree over?"

"What do any business partners disagree over? Money."

I sneaked a look at Vaughn and gauged his expression. I knew he had been raised with money. He knew I had not. It was a subject that had come up between the two of us on more than one occasion and kept me wondering if time spent with Vaughn was time wasted. I didn't know if I'd ever fit into his world. I only knew I didn't want to ever become so comfortable that I took money for granted.

I changed the subject. "So, garden parties, beauty pageants, and men in orange. Anything else I need to discover about this town?"

"Wait a couple of weeks. I'll take you to Gnarly Waves, our very own water park."

"For real?"

"For real. Independently owned and operated since 1971. Best corn dog in the state. Good onion rings, too. And the only place you can get a Tangorli Creamsicle."

"Sounds righteous," I said with a laugh.

The couple in front of us moved along the path. I started to follow them, and Vaughn's hand shot out, grabbed my hand, and pulled me to the left under a weeping willow tree. I stumbled slightly. He reached out and caught me around the waist and pulled me closer to him.

The hanging branches, covered in white blossoms, swayed ever so slightly in the midnight breeze. Now that we were off the path of the other partygoers, we were partially hidden. I put my hands around Vaughn's neck. He leaned down and brushed his lips against mine. I felt exposed by his public display of affection. I looked to my left to ensure that we were alone.

But we weren't. On the path, also partially hidden, but this time by the blooming ground cover, was the thin man with the white ponytail Charlie had been talking to earlier. He was engaged in a heated discussion with a man with bright orange hair dressed in an orange tuxedo.

"Do you know who that man is?" I asked.

"That's Harvey."

"No, I mean the other man."

"I don't think so. A lot of people come to San Ladrón for the night. That's how the Waverly House gets exposure to new business."

A silver chain hung down on the side of the ponytailed man's pants. He lit a cigarette with a chrome lighter, then flipped it closed and tucked it into his pocket. After he inhaled, he raised the hand that held the cigarette and pointed at Harvey with his fingers, the orange tip of the cigarette—that so perfectly matched Harvey's outfit—bouncing around in the darkness as he did so.

"I don't think they know we can see them," I said.

Harvey raised a glass to his lips and drank. The other man seemed to be waiting for a response. A few seconds passed. Harvey lowered his glass and took a step backward. He stumbled a few steps, dropped the glass, and crashed to the ground after it.

The man with the ponytail looked stunned. He bent down and reached into Harvey's orange tuxedo jacket.

"He's robbing Harvey," I said. I stepped out from the cover of the tree. "What are you doing?" I called. The man with the ponytail looked up at me. He turned around and fled. Vaughn and I ran to Harvey. He was still on the ground, but he appeared conscious.

"Help me," he croaked.

I hiked my dress up and moved to his side. "Do you have your phone?" I asked Vaughn. "Can you call the police?"

Vaughn already had his phone out. I knelt down and felt Harvey's wrist. His pulse was uneven, but it was there. "Sir, can you hear me? I'm Poly Monroe and we're going to get help." He tried to lift his head but winced in pain. "Don't move. Don't do anything. Can you talk? Can you tell me your name?"

"Harvey," he said. "Halliwell," he finished. His fingers wrapped around my wrist and he looked at me with watery blue eyes. "He's not far," he said.

"Who? The man who was talking to you?"

He closed his eyes and was silent. I wanted to find out the identity of the man and what they'd been talking about. I wanted to tell him to check his pockets and see what was missing. But more than any of that, I wanted to make sure he was okay. If Vaughn and I hadn't stepped off the path at that point, we might never have seen Mr. Halliwell drop to the ground. Who knew what might have happened if we hadn't come along? Vaughn took off down the path.

I'd been trained in basic CPR and knew it was best to keep Mr. Halliwell talking. "Sir? Can you tell me where you live?"

"Why? So you can rob me while I'm recovering?" he said. He struggled to sit up.

I put my hand on his orange lapels and gently pushed him back down. "Please don't try to move. Help is on its way."

"I'm a tougher old coot than he thinks I am." He pushed my hand out of the way and sat up. "Gonna have to slip me more than a mickey to get me out of the picture."

I looked around for someone—anyone—else, and was surprised to discover that I was alone with the injured man. Many of the attendees had migrated to the opposite end of the gardens or inside for one last glass of champagne, but the Waverly House had been planning to leave the grounds open all night. Guards and volunteers had been stationed around the exterior of the property. Adelaide would be manning the yard, greeting people, circling through, making connections with potential donors, young lovers, and families.

So where were they all?

Mr. Halliwell reached for a cane that I'd mistaken for a branch of the tree behind him. He held it in front of himself, pushing me backward. I was torn between restraining him—or at least trying to, since I had no idea just how tough an old coot he really was—and letting him leave. As far as I knew, there was no law against him leaving before paramedics showed up, though I didn't know why he'd want to do such a thing.

"That's what happens when you let someone bring you a drink. They're all out to get me. Me and my money. You probably are, too. Now get out of my way."

"Don't you want to wait until the police arrive and fill out a statement? They'll need it to find the person behind this."

"Missy, this town has been out to get me for years, and the leader of the pack is that man's father." He pointed the end of his cane in Vaughn's direction. "If he ever succeeds, the joke will be on him."

I heard footsteps behind me and turned. Vaughn was headed in my direction. When I turned back to face Harvey, he was gone.

Vaughn reached me. "Where is he?" he asked, looking around the ground.

"He left. He said— He said he was a tough old coot and he didn't want to wait to make a statement." I looked behind Vaughn. "Did you call the police?"

"No."

"We have to report what we saw."

"What did we see, Poly? Two men having a discussion. One man fainted. He regained consciousness and left of his own volition."

"But the other man took something from him. Didn't you see that?"

"It's dark and I don't know what I saw. If Harvey wanted to get up and walk away, we can't really stop him." He ran his hand through his hair. "Besides, I didn't want to spoil my mother's event. I went inside hoping to find Sheriff Clark."

"I don't think he's here." I thought back to Sheriff Clark at Tea Totalers, and Charlie leaving him there. I didn't know if Vaughn knew about that relationship. If it even *was* a relationship.

"Neither is Mr. Halliwell."

"I don't understand it. He looked so weak, and then when you went for help, he got up and left. I told him to stay so he could give the police a statement, but he didn't want to. And he just disappeared. How could he vanish in that orange tux jacket?"

"I don't know."

I stepped back onto the lily pad pavers and walked around the gardens. The temperature had turned chilly, and with the drought we'd been experiencing, it was borderline cold. The surreal aspect of the garden stroll combined with the victim who had gotten up and walked away left me with a disoriented *Alice in Wonderland* feeling of having sipped from the container that said "Drink me."

The grounds of the Waverly House had thinned down to almost nobody. Here and there a couple stood, arm in arm, pointing to the white trim on the restored blue-and-white Victorian house, or the gazebo that sat at the edge of the property, or the paths that were illuminated with small, battery-operated tea light candles, providing light without risk of fire hazard. The families had long gone home, and the waiters and waitresses who had woven through the crowd offering flutes of champagne had long since packed up their stations.

Something shiny rested in the grass where Harvey had been. I bent down and found an amber pill vial. The prescription was for nitroglycerine, but the name on the label had been smudged beyond legibility.

Three

I slept until eight the next morning and was showered and dressed by eight twenty. My short layered auburn hair and minimal makeup application kept my routine under thirty minutes, as did my all-black wardrobe: today a tank dress and gladiator sandals. The glorious dress from last night was still spread out on the chaise. It spoke of a side of me that I wasn't ready to acknowledge. I tossed a throw blanket over it, fed the cats, Pins and Needles, and headed out to Lopez Donuts to grab a bite before opening the store.

Lopez Donuts was a small shop about three blocks east of Material Girl. It was owned and operated by Big Joe Lopez, the nicest former Marine I'd ever met. His wife, Maria, ran a cleaning business called Neato but kept enough of a hand in the donut business to let everyone know who really wore the pants in that family. They were the go-to destination for anyone who needed sugary glazed treats or powdered puff pastries filled with cream to start off their day. My eating habits ran toward local fare, but the way I saw it, the Lopez glazed donut ring was as local as the citrus the city had been known for. My status as a locavore would not be threatened, at least not until the next time I was pressed for time and opted for a burger and fries from The Broadside Tavern.

Big Joe stood behind the counter straightening a wire bin of donuts. The case was already full, and he had to maneuver the tray to fit it between the others. He looked up when I walked in and the tray tipped precariously. Parchment paper slid to the side and several donuts plopped from the tray, bounced off his pant leg, and landed on the floor. He shook his leg repeatedly, then stood up straight, set the tray on top of the counter, and shook his head.

"Darn party made everybody sleep in. Now I have too many donuts. Sure wish you were a family of ten," he said. "Not that I'm not happy to see you."

"Tell you what. I'll take two dozen iced with multicolored sprinkles and a carafe of coffee. I bet anybody who trickles into the fabric shop would appreciate the pick-me-up."

His brow furrowed. "Since when do you like iced with multicolored sprinkles?"

"I don't. This way I won't eat them all by myself."

Big Joe assembled a pink bakery box and used the handy metal tongs to transfer the donuts from their tray. After the unfortunate donut drop that had taken place upon my entrance, I thought it best not to distract him with small talk.

"You have fun at the party last night?" he asked as he poured fresh coffee into a black-and-silver urn.

"Tea Totalers was so busy I didn't have time to think about whether I was having fun. Were you and Maria there? I didn't even see you."

"We had to wait until the boys were tucked in before we could leave. We missed Genevieve's but went straight to the Waverly House."

"Those gardens sure were pretty, weren't they?"

"Not as pretty as you in that gold dress." He flashed a broad smile, white teeth that stood out against his dark skin. "If you'd worn black like you always do, I might not have seen you in the dark. You should wear gold more often."

I sank into a booth and he joined me. We were the only two people in the shop and by the looks of things, it was going to remain that way for a while.

"Did you see a man in an orange tuxedo jacket? With orange hair?"

"Harvey Halliwell? Nope. Was he there? Makes sense, I guess. His pageant's coming up soon, so he'd want to make an appearance. Why are you asking about him?"

"Vaughn and I were there pretty late, and we saw Harvey pass out. But then he got up and walked away like nothing happened."

"Did you call the police?"

"We tried to get help but Mr. Halliwell didn't want it. He grabbed his cane and took off."

Big Joe crossed his arms over his broad chest. "You got something on your mind. Let me get us a couple of crullers and some coffee and we'll talk."

He went to the counter and returned with a dark green plastic tray that held two disposable cups of coffee and two paper plates with a glazed donut on each. There wasn't a multicolored sprinkle in sight. I took a plate and a cup, added some half-and-half to my coffee, and bit into the donut. Man-made perfection.

"If donuts like this grew on trees like Harvey Halliwell's fruit, you'd be a very rich man."

"I'm rich in the ways that count. What's on your mind, Poly?"

I sighed. "Do you think Mr. Halliwell is of sound mind? He seemed a little kooky."

"You said he passed out?"

"Maybe he's not well. It just seemed so strange that one

minute he was talking to someone, and the next minute he was on the ground."

"He collapsed? Just like that?" Big Joe snapped his fingers.

"He had a glass of orange juice, or at least that's what it looked like. He drank it and then stumbled backward, and then he collapsed." I pulled the amber pill vial out of my pocket. "And I found this on the ground."

Big Joe looked at the amber vial. "Nitroglycerine tablets. Standard for anybody who's had a heart attack, but I don't remember hearing anything like that about Harvey Halliwell. He's been the picture of health around these parts. Credits that darn Tangorli juice he's always drinking. You say Harvey dropped this?"

"I found it on the ground where he fell. I assumed he dropped it, but maybe it wasn't his."

Big Joe pursed his lips and seemed to consider this. The chimes over the door rang. Duke maneuvered his wheelchair inside.

"Hey, Big Joe," Duke said. "Can I get four chocolate glazed?"

"You keep packing away these chocolate glazed, you're gonna need a bigger chair."

Duke wheeled himself backward and forward a few times. "Maybe I'll trade up to the Rolls-Royce model for the Miss Tangorli pageant."

"You're involved in the pageant?" I asked.

"You're looking at one of this year's judges." He looked at me and winked.

Duke owned and operated The Broadside Tavern, which sat almost directly across the street from Material Girl. I'd been inside on more than one occasion and had determined that while they served a good burger, the regular clientele was slightly too threatening for my tastes. But despite the atmosphere of his bar, I liked Duke. He was a straight shooter like Big Joe. If I needed backup in a dark alley, these were the two men I'd call. But only if Charlie was unavailable, because I had a sneaking suspicion she had a mean left hook.

"Polyester Monroe," Duke said, pointing a finger at me accusingly. "You cleaned up pretty nice last night. Don't see many dresses like that around here. What do you call those beads?"

"Bugle beads."

"Yeah, those. You don't see many bugle beads around here." He looked at Big Joe and they both smiled. "I know one person who was happy you wore it."

"I don't want to talk about Vaughn McMichael," I said.

"Vaughn? I'm talking about Nolene Kelly. When she heard you designed the thing, she got very excited."

"Why would she care about my dress?"

"Maybe she wants you to make her one."

"But I didn't make my dress," I said. "I only designed it."

"Then maybe she wants to employ the birds and the mice you keep in the store who turned your sketch into reality," Duke said.

Men.

"Why don't you ask her?" he continued. "She's been standing in front of your shop for the past twenty minutes."

"How do you know?" I looked out the window toward the store, though it was too far to see.

"I passed her on my way here."

I stood up. "Business awaits, gentlemen." I loaded myself down with boxes of donuts and the carafe of coffee and backed out the front door. "Big Joe, put this on my tab," I said.

"You got it."

Bonita Avenue was empty, so I cut across the middle of the street, covered the blocks between us, and called out a greeting to Nolene when I got within what I hoped was hearing range. She followed me into the store and waited while I set the box of donuts up on the wrap stand. She glanced to her left and right, scanning the shelves, and then advanced to where I stood.

She idled by the register, picking up flyers I'd printed with coupons and craft ideas, then setting them back down. The last thing she picked up was an announcement about the Midnight in Paris party at Tea Totalers and the afterparty at the Waverly House.

"May we sit?" she asked.

"Sure. Follow me." I led her to the front corner of the store where I had set up sewing tables and sewing machines. There were twelve in all. Initially, I had hoped to fill the space with women who were eager to learn how to sew, but I had yet to figure out the right time slot to try to draw in a crowd.

I sat in one of the chairs and swiveled to the side until I faced Nolene. She tapped her square-cut fingernail against the side of the sewing machine—*tap tap tap* pause, *tap tap tap* pause—through several cycles, until finally she dropped her hands into her lap and faced me.

"You indicated that you're not familiar with the beauty pageant circuit, so I'll apologize now if I tell you things you already know."

"I don't think an apology is going to be necessary," I said.

"I've been involved in the planning and management of the Miss Tangorli pageant for the last twenty years. What I've seen appalls me. Every year the competition to outdo each other becomes more and more fierce, to the point where the young ladies who should enter the pageant don't because they can't afford to."

"How much does it cost?"

"There are entry fees, of course, that run about five hundred dollars. That's to be expected. But when you add on gowns, costumes, salon services, coaches, well, that number gets well into the thousands."

"Thousands of dollars?"

"Yes. And that's just the opening figure. Frankly, it's gotten out of control."

I started to get the uncomfortable feeling that Nolene Kelly was inching her way around to asking me for something, though I couldn't figure out what. She'd already said she had her judges, and Duke said something about my dress.

"Nolene, I'm not sure how I can help you with your pageant," I said.

"Your fabric store is new to the area, and from what I saw last night, I can tell you're interested in gaining exposure and trying things that are outside the box. Would you consider making dresses for the contestants?"

"How many are we talking about?"

"We usually get about a hundred entrants, but by the time the screening is over, we're down to about twenty."

"I can't make twenty dresses myself. Not to the level the contestants would want." I'd left the pageant dress business behind when I quit my job at To the Nines, a cheap dress shop in downtown Los Angeles. To the Nines' business had depended on moving inexpensive gowns quickly in order to make payroll. What Nolene suggested would have been a snap if I had the ladies of the To the Nines workroom at my disposal. My job as senior concept designer had been to do just that. My great-aunt Millie had taught me about fabric at an early age. Soon after that she taught me to frequent thrift shops for damaged dresses that could be used to create patterns. It was that skill that had gotten me a scholarship to the Fashion Institute of Design + Merchandising, known as FIDM, and ultimately landed me the job at To the Nines.

"Nolene, some people have a natural aptitude for design and others don't. I can oversee the sewing and I can make sure a garment is crafted properly, but the dress design will be limited to the imagination of the contestant. Would that be fair?"

"It will be more fair than allowing a contestant in a five-thousand-dollar dress go head to head with a contestant in a hundred-dollar dress. These young women are competing for a once-in-a-lifetime opportunity. It is my job to make sure they each feel like they have a chance to win. Limiting the expense of the dress won't make that much of a difference. People can easily rent, borrow, or claim hand-me-downs. Two years ago we had a scandal when one contestant wore her dress and returned it to the store when the competition was over."

"You should know that construction isn't my strong suit. I can design, but I've always had a staff of sewers at my disposal to turn my designs into wearable garments. What if each girl got an allotment of fabric and I consulted with them on color and design? I can sketch out each concept and someone else can make the dress for them."

"They are young ladies, not girls," she said as if it was a trained response. She tipped her head and looked just past me, apparently at nothing in particular, while she thought. "I see a unique learning opportunity here. You tell me what kind of workers you need to make this happen, and I'll talk to the board about funding."

"The board? I thought Mr. Halliwell was in charge of the pageant."

She laughed. "Poly, that man hasn't been in his right mind for years. We don't need him to make decisions. We don't even need him to be present. If we could convince him to give us power of attorney, we wouldn't even need him to sign the checks."

"Is that a possibility? That he'd give your board the power to write checks in his name?"

"Officially? Not that he'd ever agree to, but unofficially? I have a stack of signed checks in my desk and I've been using them for years. And trust me, if those ever ran out, I know his signature well enough that I could fake it in my sleep."

Four

Having only worked for a cheapskate like Giovanni, who ran To the Nines, I couldn't imagine working for a millionaire who trusted me with a stack of signed blank checks. Giovanni locked the drawer of his desk that held the loose change.

"Now, I better get moving if I want to lock in a third judge," Nolene said.

I had an idea. "Have you considered another local business owner? Maybe one of the ladies who runs the antiques shop next door?"

"That would be a cruel joke, Poly. No, I won't be asking either of them."

"What about Maria Lopez?"

"The cleaning lady?"

"She started her own business and employs over fifteen people now. She's a real inspiration to the women of San Ladrón."

"You might just have something there. Think her husband would mind?"

"You already said you can't have three male judges."

"Settled. I'll go see her right now."

I sank into the chair by the desk and glanced at the clock. Nolene Kelly had accomplished more in a twenty-minute conversation on a Sunday morning than most people accomplished in a week.

I walked Nolene to the front door. When we reached the sidewalk, the door to Flowers in the Attic opened and Violet Garden, one of the two sisters who ran the antiques shop, came out. She gave Nolene a nasty look, then went inside the fabric store. Nolene made a face at her back.

"I don't envy you being her neighbor. Nothing's ever good enough for her."

"Violet's been nothing but nice since I arrived." Mostly.

"I'm sure it's an act and it can't last forever."

Nolene left. When I went back inside, I found Violet carefully studying a bolt of marked-down tweed.

"Violet, how are you?" I asked.

The woman stood up and ran her hand over her long ash-blond ponytail. "Poly," she said, "I'd stay away from that pageant if I were you."

"Why?"

"For starters, Nolene's a bit sexist in her choice of judges for the pageant. I understand why she'd go to Vaughn McMichael, but Duke? That's a stretch. I was hoping she'd tapped you to keep things balanced."

"What's wrong with Duke as a judge?"

She cut me off. "Duke is a *bar owner*"—she said the words like she was saying he had leprosy—"and The Broadside isn't the nicest bar in San Ladrón. Have you seen the clientele?"

"As a matter of fact, I have."

"You've frequented The Broadside?" she asked. Her hand fluttered to her chest and her eyes went wide.

"Yes. They serve a good burger."

"I didn't realize you liked to fraternize with the dark side, but I should have known when I saw you spending time with that mechanic across the street. Honestly, Poly, you should think twice about who you become friends with. My sister and I are just on the other side of that wall and we're more than happy to help you out when you need it."

"Violet, was there something specific that you were looking for today?" I asked. "I saw you looking at the clearance bin."

"Just being neighborly," she said. I suspected there was a better chance that she was trying to overhear our conversation. "So, what did she want to talk to you about? Something to do with the pageant? That woman does have a one-track mind," Violet said.

She wasn't the only one!

"She was impressed with what I accomplished by using fabrics at the tea shop," I said. It was true, and I didn't think it wise to tell Violet any details about my conversation with Nolene.

"Yes, it was impressive. Lilly was surprised you gave away that much fabric, but I told her you were probably just being nice, considering the poor French girl's husband had been murdered."

I refused to engage in Violet's gossip. "Is Lilly running the store today?" I asked, hoping to prompt Violet to leave.

"That's what I wanted to tell you. We're not opening today. Nobody shops the day after the garden party. Everyone who is anyone brunches at the Waverly House. That is, anyone who gets up before noon."

"Are you headed that way?"

"Of course," she replied, as though I'd suggested she didn't count. She pulled a pair of tortoiseshell cat-eye sunglasses out of her small handbag and left.

Even though I considered closing the store after Violet's visit, I didn't, and it was a good thing. I sold two sewing machines to a pair of women who had been impressed with the transition of Tea Totalers, and ten yards of purple ultra suede to a couple who wanted a wall of fabric in their bedroom. My fourth customer would prove to be trickier than the first three. It was Harvey Halliwell.

Today he wore a white linen suit and orange bow tie. "Good morning, Mr. Halliwell. Welcome to Material Girl," I said.

"So you're Polyester Monroe," he said.

"Yes, but I go by Poly," I said. "Mr. Halliwell, how's your head?"

"My what?" His eyes rolled up as if he were trying to see what might be wrong with his head.

"I saw you last night in the Waverly House gardens. You said—"

"Never listen to an old man with a flair for the dramatic. I'm fine, my head's fine. Everybody's fine. Now listen. Nolene told me about your idea and I think it's a squeeze!"

"It's a what?" I asked.

"A fine squeeze—like a perfect piece of fruit ripe for the picking. Our pageant is ripe for your idea. Ripe, ripe, ripe, I tell you! I love it and I came here to give you the green light personally."

"Mr. Halliwell, are you sure you're okay? Maybe you should be resting."

"No time to rest, young lady. Not when there's work to be done. Do you think the fruit takes a day off?"

"No."

"That's right. My business is built on fruit. If the fruit doesn't get a day off, then neither do I."

I hoped the expression on my face didn't give away my thoughts, namely, that Mr. Halliwell was as fruity as his produce.

"Now, the pageant. I've decided to create a second prize

this year. The winner will receive a seat on the board, like always, but the runner-up will get a chance to work as my traveling companion. Right on the front lines, I tell you."

"I mean no disrespect, sir, but do you think that's fair? The winner is on the board but the runner-up is your assistant?"

"My dear, the board position is an unpaid seat with no voting privileges. My current assistant gets a six-figure salary. Which would you prefer?"

"And the trip to China?"

He studied me for a moment. "You know quite a bit about our little pageant, don't you? Too much?" He smiled and rocked backward on his feet. "Just kidding. Yes, the winner goes to China for a publicity opportunity. Four days of press junkets, interviews, and staged photos. But I fly to China four times a year and I don't like to travel alone. Nolene's been coming with me, but I believe it's time to branch out, like a Tangorli tree! And offer the experience to someone new. And let's just say, whoever travels with me doesn't have to keep track of their expense account." He winked.

"I had no idea," I said.

"Not many people do. Now, let's talk about your role in the pageant. Something about silk?"

I walked Mr. Halliwell to the wall of silk. The colors popped against each other like colored pencils in an artist's tool kit. I couldn't resist a new bolt of silk in a pretty color and had stocked us with sixty-four different shades. Thanks to my experience working with silk at To the Nines, I could speak to the ease of working with the luxurious fabric but could also steer customers away from typical mistakes like using too big a needle or too thick a thread.

"You wanted something to help level the playing field, so to speak. My idea was that each contestant sketches a dress and buys ten yards of silk to make it from."

"They aren't all sewers like you."

"That's the thing. I'm not the best sewer in the world. To keep things equal, I think the contestants should not have to worry about making their dress, only about designing and selecting the fabrics. After all, that speaks to taste level and them each knowing what suits their individual style. If someone is skilled in sewing, then of course they should be able to make their own garment, but I don't think that should be a requirement."

"Where do you expect these seamstresses to come from?" He looked around, his sights settling on the empty chairs by the sewing station.

"I have contacts in Los Angeles, and I can arrange for some of them to come here for a week," I added.

"Do you think your former employer would be willing to work on this?"

"If you were willing to give his workroom credit for the gowns, I think he might. In addition to reproduction rights of the gowns."

"Tell you what I'm going to do. How much does this silk cost?" he asked.

"Twenty dollars a yard," I said.

"At ten yards per dress, that's a two-hundred-dollar investment." Harvey Halliwell got a faraway look in his eyes. "How about you sell it to these women for ten dollars a yard and I make up the difference direct to you?"

My mind raced to keep up with what Mr. Halliwell was offering.

"If you get low, you order more. I'm a gambling man, Polyester, and I'd be willing to wager that you get your fabric for a lot less than you sell it for. You'll get your twenty dollars a yard. That's four thousand dollars gross, minus your costs, guaranteed. In exchange I want you to consult with these women, treat them fairly, and make sure they all have use of equally talented seamstresses. You got that?"

"Sure," I said. My head was spinning from the calculations and the potential profit.

"Good deal." He shook my hand. "I'll have my lawyers draw up the paperwork and drop off a contract. If you have any questions, you can come to me."

"Sure," I said again.

Mr. Halliwell was halfway to the door when I remembered the prescription vial I'd found the night before. "Mr. Halliwell," I called out. I pulled the vial from my pocket and held it out to him. "I just remembered. I found this on the ground last night. You must have dropped it when you stood up."

He took the vial and stared at the illegible label, then tucked it into the inside pocket of his linen jacket. "Good day, Ms. Monroe," he said.

A handful more customers, tipsy after their champagne brunch, pushed me over my sales quota. I closed the shop fifteen minutes early. Curiosity had gotten the best of me and I wanted to check out the events at the Waverly House.

I corralled Pins and Needles from where they were swatting a felt mouse by the tables of fake fur and secured them in the wrap stand. Pins jumped from the floor up to the counter and meowed. He was a striped tabby like his brother, only Pins was gray and Needles was orange.

"Take care of each other," I said to him. He meowed again and jumped to the ground, where he nosed his brother Needles, who swatted him like a southpaw.

I headed out the back of the store and walked through the alley. After moving into the apartment above the fabric shop, I quickly learned that the alleys were the best shortcuts for getting around town in a jiffy. They ran behind all of the businesses, and the shrubbery had been trimmed back to allow people to pass through from one property to another. I cut through the bushes and ended up behind the majestic Victorian mansion.

The landscapers who had taken such care to turn the gardens into the impressionist floral masterpiece it had been last night were tending to the flowers, replacing last night's lilies with new ones in each of the glass vases. The head landscaper, a heavily tattooed bald man with a patch of beard in a neatly shaved line that ran down his chin, instructed the other men in Spanish. He saw me watching them and approached me.

"*Si? Hay problema?*"

"*No problema.* Are you in charge of the gardens? They're beautiful."

His expression changed from wariness to pride. "*Si.* I'm Xavier. I designed the landscaping for this year."

"It's amazing," I said. "How long will it stay like this?"

"We'll be maintaining it for a week, and then it's up to the Waverly House whether they want us to tear it down."

I watched the men move their tools and leftover lilies to the wheelbarrows that lined the far end of the property. Xavier smiled at me, and then turned away and joined the others by a pile of sod squares. A few men knelt down and swapped out an existing patch of sod for a new one. The seams were visible, leaving the appearance of a patchwork blanket—at least the parts that weren't bald patches of brown dirt did. Now, that would be a great idea for a backyard, I thought. Patches of sod in varying shades of green, whipstitched together with a biodegradable twine to look like a quilt!

The alley had been handy for getting me from Material Girl to the Waverly House grounds, but I hadn't given much thought to my gladiator sandals and the exposed soil. Already grains of dirt had found their way under my toes. I took a long step over a patch of overturned ground and put my hand against the tree where Vaughn and I had stood last night. I held a branch for balance and tapped the toe of my foot against the trunk, trying to shake the dirt loose.

And that was when I saw that I wasn't alone. Lying on the ground behind the tree was Harvey Halliwell.

His white linen suit was rumpled in a way that only linen can be. His tangerine bow tie now dug into the folds of his skin. An orange knife jutted out of his side.

Five

I knelt down beside Harvey. His head fell to the side. I felt for a pulse at his wrist. There was none. Something dark and sticky transferred from his body to my arm. I moved my fingers to his throat, hoping to find some sign of life, but already I knew I wouldn't find any.

I looked around for someone—anyone—whom I could instruct to call the police. Two landscapers stood by the far corner of the grounds. I yelled as loud as I could, but neither looked up from his task. Wires ran from their ears to their pockets and I knew they couldn't hear me.

Gently, I set Harvey's head back down on the ground and ran to the front of the Waverly House. Once inside, I found Sheila Bonham, the red-haired hostess in charge of seating people, and pulled her away from the crowd. "You have to call nine-one-one. Harvey Halliwell is out back and he's—" I paused. "Call nine-one-one. We need the police."

She stared at me, her eyes wide with disbelief. "He's what?"

"He's dead. I'm going back outside to wait with him. He's behind the weeping willow tree. Hurry."

I didn't wait to see Sheila make the call. Already, my actions were alarming patrons of the restaurant. A crowd of tipsy brunchgoers trying to sneak a peek at the dead man would be the worst thing for Sheriff Clark to discover when he arrived.

I ran down the hallway, out the side exit, and down the exterior staircase. I raced over to Xavier and pulled at the headphone cords until the ear buds fell out.

"What are you doing?" he asked.

"There's a man over there under that tree. He's dead. Can you help me block off the area so people can't get too close when they come out of the restaurant?"

"How much champagne did you drink, lady?" he asked.

I heard the sirens in the distance. "Please. That's for him. I'm not lying." I tipped over a garden gnome and lugged him to a spot ten feet from Harvey's body. The landscaper followed and laid an assortment of small gardening tools down end to end. I added the rake and the hose to the chain of items. When we were done, we'd effectively completed three quarters of a circle around Harvey's body. The intersecting hedge behind the tree served as the barrier behind him.

Patrons trickled out of the Waverly House and approached our makeshift crime scene barrier. What started as a few people soon turned into a crowd. A black-and-white pulled up alongside the curb and Sheriff Clark got out of the driver's side. A young man in a brown sheriff's uniform got out of the passenger side and followed Clark to where we stood.

"Ms. Monroe," he said. "You made the nine-one-one call?"

"No, Sheila did. Inside. I'm the one who found him. He's behind the tree."

He glanced down at the makeshift barrier of gardening utensils and gnome that lay on their sides, marking off the circle around Harvey's body, and then looked up at me.

"I didn't want people to get too close," I said.

A woman with short spiky gray hair and earrings made of fruit clusters broke away from the group. "Mr. Halliwell?" she cried. "Mr. Halliwell!" She dropped to her knees on the ground next to his body. Sheriff Clark ran forward. He put his arms on her shoulders and said something to her. He helped her stand, put an arm around her, and led her back to the sidewalk to the other officer, who escorted her to a wrought-iron bench away from the view of the body.

Sheriff Clark stepped over the rake handle and walked to the tree. Harvey's feet stuck out in front of him, two orange socks showing from between the cuffs of his white linen pants and the brown oxfords on his feet. Clark turned around and waved the uniformed officer forward. The young man stepped over the gnome and the two of them spoke in hushed tones. The new guy nodded and turned around to the crowd.

"I'm going to need to get the names and contact info for everyone here," he said. The crowd groaned collectively. "If you could all join me over by the steps to the Waverly House I'll get started."

A few couples started to back away toward the street. Charlie appeared from the curb. She held her arms out on either side of her and blocked their path. "I don't think you heard the officer correctly. He said to meet *by the steps*," she said. The grumbling continued but the patrons turned back and followed the officer. Charlie looked past me to Clark and flashed him a smile.

"What's happening?" she said to me.

"Harvey Halliwell. Did you know him?"

"Used to. Drove a silver Infiniti that had all kinds of problems. Traded it in for a hybrid and now I never see him. Electric cars are going to be the death of my business."

I cringed at the use of the word *death* and told Charlie what had happened. "I cut through the shrubs between the alley and the Waverly House and there he was. Who knows how long he's been there."

"Could have been there since last night," she said.

"No. He was at my store this morning. Only a couple of hours ago."

I studied her face for signs that she knew something. She met my stare and held it. If I hadn't had a chance to learn Charlie's body language, I might not have noticed how tense she was when I told her about Harvey, and the subtle shift that occurred when I mentioned that I'd seen him alive and well today. Her eyes dilated for a second and she bit at her lip.

"You said you talked to Harvey Halliwell earlier today?" asked Sheriff Clark, approaching us.

"That's my cue to leave," said Charlie. "Come on over when you're done here," she said to me. She finger-waved at Clark, who turned red, and then walked away.

Clark watched her leave, then turned to me. "What can you tell me?"

"Harvey was at my store earlier today. We were meeting to discuss the pageant. Who was that woman?"

"Which woman?" Clark asked.

"The gray-haired woman who broke down."

"Beth Fields. Works for Halliwell Industries."

"She seems pretty shaken up."

"Sometimes that happens when people see a murder victim." He moved a few steps to his right, blocking my view of the woman. "What time did Mr. Halliwell leave your shop?"

I thought back over the morning. "I'm not sure. I had customers before he got there and a few after."

"Can you do better than that?"

"I can check the time stamp on the receipts of the customers before and after him, but that's still going to be pretty vague."

"Not necessary."

"Sheriff, last night I saw Harvey collapse at the party." I looked behind me, in Charlie's direction. She was half a block away but stood on the sidewalk, watching Sheriff Clark and me talk. I turned back to Clark. "He fainted. Vaughn went to get help. Harvey snapped back to consciousness and got up and left. Do you think that's relevant? Or coincidence?"

"I don't believe in coincidence," he said.

"I found a pill vial on the ground next to where he collapsed."

"Do you still have it?"

"No. I gave it back to him when he was at my shop this morning. Was he on any medications? Maybe somebody tampered with his prescription."

Clark reached out and turned my arm over. Traces of blood had transferred from Harvey's torso onto my arm. "That's from a knife wound, not a prescription."

I turned my head and watched as men in white uniforms moved Harvey's body from the ground to a flat metal cart on wheels. The lone officer had moved the crowd away from the scene and appeared to be doing a fair job of keeping them under control.

"You have help today," I said.

"Crime's been on the rise in San Ladrón. The county approved my request for part-time help. The kid's a little green, but he'll do." He turned back to me. "You said Harvey met with you to discuss the pageant. Tell me about that conversation."

I told him what I could. "Nolene Kelly sent him my way. She didn't like how the pageant was becoming a competition for the wealthy. She must have told Harvey we talked and that's why he came to my store. We brainstormed an idea for the contestants, that each competitor design her own dress, get an allotment of fabric from my store to make it." I paused for a moment, thinking about how only hours ago the pageant had seemed to be a financial boon for me.

"You know, it's not a bad idea. Might have helped put this whole thing into proportion. Did either of them say anything else?"

I thought back to what Nolene said about Mr. Halliwell. "Not really."

The men in white pushed the wheeled gurney past us and loaded it into the back of a waiting ambulance. The vehicle drove off in the direction of the hospital, leaving only the presence of the police as evidence that something untoward had happened.

"You say Nolene was at your shop this morning before Harvey? Doesn't take long to get from there to here, does it?"

"A couple of minutes if you cut through the alley and the hedges," I said. "But after last night's party, you can access the yard from almost any angle. The gardeners have probably been working back here for hours. I don't think many people would notice someone coming and going."

"Let me know if you remember anything else," Clark said. He handed me one of his business cards, a formality since I practically knew the number to the police station by heart. I took the card and slipped it into the pocket of my dress.

"Do I need to talk to him, too?" I asked, pointing at the younger cop.

"No, you're free to go."

The hot, dry June temperature that kept most of us roasting during the day had broken as the sun went down. Californians referred to this time of year as June Gloom. It should have felt like summer, but the days were often overcast and gray. The temperatures rose to the nineties during the day, but when the sun went down, the nights dropped to the sixties. The town was sorely in need of rain, but there were no signs of it. I was unprepared for the chill in my sleeveless tank dress, so I wrapped my arms around myself and headed home. I showered off the blood that had transferred from Harvey to me, changed into black jeans and an oversized sweater, and headed out the door to Charlie's.

Early Van Halen spilled from Charlie's office onto the street. I followed the sound of David Lee Roth's voice until I saw the strange man with the white ponytail inside her office. They were arguing. Charlie's back was to me. I stopped on the sidewalk out front, unsure if I should barge in.

The man looked to be in his late forties. Mirrored aviator glasses were clipped to the front of his black T-shirt. I could tell from their body language that they were on opposite sides of whatever it was they discussed, but their voices must have been lowered because, aside from the occasional word, I couldn't make out anything they said. Charlie caught me watching them. She said something to him. He put on his sunglasses and stormed out of her office, past me, and out the door.

"Did I interrupt something?" I asked.

"Old friend. He doesn't like my choice of transmission fluid. What's up?" she asked.

I watched the man with the ponytail enter the gas station across the street. "That guy was arguing with Harvey Halliwell at the party last night. Now Harvey's dead. Charlie, I know you know him. I saw you talking to him before they argued."

"I talked to a lot of people last night. Ever hear of mingling?"

"That wasn't mingling. You know him. Who is he?"

Charlie stared out the window for a long time. "I can't talk about him. Not yet."

"You better talk about him soon. I have to tell Clark what I saw. He could have something to do with the murder."

"He didn't."

"Then tell me who he is. Tell me why he was arguing with Harvey." She was silent. "Charlie, this doesn't look good."

"Did you hear what they were arguing about?" she asked.

"No."

"Did he see you?" she asked.

"He had to. He looked right at me when I tried to stop him."

She tapped a pen on the mouse pad and then threw it at the wall. It bounced off and landed on the desk, and then rolled to the edge and fell to the floor. Charlie punched her fist into the mouse pad and the whole desk shook.

"Charlie, what's going on? Who is that guy?"

"That guy is the closest thing I have to family."

Before I could react, Charlie held up her hand to stop me. "Remember how I told you once that I bounced around different foster homes after I was given up for adoption?"

I nodded.

"The older I got, the less anybody wanted me. Eventually I took off with everything I owned, which wasn't much, and hitchhiked until I ended up in Encino. I moved in with a mechanic because he said he had a room for rent. His name was Ned Rains." She tipped her head toward the street, and even though the man with the ponytail wasn't there, I knew who she meant. "He wasn't much older than I was—twenty-two to my fourteen. It was his auto shop. I didn't have any money, so I took care of the food and laundry and stuff, but that got real boring real fast. I started hanging around while he worked on cars, helping him when I could. He taught me about engines and oil changes and transmission flushes."

"Were you and he— I mean, did he— I mean—"

"No. He understood that I'd had a hard life up to that point, and he took me in. He even helped me try to find the people who gave me up for adoption. When it was time for me to leave, he gave me two thousand dollars and said I should forget the past and start a life of my own. I moved here, got a job at the auto shop, and saved up until the owner was ready to sell to me. This has been my shop ever since."

"But you and Ned kept in touch."

"Yes. When you first came to town and found out my secret, I needed to get away. I showed up on his doorstep without much more than I did the first time."

"Does Clark know any of this?"

"What does Clark have to do with it?"

"You're having a relationship with him, or I think you are. There's this thing people do when they're in a relationship. They talk about what made them the person they are. It's sometimes referred to as 'getting to know each other,'" I said, using finger quotes.

"Clark knows I'm a private person, and he knows if he so much as glances at a background check of me, I'll kick him to the curb."

"Clark's not dumb. He's going to look into anybody connected to Harvey Halliwell, and it won't take long for him to start asking questions. Why is Ned here? Why now?"

"I told you, I can't talk about that." She looked up at me. "You're not going to turn this into your latest rescue mission, are you?"

"I'm just trying to find out the truth. Somebody killed Harvey Halliwell."

"Ned didn't do it. Their argument was about something else. Let me talk to him first before you go to Clark."

"I don't feel good about this," I said.

"Ned's not a killer," Charlie said. "I'd risk my auto shop on that."

"Charlie, I have to tell you something about Ned that you might not want to hear." I paused for a second to gauge how she would react. "After Harvey fainted, Ned took something out from Harvey's jacket. That doesn't look good."

"What was it?"

"I don't know. It was dark and I couldn't see."

"Did Vaughn see?"

"He said he didn't see anything."

Charlie stood up and slammed her open palm down on her desk. "Did you tell anybody else about this?"

"No."

"Maybe you should have," said a male voice from the doorway. We both looked up and saw Sheriff Clark standing there, listening to our conversation.

Six

"How long have you been standing there?" Charlie asked.

"Long enough to hear what Poly said." He turned to me. "Why didn't you tell me this before now?"

"Because I don't know what I saw. And Vaughn didn't see anything, so maybe it was my imagination. And what difference does it make? Harvey stood up and walked away. He was fine. I told him we were getting help and he said he was a tough old coot and not to make a fuss. And then he grabbed his cane from the tree and walked away."

"How can I get in touch with this man?" Sheriff Clark asked. He looked at me, but I knew his question was directed toward Charlie.

I looked at Charlie. Her face was flushed a dark shade of red. "You have no jurisdiction outside San Ladrón. When Ned comes back, I'll tell him to call you. Until then, maybe you should try to find the real killer."

Sheriff Clark's face went stone cold and his eyes went

dark. His brows lowered over his dark eyes and gave him a serious appearance. Whatever he might have felt for Charlie, it didn't involve her breaking the law or becoming an accessory to murder.

"Ms. Brooks, Ms. Monroe, I'll be in touch." He turned around and left.

I was afraid to look at Charlie. First I'd told her Ned might have harmed Harvey Halliwell, and that caused her to suppress information to the police. Then Clark had referred to her as "Ms. Brooks," all but eliminating the personal connection they had by adopting police formality. Any anger she might have felt five minutes ago would be magnified by a gazillion percent by now.

"Charlie, listen to me. I don't know anything about Ned. I only know what I think I saw, and that wasn't much. Why not let Clark worry about Ned? He may have had something to do with Harvey Halliwell's murder," I said softly.

"You don't know what it was like to be all alone in the world, Polyester. Ned changed all that. I'm not going to let him take the fall for something he didn't do."

She turned around and stormed away, leaving me and David Lee Roth alone in her office.

I left the auto shop and jogged across the street. There were no cars on the road and I assumed the police wouldn't mind a little jaywalking. They had more important things on their mind.

The thing was, I did, too. Charlie's relationship to Ned raised more questions than before. What exactly had transpired between him and Harvey? And when Harvey came back to consciousness, why hadn't he insisted that we get him professional help?

There was one reason people didn't want to involve the police. Because they were hiding something. But what could Harvey possibly have been hiding? And what had Ned taken from him? I didn't like it. I didn't like any of it. Was Charlie so sure Ned didn't do it because she knew something I didn't, or was her total belief in his innocence because she couldn't bear to acknowledge he might be guilty?

I unlocked the fabric store, collected Pins and Needles, and went to my apartment above the shop. I carried a glass of wine and a blank journal to the living room, curled up under a quilt my great-aunt had made in the seventies, and jotted down everything I could remember about my conversations last night and this morning.

I woke up Monday morning on the sofa, my wineglass still mostly full on the table in front of me. Needles was asleep by my knees. The sounds of early-morning commuters floated up from street level: horns, engines, and the occasional talk radio station mingled with a top forty hit.

Something tugged at the side of the quilt. I looked down. Pins had his claws caught and was trying to free them. He yanked on the fabric, pulling it off me. Needles picked up his head and let out a lazy meow.

"Don't blame me, blame your brother," I said. "I was going to let you sleep in."

Needles meowed again. I leaned over and freed Pins's paw from the threadbare cotton, and he jumped up onto my chest and nudged me with his cold nose. Needles stood up, stretched, and walked up my torso until he was jockeying for attention, too. I bent forward and kissed them both on top of their heads, then got up.

After the cats were fed and I was suitably showered, dressed, and coffeed, I headed downstairs. My commute was a lot shorter than that of the people in the cars out front, but I used that time wisely. My contacts at the fabric wholesalers were on the East Coast, so if I wanted a chance to put in a bid on their closeout fabrics, I had to let them know before someone else in their time zone swooped in and bought their inventory out from under me.

The apartment over the store had belonged to my great-aunt and great-uncle back when they ran Land of a Thousand Fabrics. I loved the feeling of living in a time warp and so, for the moment, I kept technology restricted to the fabric shop, where my day-to-day business needed it. I set my coffee mug on my desk and cued up my e-mail. And there, in the middle of the twenty-seven unread messages, was an e-mail from Nolene.

Dear Poly,

Your check is ready to be picked up. I hope you're prepared to deal with a small army of pageant contestants!

Nolene Kelly

In light of the murder, the note took me by surprise. I called the number in Nolene's signature block.

"Halliwell Industries," said a female voice. The words came out slightly nasally.

"Hello," I said. "This is Polyester Monroe. I have an e-mail from Nolene Kelly that I wanted to clarify."

"Nolene's out of the office right now. I'm Beth, her secretary. Hold please." A button tone sounded in my ear, and then I heard her blow her nose. After a few more clattering sounds, the tone sounded again and she came back on the call. "Are you still there?"

"Yes," I said. I didn't bother telling her that she hadn't succeeded in putting me on hold in the first place.

"Maybe I can help. What did the e-mail say?"

"It's about the pageant. I own a fabric store on Bonita, and—"

She cut me off. "Yes, the fabric store. Nolene told me all about your idea. What was your question in reference to?"

"I thought maybe she sent the e-mail before Mr. Halliwell

was murdered." The other end of the phone went silent. "Hello?" I prompted.

"I'm still here, just shaken up. The e-mail is for real. The pageant was always so important to Mr. Halliwell that we're proceeding with it as his legacy. Are you okay with that?"

"Sure," I said. Despite the circumstances, I welcomed the role I'd play in the pageant. Fabric was my business, and this was another opportunity to become a part of the San Ladrón community. Twenty young women would be consulting with me on the dress they planned to wear when the crown of Miss Tangorli was awarded. From what I'd been hearing, it was a big responsibility.

"Come by Halliwell Industries later today and I'll see that your check is by the front desk."

I wrote down directions, then closed my e-mail and moved on to other business, which included thirty minutes studying a catalog of Christmas fabrics to determine what I thought I'd need to have in stock to get us safely through the holidays. I followed that up with phone calls to my favorite suppliers and scored several end-of-production bolts of designer material. The arrival of those fabrics would feel like Christmas, having purchased them sight unseen. But that was half the fun of running a fabric shop!

I opened the front gate at ten on the nose and glanced at my two neighbors. Flowers in the Attic didn't open until eleven, but Tiki Tom had the door to his Hawaiian ephemera shop propped open with a lava rock. Tom himself was in the window setting up a display of hula girl collectibles.

"Aloha, Poly," he said. He backed out of the window, picked up a skull-shaped coffee cup, and met me outside. "Good day for a luau, don't you think?"

"You think every day is a good day for a luau," I said.

"True. There's something special about a luau."

I studied his face and wondered for a second if it was really coffee in his mug.

"I guess you heard about Harvey, didn't you?" he asked.

"Yes," I answered. For the moment, I kept quiet about being the person who found the body. "Was it on the news?"

"Anything that has to do with that darn pageant is news these days. If it weren't Harvey's murder, it would be a sneak peek at the pageant setup, or the judges, or a spotlight on a former winner."

"How do you know so much about this? You're not exactly the pageant type."

"If you spend any time in San Ladrón, you learn about the Miss Tangorli pageant. There was a big scandal when one girl lied about her age. They had to incorporate background checks, letters of recommendation, all sorts of stuff."

"When was that?"

"Ten years ago? Maybe more? It was a big deal. All of a sudden the applicants had to have sponsors, pass psychological evaluations, provide legal documentation of their ages, the works. It's harder to qualify for that thing than to get a government job. High stakes don't always bring out the good in people, if you know what I mean. Ask Violet. Not a lot of love lost between her and Harvey. Can't say I'm surprised by what happened. She's had it in for Harvey Halliwell for years."

Seven

"Violet? What's her connection to Harvey Halliwell?"

"She's always blamed Harvey for what happened to her daughter."

I must have looked confused, because Tiki Tom continued without my asking. "Her little girl was a contestant in Harvey's pageant. Elizabeth wanted no part of it, but Violet entered her anyway. She thought Elizabeth was going to win the pageant and get all kinds of opportunities that she never had herself. That's all Violet talked about. I used to hear them fighting over it from my shop two doors away."

"Her daughter could have just said she wasn't going to participate."

"Well, truth be told there's a little more to the story than what I've told you." He took a sip from his mug. "I don't think it'll do anybody any good to stand around here gossiping about it. Best let sleeping dogs lie." He pointed behind me with the hand that held the skull mug. "Besides, looks like you got your first customer."

I wanted to press Tiki Tom for more information, but he was right. A woman who looked to be in her midthirties entered the shop with a nervous Chihuahua in tow. The woman had brown hair streaked with chunky copper and blond highlights. Large square vintage sunglasses covered her eyes. I followed her and said hello. She turned and smiled a tight-lipped smile that told me she wasn't interested in small talk. She stopped by a fixture of green-and-white floral cotton twill.

I took a dog biscuit out of a Tupperware container that I kept at the wrap stand and carried it to the Chihuahua.

"May I give him a biscuit?" I asked. The woman nodded. I snapped the biscuit in half and the Chihuahua stood on his hind legs and reached for the treat.

"I'll take four yards," she said, handing me the bolt of floral fabric.

I carried it to a cutting station. "I'm Poly Monroe. This is my store," I said, and held out my hand. "What are you planning to make?" I asked.

The woman held out the hand not holding the dog's leash. "A tablecloth. I knew I could find something in here that would be prettier than anything I can find in a department store. Did you just open?"

"I inherited the shop from my great-uncle. It's been closed for ten years, so in a way, yes, I just opened."

She looked around. "There are so many pretty fabrics in here. Lots of possibilities."

"Yes. Do you sew much?"

"Oh, I can't sew!" she said. "I'm going to fold this over to hide the raw edge. When I want something made, I take it to a tailor. There's a lovely lady on Magnolia Lane who can make just about anything."

Considering she was buying fabric, which was my trade,

I was happy for her purchase. I stooped down and fed the rest of the doggie biscuit to the dog.

"Who's this little guy?" I asked, ruffling his fur.

"That's Archie."

The woman followed me to the register, where I rang up the fabric. I suggested she look at pattern books and notions, but she said she didn't have the time. After she paid, I thanked her and offered her a discount coupon if she'd sign up for my e-mail list. She wrote her name in and left.

That hadn't been the first customer who had purchased fabric to take to a tailor. A sale was a sale, but if I could find a way to help people discover the joy of turning their favorite fabrics into something themselves, I'd have a much more loyal customer base and I bet sales would soar. If only I knew how to do that.

I folded up the floral cotton twill and returned it to the fixture. I thought back to what Tiki Tom had told me. He'd hinted that Harvey had enemies because of the pageant. And here I was, officially employed by the pageant committee. If I could figure out who Harvey's enemies were while doing the job I was hired to do, then I could divert Clark's attention from Ned.

But no matter which way things went, one was certain. If I were to get involved with the pageant, the day-to-day running of the fabric store would suffer, and I couldn't let that happen. Even though things had been running smoothly for the past four months, I wasn't bringing in enough net profit to cover a second employee's wages. And that meant there was only one place I could turn.

Family.

I picked up the phone and called home. My mom answered halfway through the fourth ring.

"Hi, Mom, it's Poly."

"Hi, Poly," she said, panting heavily between words.

"Mom, are you okay?"

"I just finished taking out the trash. Almost didn't make it to the phone."

"Why are you taking out the trash? Where's Dad?"

"Your dad and I have swapped household duties for the week. I wanted to prove to him that what I do around the house is just as difficult as what he does."

"Okay, sure." Every once in a while my mother flexed her equality muscles and used my dad as her opponent. I would have thought it was funny if I didn't recognize a little of myself in her actions. "Listen, Mom, I have to ask a favor. Do you think you could spare a couple of days to help me out at the store?"

"Sure, but if you've gotten that busy, maybe you should hire someone else?"

"It's not that." I gave her a thumbnail sketch of the situation. My parents lived halfway between San Ladrón and Los Angeles. Every once in a while they threatened to up and move to one of the square states in the middle of the country, but I figured if they'd made it this long, mortgage paid off and standing Bunco games with the neighbors on Saturday night, they weren't going anywhere.

"How's tomorrow? I told your father I'd change the oil in the Ford this week. I watched a YouTube video on how to do it, but I need him to leave the house before I get started in case anything goes wrong."

"Mom, I'm friends with the mechanic across the street. Drive the Ford here and I'll get Charlie to change the oil while you're working. Deal?"

"I'm not sure that's the proper way to prove my point."

"Why not? Dad wants the oil changed. You're going to have the oil changed. He doesn't need to know the details."

"Can you get me a little 10W40 to rub on my fingernails, make it look like I did it myself?"

"Mom . . ."

"You're right, too far."

"Do you still have the keys to the shop I made up for you?"

"Right here. I'll be there after lunch."

After we hung up, I checked my e-mail. Buried in my inbox among a conversation about tweed in my Yahoo fabric group was my monthly notice about my business loan. The first payment wasn't due for a few months, but I would need more than a steady trickle of customers to make the payment.

I dug a calculator out from a drawer under the register. Mr. Halliwell had been right about the cost of my fabrics. On average, I had a 60 percent markup from cost. That meant a twenty-dollar-a-yard silk cost me eight dollars a yard. His proposal would guarantee me the retail price for two hundred yards of silk. That was four thousand dollars, minus a cost of sixteen hundred dollars—click click click—equals a profit of . . . twenty-four hundred dollars.

Not too shabby!

I stared at the calculator for a few seconds, then typed the numbers in a second time to make sure I hadn't hit a wrong key. Same answer. Same answer! My involvement in the pageant would net me enough to exceed the first payment on my business loan. I stood up and spun around in a circle.

"Good news?" said Vaughn from the doorway. He held a paper take-out bag from Tea Totalers. "I know it's early but I thought maybe I could interest you in sharing your lunch break with me?"

I was so caught up in my happiness that I forgot my usual reserved nature. I danced across the floor to him, took his hands, and hopped up on my toes. "Halliwell Industries green-lighted my proposal for the pageant!"

Vaughn's smile froze on his face. "Your proposal?" he said. "I didn't know you were going to be involved in the pageant."

"I'm not, I mean, I didn't know I was." I dropped his hands. "Why, is that a problem?"

"I just thought, when I heard about Harvey, and about you finding him . . ." His voice trailed off.

At the mention of Harvey, my enthusiasm evaporated. It felt wrong to be happy in light of his death. "You're right. I shouldn't get involved."

"I didn't say that. Maybe if you told me about the proposal, it would be different."

"You're going to be a judge, right?" He nodded. "So you're involved with the pageant. But it's not a secret, and I can't see how it would hurt to tell you." I stared at him for a second. "Okay. Really, it was Nolene's idea."

I led Vaughn to the wrap stand. He unpacked the paper bag and doled out two roast beef sandwiches on a French baguette, a plastic cup of *jus*, and a small carton of *pommes frites*. The scent of the French dip mingled with the salty potatoes.

My mouth watered and I unwrapped a sandwich while I told Vaughn about the agreement I'd reached with Harvey Halliwell.

"When was this?"

"She talked to me on Saturday night, and Harvey and I finalized things on Sunday morning."

"I don't want to be the voice of doom here, but in this particular case, a handshake agreement isn't worth the paper it's printed on."

"That's what I thought, but I just got off the phone with Nolene's secretary, Beth. She promised me a check by the end of the day."

"I'm surprised. I didn't expect you to be so excited about participating in the beauty pageant."

"Mr. Halliwell guaranteed me I'd make retail on two hundred yards of silk. The profit from this one event will help me pay back the first installment on my loan."

"Your loan," he finished quietly. He reached forward and tucked a curl behind my ear. "It's okay. It's business. I wish you'd come to me for a loan, but I know you have history with other people in the financial world."

Vaughn was referring to my ex-boyfriend, a financial

analyst in the heart of Los Angeles's business district. Which meant he didn't know the truth—that his own father had intercepted my loan application from the bank and cosigned it himself. I felt uncomfortable keeping a secret from Vaughn. I already knew the subject of money was a touchy one between us.

"The loan didn't come from Carson," I said. "It came from your father."

"You went to my father for a loan instead of coming to me?" Vaughn asked.

"No. It's not what you think. It didn't happen that way."

Vaughn's face went pale and his jaw went rigid. "I have to go." He set down his sandwich and walked out.

I watched his back as he left. There was no good-bye, no *Oh, okay, well that explains everything.* I wasn't sure what I'd expected, but whatever it was, I sure didn't get it.

Between wealth and working class, Vaughn and I had met somewhere in the middle. I never knew if our disparate backgrounds would keep us from sharing anything more than a couple of dates.

I wrapped up what was left of my sandwich and the fries, put the lid on the *jus*, and packed it all back into the carryout bag. My appetite was gone. Two days ago I'd been getting ready for the Midnight in Paris party and everything had felt perfect.

And it was all because of that accursed dress.

I didn't know why I'd worn the champagne dress instead of any of the others in my closet. When I first came to San Ladrón to sign the paperwork to inherit the fabric store, I'd been surprised by how inspired the luxurious fabrics inside the shop made me feel. They were a far stretch from the cheap poly satins that I'd grown familiar with at To the Nines, and one night, needing a respite from the drama that surrounded my arrival in town, I had let my mind wander into fantasy territory and I designed a dress for the likes of a glamorous starlet from the thirties. I had set the sketch aside and returned to my real life filled with black, black, and black. Good for hiding grease, dust, dirt, and the glue stick messes that were so frequent in my former life.

Vaughn had seen the sketch. He'd had it made for me. I still didn't know who the seamstress was who had turned my sketch into a reality. And it struck me that the person he'd hired to make my dress would be perfect for helping with the pageant dresses. Only now, calling him would feel awkward, like I'd made up an excuse to talk to him.

Curses. I felt like I was in tenth grade.

By the time my mom arrived at the store, I'd placed all of my orders, restocked the thread fixture, and set up a display of bright floral cottons on a round fixture by the front door. Next to the fixture I moved a bust form. I cut two lengths of roughly six yards each and draped them over each shoulder of the form, cinching the fabric around the waist with a triple wrap of inch-wide yellow ribbon. I knotted it off and tied the ends in a big bow. Next to the form I placed a sign that said, *How does your garden grow? Summer florals, $9.99/yard.*

"That's a nice display," she said, and kissed me on the cheek. "But maybe if you actually sewed a dress out of the fabric, people would be more impressed. Who's going to drape fabric over themselves and tie it with a ribbon?"

I thought about the customer from earlier, who had purchased four yards of floral to use as a tablecloth. "That's not the point, Mom. Why do people need to start with the pattern? Why can't they fall in love with a fabric and just buy it and figure out what to do with it afterward?"

She held her hands up. "It's your store. You do what you want." She walked to the wrap stand and tucked her small handbag behind the counter. "Do I smell roast beef sandwiches?"

"Help yourself. I have to run an errand and I'll be right back."

I pulled my car around from the lot behind Material Girl to the curb in front of Charlie's Automotive. Charlie was on the floor, knees bent, running a dirty rag over a wrench. Black grime coated her palms. Not all that different from the sewing machine grease that ended up under my fingernails.

"Uncover anybody else's dirt today?" she said. "Or is that why you're here. Trying to make your quota?"

"Actually, I'm here for business. Can you squeeze in a secret oil change on a Ford Taurus this afternoon?" She raised her eyebrows. "My mom's helping out at the store."

"Tell her to bring it over in the next hour. There's something I have to do this afternoon and I won't be back until tomorrow."

"Anything I can help you with?"

"Nope. Solo mission." Despite our friendship, there was a wall between us that I didn't know how to scale. I wanted Charlie to open up to me, to trust me, but that wasn't something I could force.

"I'll send her over now," I said. Halfway out the door, Charlie called behind me.

"Yo, Polyester. Thanks for not asking a bunch of nosy questions."

"Sure."

"Keep an eye on Clark for me while I'm gone, would ya?"

"You got it."

Halliwell Industries was about two miles north of the heart of San Ladrón. The farther I drove, the more I felt like civilization was behind me. Ahead of me was a stretch of green land, and then a mountain range. The sign for Halliwell Industries sat off to the right-hand side of San Ladrón Avenue and marked off a large parking lot. There were several buildings attached to the lot, and Beth hadn't told me which one to enter. Before parking, I slowly drove around the perimeter and looked for something that would point me in the direction of the main offices where they held my check at the front desk.

No smarter after circling the lot twice, I parked next to a small brown Fiat and approached the buildings on foot. I followed the signs to the main office and approached the woman behind the desk.

"I'm Poly Monroe," I said. "Are you Beth?"

She nodded and held up a finger and pointed to the phone. I spotted a small earpiece next to her dangly earrings. Today they were lemon wedges that coordinated with her pale yellow dress and matching cardigan. She pressed a button on the phone and looked up at me.

"We spoke this morning about a check for my involvement in the pageant?"

Beth sniffled a few times. "Poly, I don't know how to tell you this. There's not going to be any pageant. Nolene Kelly cleaned out Mr. Halliwell's bank account and disappeared with all of his money!"

Eight

Beth sniffled again. "Nolene was the only one who had control over Mr. Halliwell's bank account. We all knew it. She came in this morning and said we were to continue planning the pageant as if nothing had happened. When she left for lunch, I noticed a bunch of suitcases in the back of her blue convertible. And when I tried to use Mr. Halliwell's account to pay the caterer, they said there was nothing left!"

"Try to calm down. There's a very good chance the police or the bank froze his account because he was murdered." I fought to keep my tone clinical, but no matter how many times I said the M word, it didn't get any easier.

"But the phones won't stop ringing. We were supposed to release the results of the preliminary screening exams to the pageant entrants tomorrow and I can't even find them. The newspaper has been holding space for us to announce the contestants. And if word gets out that there's no money for the pageant, the whole thing will fall apart. What am I going to do?"

"Don't answer the phone, don't send any e-mails. Don't try to pay anything."

"For how long?"

"I don't know." I thought for a second. If there was no pageant, there was no proposal and no money to pay off my first loan payment. But a canceled pageant would affect far more people than me. The businesses around San Ladrón. The hopes and dreams of the women who had wanted to compete. And the legacy of Mr. Harvey Halliwell, who had brought so much to the city.

"Beth, can you close Halliwell Industries early today? I don't think anybody would question it considering what happened to Mr. Halliwell."

"I could do that. There's only a few of us here, and I do have to get to a doctor's appointment."

"Cold?" I asked. I stepped back in case she was contagious.

"No. I have a condition." She sniffled again.

I took down her personal cell number and e-mail and promised to be in touch. I hung up the phone. There was a definite disconnect between what Nolene had told me and what everyone else said. It occurred to me that I knew as much about her as I did everything else connected to this pageant, which was not very much at all.

The door to the fabric store was held open with a vintage black iron sewing machine. Inside the store the lights were bright. My mother had rearranged the wall of quilting cottons by color. The top shelf was green; the second shelf yellow. The third and fourth shelves were bare, and colorful blue and pink bolts of fabric were scattered around her on the floor. The customer with the Chihuahua was back. She stood by the floral cottons again, this time unwrapping each bolt, letting the fabric fall from her fingers while she assessed the pattern, and then moving on to the next.

"She says she's just looking," my mom said. "You should go chat her up."

"I got this one. Why don't you take the Ford across the street for that oil change we talked about?"

"Okay, fine, but I'm prepared to let you boss me around if you need to."

"That won't be necessary. Go." I pointed at the door. My mom had the best of intentions but Charlie was waiting. I only hoped she wouldn't give my mother any ideas about doing her own transmission flushes.

I approached the woman with the Chihuahua. "Back so soon?" I said.

"I shouldn't even be in here. I was planning to visit the antiques shop next door. Your employee approached me before I entered and told me to come in."

"Did she badger you?" I asked, casting a wayward glance at the door.

"I wouldn't say badger, but she was persistent. This really is a cute shop. If I knew how to sew I'd spend a lot of money here."

"You can always learn," I said.

"I don't really need any more fabric right now. I should really be going," she said. She tugged on Archie's leash and they left. I followed her out front. She glanced at Lilly, who was arranging vintage umbrellas in a tall narrow vase in front of her shop, and then hurried in the other direction down the street.

"Hi, Lilly," I called out. "Just a heads-up, my mother—Helen—is going to be helping me out at the store over the next week or so."

"Oh? Business is that good?"

"It's not that. My time is going to be split. I'm involved

with the pageant and she's going to handle the day-to-day sales in the fabric store."

Her head snapped up. "You're working on the pageant? Does Violet know?"

"I don't know who knows. Why?"

"I can't believe that pageant keeps on going after what happened."

I stepped forward. "I admit, I was surprised, too. Did you know Mr. Halliwell?"

She picked up the metal umbrella stand and slammed it back down on the ground. "Harvey Halliwell was as much a part of the problem as anybody. To think how he profited from that dog-and-pony show. He deserved what he got, and now maybe somebody will shut that pageant down for good."

She stormed inside. The fabric shop was empty and there was no sign of anybody on the street. I followed Lilly inside her shop. "What did you mean by that?"

"That man profits from putting young women on a stage. Once a year his pageant turns our town into a big orange joke. Those young ladies should be thinking about graduating high school or entering college, not becoming a beauty queen and taking off for China to hang off a rich man's arm in photo opportunities. At least it's all over now."

"It's not over. The pageant is going to continue without Mr. Halliwell. In fact, Halliwell Industries considers the pageant to be his legacy."

She glared at me, her eyes narrowed into slits. "That can't be true," she said.

"It is. That's one of the reasons I need more help this week."

Lilly picked up a rag and turned her back on me. I stood there for a few seconds but finally said an awkward good-bye. I needed to find out what had happened to make the Garden sisters hate Harvey Halliwell as much as they did.

* * *

The afternoon was quiet. My mom returned at four, and I ran upstairs to the apartment to use the bathroom. When I came out, I saw the champagne dress on the chaise lounge. The throw blanket I'd tossed on top of it was on the floor, and curled up on top of the blanket were Pins and Needles, sleeping in a patch of sunlight. The dress reminded me once again of Vaughn, and, once again, I questioned whether we could get past our differences.

But then I thought about why Vaughn had been upset. His area of expertise was money, and on more than one occasion, when I'd had money problems or questions, I'd gone to someone else. Was he hurt by that? Did he think I didn't respect him?

I considered things from a different angle. Vaughn and I were still just getting to know each other. But if he had questions about fabric or about making a dress, I would like to think he'd come to me. How would I feel if he didn't? I didn't even have to finish the thought to know the answer. It seemed I owed him an apology.

I cued up his office number and stared at the screen for a few seconds before making the call. His secretary answered.

"Hello, I'd like to make an appointment with Mr. Vaughn McMichael," I said. "To discuss a private business matter."

She hesitated for a moment. "He has an opening tomorrow morning at eleven and tomorrow afternoon at three."

"Does he have any time today?"

"I can fit you in at four forty-five, but that doesn't give you much time," she said.

"I'll be there." I gave her my name and phone number and hung up. I knew as soon as Vaughn saw my name he'd think something was up. The sooner I arrived, the less time he'd have to cancel.

I pulled a blazer over my tank top and traded my jeans for a pair of trousers. Already the temperature had been hitting the eighties, but I knew if I wanted him to take me seriously, I had to take myself seriously. I stepped into low-heeled shoes, put pearl stud earrings in my pierced ears, and moved my wallet, keys, and money from my messenger bag to a small leather purse. I was back downstairs fifteen minutes later, and I had less than twenty to get to Vaughn's business and find a parking space.

"Mom? I have to run to the bank. It's a last-minute thing. You can handle things?"

"I think I can manage to not badger any more customers," she said with a smile. "Besides, I think you lost your window of sales to happy hour. I just watched four people go into the bar across the street."

I glanced outside. Duke was outside The Broadside with a tent sign on his lap. He rolled himself to a spot on the sidewalk and set up the sign, then rolled himself back into the bar.

"You can close and lock up at six. I'll be back as soon as I can." I kissed her on the cheek. "Thank you for helping me out today."

I made good time to Vaughn's office. McMichael Investments was only a couple of miles from the fabric store, almost a straight shot down San Ladrón Avenue. It was a two-story office building, beige siding with dark brown trim. The parking lot sat off to the side, only a handful of cars occupying the numerous spaces. Vaughn's car was parked next to his father's in the lot, the full size and the mini-me versions of silver BMWs. His father's plates said *MCM*; Vaughn's had the combination of letters and numbers that had been assigned to him by the State of California. The space next to Vaughn's was marked *Visitor*, so I pulled in, hoping he didn't have a view of the parking lot from his office. I'd at least like to make it inside before I was asked to leave.

I signed in with security and was directed to the second

floor. The lobby was quiet. I gave myself a pep talk as the elevator climbed. When the doors opened, Vaughn stood in front of them, arms crossed.

"Security called and said you were on your way up. What are you doing here?" he asked.

"I have an appointment." His face went blank. "With you."

"No you don't," he said.

"Ask your secretary," I challenged.

He turned around and walked down a blue-carpeted hallway. I followed, assuming this was the way to his office. He stopped by a woman in a blue sundress. "Do I have an appointment this afternoon?" he asked her.

"Yes, sir, with Poly Monroe."

"I'm Poly Monroe," I offered.

"Oh!" she stood. "Can I get you anything? Water, coffee, tea?"

"Poly doesn't need anything," he said. He turned back to me. "Do you?" he asked.

"Only my appointment."

"Follow me."

Vaughn led us past his secretary to a large room with floor-to-ceiling windows. Outside I could see the row of purple jacarandas spilling their blossoms onto the parking lot.

"Don't you think this is a little extreme?" he asked.

"I don't know what you're talking about. I have a financial matter to discuss, and I've heard you're good with money."

He stared at me. The sunlight from his windows picked up the gold flecks in his otherwise green eyes and highlighted strands of his light brown hair that had been bleached by the sun. I sat straight and pretended I was on a job interview. No jokes, no flirtation. Just business.

Vaughn stood up and walked past me, and, for a second, I thought he was going to open the door and ask me to leave. He didn't. He opened a small refrigerator and pulled out two bottles of water. He handed me one, set the other on his desk blotter, and pulled two cut-crystal glasses from a cabinet.

"Tell me about your financial matter."

"It's not my financial matter. It's Harvey Halliwell's financial matter."

"Harvey Halliwell isn't one of our clients."

"Harvey Halliwell isn't anybody's client anymore," I said, "but that didn't stop somebody from cleaning out his bank account today."

"What?" he asked, leaning forward with interest.

I relayed to Vaughn what I'd learned from Beth at Halliwell Industries. "I went to pick up my check and Harvey's secretary was hysterical. She said she tried to pay the caterer and was told there was no money in the account. She also saw Nolene with a car filled with suitcases, and apparently Nolene was the only person with access to Harvey's money."

"That doesn't sound good," he said.

"I know. So now it's not just a murder, but add to that a freaked-out staff and a very big pageant that draws national attention. You have hundreds of thousands of dollars of business revenue at stake, and the dreams and aspirations of women who were supposed to find out whether they were in contention to win the Miss Tangorli title and everything that went with it."

"What do you mean, 'supposed to find out'?"

"You know there's a pretty heavy screening process used for the competition, right? The results were in and the competitors were going to be published in tomorrow's paper."

"That's interesting timing," he said.

"That's what I thought, too."

Temporarily, the tension that had existed between Vaughn and me disappeared. I leaned forward to mirror his body language.

Vaughn stood. "Wait here," he said.

He left me alone in the office. I poured my water into the

glass and drank. It was refreshing on a hot day. I held the empty glass up against my forehead and closed my eyes. If it was this hot now, what would it be like in August when the high averaged in the nineties?

I stayed in Vaughn's office for the better part of an hour. Curiosity led me to inspect the diploma on the wall and the photos on his desk. When the door to Vaughn's office finally reopened, I turned around. Vaughn had returned, but he wasn't alone. This time he was followed by his father on one side and Sheriff Clark on the other.

Nine

"I'm sorry we took so long, Ms. Monroe," Vic McMichael said. "I understand you learned some information about Harvey Halliwell's estate. For the purposes of finding out who killed him, I asked Sheriff Clark to come here so we could discuss it together."

Clark wore his discomfort like a Halloween mask that pinched his nose. He took off his hat and stood by the side of the room. Mr. McMichael gestured to the glass table and chairs that sat in the corner of the room and Clark took a seat. Vaughn looked at me and tipped his head that direction, too. I moved from the chair opposite the desk to a chair at the table. Vaughn stood behind me and pushed my seat in. I blushed and looked up. Mr. McMichael watched his son but didn't say a word.

When we were all seated, Mr. McMichael spoke. "Sheriff Clark knows he has my full cooperation in the investigation of Harvey's murder. Harvey was my first business partner.

We parted ways early on, but that doesn't mean there was bad blood between us. On the contrary; I respected him immensely. He was a risk taker, a gambler, and a man who built an empire out of a trip to China and a transplanted tree."

"The Tangorli tree," I said.

"Yes. Harvey and I were at a point where we needed to either invest significant money into our business with no promise of return or dissolve. We disagreed on which direction to go and so, in the spirit of leaving it up to luck, we flipped a coin. I won. I bought out his shares and he took his money and moved to China. There was a lot of revenue coming from the Far East at the time, and the government was just starting to address the tariffs. Harvey lived in China for a few years and put his money in fruit. All of San Ladrón was built on the citrus trade, though most of the original citrus fields had been replaced by buildings, many of them mine. Harvey started with a small plot by San Ladrón Canyon. He'd brought seedlings from China and set about splicing them together to create the first Tangorli trees in the United States. That was in the seventies. When it became clear that they would thrive in our soil, he came to me for a loan."

"But that would mean you were a part owner—" I interjected.

Mr. McMichael held up a hand. "No. Harvey was adamant about that, and I agreed with him. We'd been in business together once. We viewed things differently. He didn't want a partner, silent or not. He had a very specific business plan that involved the purchase of twenty acres of land, equipment, and the costs of importing the seedlings. The Tangorli tree doesn't grow overnight, so the investment wouldn't pay off for at least ten years, if at all."

"That doesn't sound like a good business investment," Vaughn said.

"Sometimes you take risks for reasons other than financial," Mr. McMichael answered softly. "Harvey was a friend who understood my drive. In many ways he was like me. In some, he was the opposite. You learn to appreciate the people who think you're normal when the rest of the world thinks you're a monster."

I was silent. When I'd first arrived in San Ladrón, I was one of the people who thought of Mr. McMichael as a monster. He had been friends with my great-aunt and great-uncle, and the friendship had dissolved along the way. I knew part of that reason was Mr. McMichael's financial success and Uncle Marius's inability to accept the subsequent generosity offered to him. And when my aunt had been murdered in the fabric store, a lot of people suspected that Mr. McMichael had orchestrated the crime as a scare tactic to gain possession of the real estate.

"A few years ago, Harvey moved his financial accounts to our firm. He suspected that someone inside his organization was embezzling money. We drew up a short list of people who would have access to his accounts in the event he was unable to make decisions for himself. Vaughn was given strict instructions to come to me if anyone asked about Harvey's money. I doubt any of us thought that person would be you."

I had been concentrating so hard on what Mr. McMichael was saying that I hadn't stopped to think about what Sheriff Clark or Vaughn thought about me showing up and asking about Harvey Halliwell's money. I looked at Clark, and then at Vaughn. Vaughn smiled.

"I just came from Halliwell Industries. Nolene's secretary said all of the checks she wrote today bounced. She said someone at Halliwell Industries had cleaned out Harvey's accounts," I said.

"In a way, that's true. Per Harvey's instructions, after his death, the business account that his employees drew upon was moved to a private account and frozen."

"Per his instructions?" I asked. "If he left instructions in the event of his death, wouldn't that include a will and inheritors?"

"In most cases, yes, it would. The problem here is that Harvey has long suspected that something like this might happen. Harvey has no wife, no children. No family to inherit his fortune. His legacy is the pageant. His instructions were designed to help identify who would try to benefit from his murder."

"But, Dad, Harvey didn't bank with us," Vaughn said.

"His banking was his business, and he asked me to make it my business, so I did."

"But he'd be in the system. The kind of money you're talking about, he'd easily rank at the top of our privileged client list. I would know about it."

"We couldn't risk anybody finding out."

The room went silent. I felt Clark's eyes on me, but I didn't look at him. Vaughn studied something in a folder. I suspected he didn't like the fact that he'd been left out of something so important that pertained to the business, especially since his father was supposed to be prepping Vaughn to take over.

"So what does this mean for the pageant? Is it going to be canceled? And if so, who's going to make that decision?" I asked.

Mr. McMichael spoke. "The pageant will continue, and it appears as though Harvey and I will do business together again."

"Meaning what?" Vaughn asked.

"Harvey left terms to ensure the pageant goes on," Mr. McMichael said.

"How are you going to do that?" Vaughn asked. I looked back and forth between their faces like I was watching a tennis match.

"Harvey was very specific about the conditions of moving

his accounts to us." Mr. McMichael paused for a second. "It seems I'm about to inherit a beauty pageant."

I was pretty sure the emotion that crossed Mr. McMichael's face was fear.

When the meeting ended, Vaughn walked me to my car. "You didn't have to make an appointment with my secretary," he said. "You could have just called me."

"Not after how things ended this morning. You misunderstood me when I told you about the loan. You thought I didn't respect what you do for a living."

"Your business is your business," he said.

"Yes, but in this case, my business is also your business. As in, money. If you needed advice on fabric, I'd like to think you'd come to me."

"So you're saying I should cancel the appointment I made with the decorator for this evening?"

"You hired a decorator?"

"I'm kidding!" he said.

I pretended to be hurt, but I couldn't stifle the smile. "Okay, fine. We're even."

"We're nowhere close to being even," he said. This time his face was serious. "You went to my father for a loan. I'm not going to pretend he's not good with money, but I never thought in a million years you would have gone to him instead of me."

"You might want to check your facts before you decide to hold that against me. I didn't go to your father. I went to the bank. I met with an advisor and turned in my five-year plan. I deposited my Vanguard fund as my start-up cash and applied for a loan to float me through the first year. When the loan application was approved, your father was the cosigner."

"You didn't know?"

"I would have gone to another bank if I had."

Vaughn looked up at the sky and squinted at the sun.

After a few seconds he looked away, in the direction of the building, and then finally dropped his gaze to my hands. He took them in his and stepped closer. "Temporary truce?"

"We're nowhere close to being even," I said, and raised one eyebrow. "But that shouldn't stop you from trying to even the score."

"Is this how it's always going to be with you?"

"Maybe."

Sheriff Clark cleared his throat on the other side of Vaughn's car. We stepped apart and dropped hands. Clark tucked his chin and stifled a smile. "Sorry to interrupt," he said. "Poly, can I talk to you for a minute? Alone?"

"Sure." I said good-bye to Vaughn. He headed back inside and I turned to Clark. "I thought you took some kind of oath to always call me Ms. Monroe."

"When I'm conducting official police business, yes. You are Ms. Monroe."

"If this isn't official police business, then what would you call it?" I asked.

"I don't want to talk to you about Harvey Halliwell or the beauty pageant. I need to talk to you about Charlie. That man that's been hanging around her shop over the past few days, I don't trust him. But like I said, I'm not talking to you as a cop, I'm talking to you as a man. Is there something I should know about?"

Ten

"I don't know how much you know about Charlie's past, but I don't think it's my place to violate her privacy," I answered truthfully. "To be honest, it's hard to say what's going on with her. There's a good chance you know her better than I do."

"No. I know her differently than you do, but not better. She and I have spent some time together, but because of my job, I don't think she'll ever completely trust me. She considers you a friend. She trusts you."

"Sheriff, if you know Charlie well enough to say she trusts me, then you should have figured out the reason she does is that she knows I won't talk about her behind her back. I know you two have something—I still don't know what it is—but I don't think it's a good idea to put me in the middle of it."

"I'm worried about her. And because of this investigation, I can't be there for her the way I normally would want to. I'm not asking you to tell me anything I shouldn't know. Just keep an eye on her, would ya?" he asked.

It was the exact same thing Charlie had asked me to do about Clark. Regardless of what was going on with her, I recognized that she wasn't just thinking of herself.

"Sure," I said. I watched Clark walk away. So Charlie hadn't told Clark about the role Ned played in her life. Why? If she wanted to protect him, she'd tell Clark who Ned was to her. She'd give him a reason to look for other suspicious people in the murder investigation. But she wasn't doing any of those things. Was it because deep down, Charlie had questions herself, questions about Ned's arrival in San Ladrón?

By the time I got back to Material Girl, it was close to eight o'clock. I went directly upstairs to the apartment and found Needles sitting on the other side of the door as if waiting for me to come home. I scooped him up and scratched his orange ears. "Did you miss me?" I asked. He meowed and nuzzled his head backward into my hand.

I followed the scent of tomatoes and cabbage to the kitchen and found my mom stirring juices in the Crock-Pot. "I didn't know how long you would be. I made halupkies."

"Just like Aunt Millie used to make," I said. I lifted the lid to the Crock-Pot and smelled the tangy tomato sauce. Halupkies—or cabbage rolls as some people called them—had long been a family favorite. Ground beef and rice, seasoned with spices, wrapped in leaves of cabbage and slow-cooked with tomatoes and sliced kielbasa. I speared a piece of kielbasa with a toothpick and popped it into my mouth. My mom rolled her eyes. I pulled a white bowl from the cabinet and scooped out three cabbage rolls before she could admonish me for eating from the pot. She poured me a glass of wine and sat in the chair opposite me while I ate.

"I hope you don't mind, but I'm going to head back to Burbank. Your father said something about painting the living room and I don't think I can let that happen."

"But I thought you two were trading responsibilities for the week?"

"Poly, I can't let him decide what color to paint the living room! Can you imagine if he chooses the wrong shade of beige?"

"Yes, I'm sure civilization as we know it will come to a screeching halt."

"You inherited his sarcasm."

"And I inherited your good looks," I said. "Go. I'll be okay here. You were a big help today."

"I'll see what I can do about coming back later this week." She kissed me on the cheek and left.

I finished my bowl of halupkies, considered having more but decided against it. I stacked the dirty dishes in the sink and then went downstairs to the store.

I tallied the sales figures for the day and put away the bolts of fabric that had been left by the cutting station. The cats ran around the store, swatting small felt mice across the expanse of concrete floor like expert soccer players angling for a goal. I let them play and opened the front door to look at Charlie's Auto. The lights were out and there was no sign of life.

The opposite could be said for The Broadside. Neon signs advertising a variety of American beers lit the windows and colored the sidewalk. A group of men covered in dirt approached the door. The one in front was Xavier, the head landscaper who had designed the gardens at the Waverly House. Strains of music spilled out the front door when he opened the door. Duke didn't have any problem pulling customers into his bar. Maybe I should take a page from his playbook to capture the afternoon shoppers.

I found my phone and called Genevieve. "Any chance you're up for a night out?"

"Poly, the tea shop has been so busy since the Midnight in Paris party. I don't think I have the energy for much more than sitting on a bar stool."

"Perfect, because that's what I had in mind."

"You want to come here and sit on a bar stool with me?"

"No. I want the two of us to go to The Broadside."

"You know something? That's just about the only place I could see going in my current state."

"Perfect. Park behind the fabric shop and we'll walk over together."

I changed out of the suit I'd worn for my meeting with Vaughn and into a pair of jeans and a black V-neck sweater. When Genevieve's car pulled into the back parking lot, I tucked my phone and wallet into a small bag, met her downstairs, and we left.

Genevieve bubbled over with good news about Tea Totalers. I wouldn't admit it to her, but after her husband had been murdered, I'd worried about her future in San Ladrón. Like me, she was an outsider when she moved to the small town. But something beautiful had happened during her mourning phase. She had blossomed in a way that only women who find themselves newly single can do. It wasn't just the new cut and color of her curly blond hair, either. Her whole personality had expanded to match her curvaceous figure and the joie de vivre that now shone through in her laughter and her gaiety. It was infectious. People who had been little more than strangers six months ago had become regulars of her shop and she counted many of them among her friends.

"Poly, you wouldn't believe how great things are. This morning the line was out the door! I can't believe it. I really can't. It's like a dream come true."

"It isn't *like* a dream come true, it *is* a dream come true. It's *your* dream come true," I said.

She wrapped her arms around herself and tipped her head back. "It *is* my dream come true!" She pulled the door to The Broadside open and followed me inside. Laughter mingled with the occasional snap of billiard balls. I led the way to two vacant bar stools. The bartender, a muscle-bound man in a tight Harley-Davidson T-shirt and torn jeans, was busy filling a row of shot glasses with tequila for a man who looked like he'd spent the day playing rugby in a muddy field. Dirt was dried and caked on his shirt and jeans. In contrast, his hands were clean, as though they were the only body part to see a bar of soap all day. One by one the dirty man picked up a shot glass and a lemon and handed it to someone behind him in a similar state of grunge.

"This place is going to be out of control in an hour," said a voice from behind the bar.

I turned to look for the voice and saw nobody. "Down," said the voice. I looked down and saw Duke in his wheelchair.

"Sorry. It's dark in here and I wasn't thinking—"

"No worries. I get a lot of that. Makes it easy to sneak back here when I need to refill the pretzel jar in my office. Can I get you ladies something to drink?"

I glanced at the row of beers on tap, unsure how Duke would manage to tap them if we were to order one. Before I could work it all out in my head, Genevieve leaned forward. "Do you have anything bubbly back there?"

"You're the French girl, right?"

"I'm not really French. I'm just drawn that way." She giggled.

"You're cute. Poly, you should bring this one around more."

"I'll see what I can do."

Duke rolled his chair to a small wine cooler and pulled

out a bottle of champagne. "Hope you don't mind. It's made in California."

"So was I," she said without missing a beat.

Duke popped the bottle, the sound only temporarily piercing the low-level noise. He poured the contents into two wineglasses—I assumed he didn't have champagne coupes or flutes lying around—and handed one to each of us. A cheer went up from the dirty men, followed by the sound of shot glasses being slammed onto tables.

"Florists," he said with a shake of his head. "They come into town every year when this pageant takes place. Commandeer the greenhouse on Mr. Halliwell's property. Next thing you know, the whole town turns orange."

"Tangorli," I said.

"What?"

"It's not the color of orange, it's the color of Tangorli fruit. Right?"

"Between us, I don't know how anybody can tell the difference."

In the background, I heard a glass break. Duke excused himself and rolled out from behind the bar. I sipped at my champagne and relaxed for the first time in days.

"He sure knows how to throw a happy hour," Genevieve said.

"His only problem is that his current clientele is going to keep him from getting a new clientele."

"What do you mean?" she asked.

"Look around. Not counting us, what do you see?"

She spun her bar stool 180 degrees so she was facing the interior of the bar. "Lots and lots of men. Big men. Dirty men. Loud men." She spun herself back. "There's a lot of flannel in here," she added.

"If you wanted to go out for a drink, would you come here?"

"We *are* here."

"Without me."

"I'm not the type to go out to a bar drinking by myself. Neither are you. For women, drinking is social."

An idea tickled the back of my mind. "Genevieve, you're a genius. You know that?" I raised my glass to hers and clinked it. After taking a sip, I grabbed a couple of cocktail napkins and a pen and scribbled *fabric store—happy hour—craft project*. If I could build off what I saw in this room but draw in my target audience, I'd have something pretty unique!

Genevieve excused herself to the restroom and I scribbled more notes on my napkin. Duke returned. "You're not stealing my secrets, are you?"

"Only the good ones."

He called to the bartender and gestured for him to refill our glasses and pour one for himself.

"So, are you still going to judge the pageant?" I asked. "I know Nolene asked you to be a judge, but with Harvey Halliwell being murdered and all, I didn't know if you were going to stay involved."

"The pageant's still going to happen, I know that much," he said.

"I need a crash course in this beauty pageant," I said, my eyes still on him. "What can you tell me?"

"This pageant makes the women around here go crazy. I know one family who took out a second mortgage on their house so their daughter could compete. And you'd think somebody would have done something after what happened with Inez Platt, but it all just got brushed under the rug."

"Who's Inez Platt?"

"Former winner. You might have seen her picture on the side of the Tangorli juice cartons. She was a very pretty young lady: exotic features, dark eyes, long black hair. Her mother was from Trinidad and her father was from San Ladrón. She looked nothing like the women you see around here today."

"What happened to her?"

"I don't know the details, but there was an accident when she was out in the Tangorli fields. Some kind of acid exploded and scarred her face and her hands. Chemical burns that discolored her skin and changed her appearance."

"Did she sue?"

"I don't think so. She dropped out of the limelight after the accident. Harvey still uses her image on the side of his products, which is odd considering how many winners there have been over the years. If I were one of the more recent winners, I'd wonder why he wasn't updating his advertising. But since then, the entrance qualifications have gone through the roof and the judges have to sign a nondisclosure agreement. This pageant has gotten more exclusive than a country club."

"I don't get it. It's a beauty pageant, right? Women get judged by how they look—"

"Whoa, whoa, whoa, stop right there. I'm going to do you a big favor and advise you to never say that outside this bar."

"But it's a *beauty* pageant, right?"

"The winner gets a position on the board of directors at Halliwell Industries. That's enough to boost anybody's résumé. And before you say it's all about appearances, it's not."

"So even though Harvey was murdered, the show goes on."

"Yep. Nolene already called to make sure I was locked in. Me, Maria Lopez, and your boyfriend."

"He's not my boyfriend."

"He could be if you'd let him."

"Can we not talk about Vaughn McMichael for one second?"

"If that's how you want to play it, sure. So what did Nolene want from you?"

"Nothing really. I'm going to donate some fabric to the contestants and consult with them on their dresses for the opening ceremonies."

His brows pulled together. "They've never done anything like that before," he said. I shrugged, like being a pioneer on the pageant program was no big deal. "You better relax now, because come tomorrow, you won't know what hit you."

"Why's that?"

"The preliminary screening is complete and the list of the final twenty contestants is going to be published in tomorrow's paper. That's one of the reasons I'm trying to kick back tonight."

"You act like the town's going to go crazy."

"Pretty much. First, you get the contestants and their families. They're happy for about five minutes and then they go into either bribery mode or watchdog mode. This bar will be swimming in muffin baskets by the end of tomorrow."

I raised an eyebrow.

"I may have let it leak that I have a thing for Genevieve's French pastries," he said.

"I don't think it's her pastries you have a thing for."

He leaned back in his chair and folded his hands behind his head. "See, now, I don't have a problem agreeing with you. She is a pretty woman."

"Back to the pageant," I said.

"Sure, the pageant. There's the unspoken belief that the judging starts from the moment the list is announced. Those young women will be on their best behavior until Miss Tangorli is crowned."

"And you're really okay with all of this? Being asked to judge a woman based on her hairstyle and how well she walks with a book on her head?"

"You're not seeing the good that comes from it, Poly. The winner doesn't win because she can walk with a book balanced on top of a hundred-dollar hairstyle. She wins because she's articulate. Poised. A role model. She demonstrates an ability to talk to people from all walks of life. She's interested in bettering herself and she's interested in representing San Ladrón. And she wins because we choose her to represent our small town when she goes out there into the world and becomes a big success."

Duke was right; I didn't get it, but I was starting to. Twenty was an age when most young women were starting to think about how to transition from girl to adult. When this winner was crowned, she'd be afforded the kind of opportunities that were rare without strings being pulled. Her life would be changed forever and the citizens of San Ladrón could stand behind her proudly.

Genevieve returned from the restroom. "This place is crazy!" she said. "No offense, Duke, but you might want to think about something other than a can of Lysol and a bar of Dial in the ladies' room."

I smiled to myself. I had a feeling Duke would be at Bubble, Bubble, Toil, and Trouble, the local bath shop, before he opened his doors for business tomorrow.

The next morning, I woke early, fed the cats, and hopped on the Internet. After making an offer on several designer remnants and updating my spreadsheet with the store sales for the previous week, I spent a little time designing our next coupon, hopped onto Facebook and updated the store page, and jumped into a conversation on Yahoo about silk charmeuse. When the clock approached ten I left the computer and unlocked the front door.

Standing out front was a small crowd of women. Each one wore a badge that said "Miss Tangorli Contestant."

This whole pageant thing was about to get very, very real.

Eleven

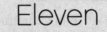

Nolene Kelly elbowed her way through the crowd until she was directly in front of me. She thrust a large wicker basket filled with citrus into my hand. "These are for you."

I leaned close and spoke directly in her ear. "Who are these people?"

"These are the contestants. I hope you're ready. Are you ready?"

"Why are they here?"

"We published the list of the twenty competitors at midnight. They were told to be here this morning. Are you ready?"

"Sure, but I thought there was a problem with the money."

"How'd you hear that?"

"Beth," I said.

Nolene pulled an envelope thick with cash from inside her folder and handed it to me. "Don't pay her any attention.

Here's your payment. Four thousand dollars, like we discussed."

"Cash?"

She waved her hand back and forth in front of me. "Easier than dealing with this bank situation. That's not a problem, is it?"

"No, I'll deposit it when I have a chance."

"Great. Take my packet, too." She thrust her envelope at me. "You'll need it to take roll call."

"Sure, yes, great." I scanned the room, which was quickly filling with energetic women in their early twenties.

"Don't worry, it's not that overwhelming. Every contestant gets the same packet. They probably memorized the rules last night. They all have a name badge that they are to wear every day between now and the event. Not identifying themselves is cause for disqualification."

"That seems kind of strict," I said.

"There's a big prize waiting for one of these young ladies. They will follow the rules. It wouldn't be fair to let them interact with the public like everyone else. They could gain favors with the judges, create a swell of public opinion for themselves or against a competitor. I want a clean competition, and this is the only way."

"I guess that makes sense."

"You bet it does. Now, the clock is ticking. I hope you ate a big breakfast. You're going to need your energy."

I checked my watch. I had about five minutes before the store was technically supposed to open. "Can you give me five minutes to make a phone call?" I asked.

I shut the door behind me and wondered exactly what I'd agreed to. I dialed home and willed my mom to answer. Instead I got my dad.

"Hi, Dad, is Mom busy?"

"She's hanging drywall in the basement. What's up?"

"Dad, I need help at the store today."

"I did the grocery shopping and the laundry yesterday. I'll be there as soon as I can."

"Dad—" I said, but he had already hung up. It seemed I was going to have to work within the confines of their role reversal.

The low-level buzz outside the shop grew, not unlike a swarm of bees growing closer and closer to the store. When I opened the door again, the crowd had doubled in size. Twenty contestants huddled close to Nolene. A group of onlookers had collected, residents who wanted first glimpse at the young ladies who would compete for the title of Miss Tangorli.

I ushered the contestants inside and answered as many of their questions as I could, until finally I gave up. I put my fingers in my mouth and whistled. The shrill sound pierced the hum of girlish excitement. When all eyes looked at me, I climbed up on top of the wrap stand and addressed the crowd.

"May I have your attention?" I said. I waved my arms around over my head and then clapped my hands twice. To the far left of the store, Nolene stood next to her makeshift table watching me.

The young women quieted and stared at me. I auditioned a couple of opening lines to my impromptu speech, but it seemed inappropriate to acknowledge that I didn't know what I was doing.

"First, congratulations to each of you. Being chosen to compete in the Miss Tangorli pageant is an honor."

"We weren't chosen. We qualified," said a blonde in a pink sweater and black cropped pants. On her shirt was a "Hello My Name Is" sticker that said "Tiffany" with a heart over the *i*.

Oops, she was right, and I knew that. "That's what I meant to say. Congratulations for qualifying. I know the exams are—" I saw a few expressions change. I glanced over at

Nolene. Very slowly she moved her head to the left and then to the right. "Let me be honest. I'm new to San Ladrón, and I don't know anything about the exams. What I do know is how to imagine a dress, and that's why you're here."

The expressions changed. I peeked at Nolene again and this time she nodded once. I continued. "My role is to consult with each of you as you sketch a dress that you'd like to wear for the opening and closing ceremonies. You will each get ten yards of the silk of your choice, and I'll have a seamstress turn your sketch and your fabric into your dress. I know—I imagine—you'll be busy with activities all week, so I suggest we start with your sketches as soon as possible. Once the cutting and sewing starts, you will schedule an appointment for when you'd like to come back for a fitting."

The young women buzzed among themselves. I scanned them collectively. Most fit the Gap ad profile: brightly colored shirt and neutral pants, or brightly colored pants with neutral shirt. Flat sandals. Hair in ponytails. They looked like young, clean-cut American women. It would be interesting to watch their transformation over the course of the week.

The front door opened and my dad walked in. I had never been so happy to see him in my life. I hopped down from the wrap stand and met up with him.

"Is this because of the pageant?" he asked.

"Yes."

"What can I do?"

I thrust the list of contestants at him. "Roll call."

I moved through the crowd and asked the young women to check in with my "assistant," John. They eagerly formed a crowd around him but quickly fell into a single-file line. I chalked their behavior up to the adrenaline rush they must have experienced from learning that they were the final twenty competitors.

While my dad checked off names, I carried a sketch pad

and a calendar to the register. Sheila, the redheaded hostess from the Waverly House, walked in and stood in the back of the line. She looked my way and I waved. I wanted to congratulate her but knew it would send a message of favoritism to the other contestants so I didn't.

It quickly became evident that I couldn't be open for business while working on pageant business. I wrote *Temporarily Closed for Private Event* on a piece of paper from the printer and taped it to the outside of the *Open* sign. I peeked across the street at Charlie's Auto. The shop was dark and a police car was parked in front.

There was no time to worry about Charlie for the rest of the day. It took an hour to check the contestants in. When they were done, they waited by the wall of silk and studied their color choices, and finally, each met with me for a fifteen-minute consultation. I answered as many questions as I could in the short window of time and made quick sketches of their initial thoughts. A few knew exactly what they wanted. Most were overwhelmed with the idea of designing a dress. I knew not to suggest ideas to them but instead advised them to take the night to think about what they wanted and come back to see me in the morning. The longer it took for them to decide what they wanted, the less time we'd have to make it happen.

Hours later, the group left. My dad tossed a clipboard with a list of crossed-off names onto the cutting table, and we both collapsed into chairs by the sewing machines.

"I can't do this by myself," I said. "Can you move in for the week?"

"I'm afraid not. Your mother surprised me with the oil change, but now she's mumbling something about replacing the fan belt on the Ford. I think I should be there in case something goes wrong."

I leaned forward, propped my elbows on my thighs, and held my head. My dad kissed the top of it. "I'm afraid you're going to be on your own tomorrow. Do you think you can handle it?"

"I'll do my best."

He went upstairs to use the bathroom and returned with Pins and Needles in his hands. He set the cats on the wrap stand. While they sniffed around for their bag of tuna treats, I walked him to the car. We said good-bye, and I went back inside.

The wall of silk looked like it had been mauled by a pack of wildebeests. I straightened the bolts, taking care to rewrap the fabric and secure the end with a small straight pin first.

When I was finished, I called Nolene. "It's done. Things got a little crazy for a while, but they turned out okay. Twenty contestants, twenty sketches, twenty fabric selections. I'm officially exhausted."

"Are you sure there were twenty? I only counted nineteen when we arrived at the store."

"Hold on," I said. I sandwiched the phone between my head and my shoulder and quickly counted the stack of sketches. "I have twenty."

"Good. That means the last one checked in."

"I bet it's a relief for you that this part is over. Now you can start your vacation."

"Vacation? Don't be silly. Who can go out of town at a time like this?"

"Beth told me your car was filled with luggage, and I just assumed you were going on a vacation."

"No vacation for me. Not for three years now, and especially not this year. She's right, though, my car was filled with luggage. I ordered a set on the Internet but the quality wasn't what I expected. I left the office early yesterday so I could get it boxed up and sent back for a refund. Now, enough about me. Go pour yourself a glass of wine and put your feet up. You'll have another day of it tomorrow. Check your e-mail for the details of your involvement and get me a signed copy of your agreement as soon as you can. If anything comes up along the way, we'll work it out. This is going to be great!"

She hung up and left me thinking about what she said about the luggage. It all made sense, except for one thing. Why would a woman who didn't take vacations need a new set of luggage?

Twelve

I took Nolene's suggestion and poured a glass of wine, but in lieu of a long shower, I filled the tub with water and bubble bath and soaked for close to an hour. The silence, after a day filled with the particular decibel level of twenty beauty pageant contestants let loose in the fabric store, was delightful. When I got out, I pulled on a thick silk nightgown and a matching duster, selected a book from the bookcase, and flopped on the sofa. I got through two chapters before I realized I hadn't registered a word from the last ten pages.

I had only been involved in the pageant for one day and already I saw what everyone had been talking about. Those young women had an energy about them. I'd heard about women who could light up a room, but that group could have lit an auditorium. The reality was, I was no match for them, and I wouldn't be by tomorrow morning. I needed backup.

Darn it, I needed my old boss, Giovanni. I found my phone and made the call.

"Poly, just the woman I wanted to talk to," he said in a jovial tone of voice. "How are things going in your lovely little fabric store?"

"Who is this and what have you done with Giovanni?" I asked.

He chuckled. "I trust you're getting along nicely. You always did have a mind for business. I heard about your involvement in the Miss Tangorli pageant."

Ding! Ding! Ding! Ding! Everything—his polite tone and his uncharacteristic compliments—suddenly made sense. In a flash, I realized our entire conversation could have a very different outcome to what I had originally expected.

"Didn't I tell you? Yes, I'm going to be working with the contestants. It'll be a nice boost of publicity for the store, don't you think? The winner is guaranteed to be photographed in a dress made with fabric from Material Girl. Isn't that great?"

"If you can pull it off, you'll see exceptional results. To the Nines made the dress for a Miss Tangorli winner back in the early days. Sales were up thirty percent for the next year."

I leaned back and put up my feet. "That's good information. I'll look forward to the additional revenue."

Giovanni cleared his throat. "Poly, have you thought about how you are going to have the dresses made?"

"It's not like I don't know how to sew," I said. I waited a few beats for him to suggest an alternative solution. He didn't. "I mean, that would be even more publicity, wouldn't it? The fabric and the craftsmanship from one store. It is a lot of work, though, and I'd probably be willing to share the credit . . ."

"Done."

"What?"

"You know what. My girls are at your disposal. We'll drive up tomorrow."

"Women, Giovanni, *women*." He grunted. "And what

exactly is it you're offering?" I asked. I suspected I knew, but in Giovanni's case, I also knew it was best to have him spell it out.

"Your fabric. My seamstresses. To the Nines will have the rights to produce the winning dress for the public. With a photo of the winner wearing her dress in our window, of course," he added.

"I'm not in a position to agree to that. What I will agree to is to give To the Nines credit for crafting the dresses. But won't you lose business by coming to San Ladrón?"

"Poly, my dear, do you remember when Inez Platt won the contest?"

"Inez Platt?" I'd heard that name before. "The woman whose face is on the side of the juice cartons?"

"Yes, that's her. She was a true beauty. That dark hair, those dark eyes, and her tan skin. She was like a native princess. When she won the Miss Tangorli pageant, the whole country sat up and took notice. She was a shoo-in to become Miss California and possibly even Miss America."

"For a dress shop owner, you seem to know a lot about her."

"She changed my life. She came to my shop and hired me to make her dresses. She came from a long line of migrant workers who eventually settled down in San Ladrón. In between helping the family, she studied. She was a true rags-to-riches story," he finished. His voice had grown soft, unlike the usual I'm-in-charge rasp and bark I was familiar with.

"So she won the pageant. What happened after that?"

"She asked me to make her dresses for the press trip to China. She had a sponsorship at that point. She could have walked into a store and paid retail for her wardrobe, but she didn't. She came back to me. She was photographed in every one of those outfits, and To the Nines got credit. That was the difference between me making it and closing my doors. Until that point I didn't know what direction to take the shop. Thanks to her, we became a destination for pageant dresses."

"Did she come back to you after she returned from China? When she went on to the other pageants?"

"She didn't come back. I heard she moved to China and worked as a public relations liaison for the man who ran the pageant. I don't know what became of her."

"She continued working for Harvey Halliwell?" I asked. I wondered if any other winners had gone on to find employment in one of his companies. And if so, what would become of them now that he was no longer alive? Had he established a contingency plan for his employees as he had for his money?

Giovanni and I hammered out the details of our joint project. He was to supply his talented staff of seamstresses and I was to supply the equipment. For the briefest moment I imagined Giovanni driving a truck filled with half a dozen women of Mexican, Polish, and Korean descent, all geared up for a road trip to San Ladrón. I wondered if he knew what he was in for.

It wasn't until after I hung up the phone that I realized I was ill-equipped to host a workroom of transplanted seamstresses. We'd be fine from the hours of ten until six, but there were small details like food and housing that I hadn't thought of. Giovanni might have expected to drive home tomorrow night much as my parents had done for the past two days, but I suspected the work would require more than an eight-hour day. For food, I could count on Genevieve. For lodging, I'd need a different favor.

I called the Waverly House and Sheila answered the phone. She was clearly stifling sobs. I asked for Adelaide Brooks and was placed on hold. When Sheila returned, she told me Adelaide was unavailable and asked to take a message.

"Sheila?" I asked. "This is Poly Monroe. Are you okay?" When she didn't answer, I continued. "You should be happy, not sad. Getting into the Miss Tangorli pageant is a very big deal."

She sniffled. "Please don't tell anybody about the pageant, Poly. If you do, I could lose my job."

"I don't see why Adelaide would fire you for participating in the pageant," I said.

"Poly, can you come here tonight? I did something really bad and I need to talk to someone."

"Sure," I said, sensing the distress in her voice. "I'll there in ten minutes."

I changed into a black cardigan and shirtdress and reapplied my lip gloss. The kitties, who had been given a chance to express their particular fondness for exploring the fabric shop, followed me back upstairs. I left the front door of the apartment open and went downstairs. Pins passed me halfway down the stairs.

"Slow down there, camper," I said. "Do I have to install speed bumps?"

Needles thumped his way down the stairs behind me. Paw, paw, jump. Paw, paw, jump. He made up for what his brother lacked in caution.

"That's more like it. A little decorum," I said. "Pins, why can't you be more like your brother?"

Needles reached the bottom step and took off across the floor. He pounced on Pins, wrapped his paws around Pins's gray neck, and flipped him over in a move that would make a pro wrestler proud. Low-level growls emanated from both of their throats.

"Boys," I said, and left them alone to play.

I left out the front. I wrapped my cardigan around my body and walked quickly down the street, picking up the pace between streetlights. On the way I passed an older couple whom I recognized as being members of San Ladrón's Senior Patrol. I nodded and smiled and kept going. If I gave them a reason to question what I was doing or where

I was going tonight, it could very easily turn into tomorrow's gossip.

I cut through the gas station parking lot by the corner of Bonita and San Ladrón Avenue, glanced across the street at the sheriff's mobile unit, and kept going. Within minutes, I was in front of the majestic Waverly House.

Having grown up in an area of Southern California that had blossomed during the tract housing boom in the fifties, I was continually impressed with the majesty of the Waverly House. The Victorian-house-turned-museum was two stories tall, topped with peaked gables, a round turret on the left corner, and at least two dozen windows that faced the street. The siding had been painted Wedgwood blue and the trim in white, like a vintage cameo. The lines of the roof had been trimmed for the garden party in tiny white twinkle lights that had yet to be removed. It gave the building a fairy-tale quality.

I walked down the sidewalk. Small tea light candles sat in glass jars alongside the edges of the path. When I reached the end, I climbed the three stairs leading to the porch that ran around the front and sides of the building. The wooden slats of the patio had been painted white to match the window casings and perfectly set off the porch swing and the wooden rocking chairs that sat to the left of the front entrance. I pulled the door open and let myself in.

Sheila stood behind a wooden lectern next to the restaurant. A brass lamp was attached to the fixture, curving around from the back and lighting the reservation book in front of her. Many restaurants had transitioned to computerized systems to track guests, but the Waverly House hadn't. I thought it was a good decision. The clicks and beeps that came with a computer would have ruined the Victorian ambiance that had been so meticulously maintained.

"Hi, Sheila," I said.

The pretty redhead wore her regular uniform of black dress and white pinafore trimmed in white lace. A white cap was pinned to the back of her head, setting off thick red sausage curls and framing her peaches-and-cream complexion. Traces of powder around her nose and eyes barely hid the redness left behind by her earlier tears. She fidgeted with her hands behind the lectern. She looked much like I'd seen her on every other trip I'd made to the Waverly House. What struck me was the one thing I didn't see.

I leaned in. "I don't know how the rules work, but aren't you supposed to be wearing your pageant name tag?" I asked. "I was told the contestants have to wear them constantly between the announcement and the pageant. I don't think Adelaide would want you to get disqualified."

She looked up at me and her eyes filled with water. A fat tear spilled down her cheek and she made no move to wipe it away. As it tracked its way down her cheek, she took a breath that hiccupped. "Poly, please don't say anything about the pageant to Adelaide or to anyone else. Please," she begged.

"Okay, but why? From what I understand, it's an honor to pass the entrance exams and be named a contestant. You should want people to know you've been selected."

This time she swiped her hand against her cheek to wipe away the tear. "But that's just the problem. I don't have a name tag because I'm not a contestant. I didn't pass the entrance exams!"

Thirteen

"You're not competing in the pageant? But you came to the fabric store today," I said.

"I didn't want anybody to know. I'm so embarrassed." She put both hands up to her face and her shoulders started to shake. I glanced into the restaurant and saw the bartender looking at us. I shrugged, like I wasn't sure what to do. He pointed to a vacant table for two off to the side.

I put my arm around Sheila's shoulders. "Let's sit down, okay?" I said.

"My shift isn't over."

"I'll take care of that."

I escorted her to the table and helped her into a chair. She remained hunched over. I took off my cardigan and draped it over her shoulders to hide her uniform. "I'll be right back," I said. I flagged down the bartender. "Sheila needs a break. Can you get one of the other waitresses to cover the front for a few minutes?"

He glanced out front. "The problem's already solved."

I followed his stare and saw Vaughn. He pointed at the lectern and gave me a thumbs-up. I returned the gesture and went back to Sheila.

Her tears had subsided while I was gone, and she'd turned stoic. She stared out the window into the blackness of the yard. I couldn't tell if she was aware of my presence or not.

"Sheila, why did you come to the fabric store today?"

"I heard the contestants were going to meet there."

"But you couldn't have checked in if your name wasn't on the list," I said.

"I thought maybe there was a mistake. When you didn't call my name, I knew I didn't get in, but by then you'd already noticed me. I was too embarrassed to tell you the truth, so I lied to the man who was checking off names. I pointed to the one badge left on the table and said that was me."

I thought back to when the young women had checked in. The energy level inside Material Girl had been high, as had the noise. My dad and I had done our best to maintain the pretense that we were organized and in charge, but Sheila could easily have waited until all of the names were called and then pretended to be the one who was last. Like me, my dad wouldn't have known who was who. Before I could ask who hadn't shown up to check in, Sheila continued.

"Mr. Halliwell was here at the Midnight in Paris party, and he told me he wanted to talk to me. I thought he was going to tell me that there'd been a mistake—but then I wasn't able to get away."

"How did you find out the truth?"

"A letter arrived today."

"Do you have it?"

Her eyes darted over to meet mine for a moment, and then she looked down. "No." She tugged on the edge of the table-cloth for a moment. "It's gone," she added.

A waitress dressed in the same attire as Sheila appeared

by our table. "Sheila, you have to get back out front. Adelaide asked where you went and Vaughn said he was covering for you while you went to the restroom. I don't want you to get into any more trouble."

Sheila unfolded the cloth napkin that held the silver utensils and used it to dab at her eyes. She balled the fabric up in her fist and pushed her chair back.

"I'll be right out," she said. When the waitress was out of earshot, Sheila turned back to me. "Please don't mention this to Adelaide. It's bad enough that some people know I entered the pageant. It's so humiliating." She passed my cardigan to me and walked back out front.

I watched Vaughn put his hand on her shoulder and say something to her. She looked up at him and smiled thankfully. My view was obstructed by the waitress, returning to the table.

"Is Sheila going to be okay?" the waitress asked.

"I don't know. Has she been upset all day?"

"She's been upset for a few days. Ever since she got that packet about the pageant on Friday."

"Friday? Are you sure?"

"Absolutely. It was the day before the garden party. To tell you the truth, I probably wouldn't have even noticed, except that she acted all weird. It was a document mailer, you know? At first she was excited, but then later in the afternoon, her whole mood changed. She put salt in the sugar canisters and set all the tables with shrimp forks. And then she started a real fire in the fireplace!"

"Is that so odd?"

"We don't burn wood in the summer because it gets too hot. Adelaide had the fireplaces cleaned out because of the garden party. We'll use the electric logs for ambiance until October. See?" She pointed to the wall behind me where the fireplace was. The illusion of a fire added to the atmosphere of the restaurant, but if the fire had been real, I would have been burning up because of my close proximity.

"What did Sheila do when you caught her by the fire?"

"She accused me of calling her crazy and she stormed off. I didn't see her again until the party on Saturday, and even then she kept disappearing."

So not only had Sheila known Harvey Halliwell was at the garden party, but now I knew she had disappeared throughout the night. What if she'd been lying about not knowing that she wasn't a contestant? What if there'd been something in the mail that arrived on Friday that told her she wasn't a finalist . . . and more importantly, told her why? If Harvey had been the one to disqualify Sheila, she might have been irrational. Harvey's body had been found in the gardens outside the Waverly House. With Sheila working here as an employee, had she orchestrated his presence and then killed him?

I thanked the waitress for her time and stood from the table. If Sheila was lying to me, I didn't think it would do me a lot of good to stick around watching her. I let myself out a side door and walked around the wraparound porch until I was in front of the front stairs. Vaughn sat on the porch swing. He kept one foot on the floor and slowly moved the swing back and forth.

"Join me?" he asked.

"Sure."

I sat down next to him and he kept the swing moving back and forth with the toe of his white Stan Smiths. I leaned back against the faded floral cushion and breathed in the scent of honeysuckle and jasmine and a few other flowers that had been planted for the garden party.

"What brings you to the Waverly House tonight?" He kept his voice light, but I sensed he was looking for more than small talk.

I closed my eyes and remembered why I was there. "I

called earlier to find out if there were any vacant rooms that I could book. My old boss is coming to San Ladrón tomorrow and he's bringing some of his seamstresses. I don't know if he planned on them staying over or if he thinks they're heading back for a day, but I wanted to make arrangements ahead of time so he couldn't spring a slumber party on me."

"And?"

"And I forgot to find out. Sheila was upset when she answered the phone. She asked if I could come over—she said she needed to talk to someone."

"Will she be okay?" he asked.

I liked that he didn't ask me to violate her confidence. "I don't know." I was quiet for a moment.

"This pageant makes a lot of people crazy. For the next couple of days, life as we know it will cease to exist. And then, on Sunday night, one of the contestants will be awarded the Miss Tangorli title." He looked up at the sky for a few seconds, then continued. "Monday will be quiet, and Tuesday, things will go back to normal. If we're lucky."

"Again with lucky. Why?"

He picked up my hand and traced along the palm side with his index finger. It tickled, but I didn't stop him. After a few seconds, he folded his hand over mine and rested it on the cushion between us. "Some people put more emphasis on this pageant than they should. Some lives have been changed forever."

"Violet's daughter," I said.

He nodded. "How much do you know about her?"

"Not much. Tiki Tom mentioned something yesterday morning, and both Violet and Lilly have no problem with Harvey Halliwell's murder."

"Harvey used to approach girls and encourage them to enter. One of those girls was only fourteen. He didn't know and she didn't tell him. That was Violet's daughter, Elizabeth. Violet thought Elizabeth would have a good chance if Harvey approached her himself, so she lied about her daughter's age to get her in. Somehow the press found out and exposed the story. Violet was judged to be an unfit mother and Elizabeth went to live with her dad. Harvey was in the hot seat for a while."

"How did the pageant recover?"

"Nolene stepped up with a very elaborate set of qualifications and stringent background checks designed to categorize applicants. It came very close to racial profiling. Not politically correct at all. Normally it would never have been voted past the board, but they pushed it through to divert attention from Harvey's indiscretion."

"So the background check and psych evaluations are a new thing. Who sees them? Who are the judges?"

"Halliwell Industries employs a fair number of professionals. There's a panel of experts who score the tests and advise him on anything that stands out on a profile. The experts' identities are kept secret for obvious reasons."

"Harvey feared retribution."

"It's not a stretch," Vaughn said. "He's faced more than one lawsuit over the pageant. One year someone torched a Tangorli field and ruined hundreds of thousands of dollars of crops. Another year someone cracked a pane of glass in his greenhouse and compromised years of research."

"But still, he kept up with the pageant."

"He always believed it did more good than harm."

I went silent, thinking about Sheila. She had shown up at the fabric store and pretended she was a contestant. Her reasoning had been that she thought there had been a mistake, but that story felt thin. If the other waitress was to be believed, she'd received upsetting news days ago. Were entrants contacted ahead of time to tell them if they wouldn't be competing? It was too much coincidence to think that Sheila's disturbing news didn't pertain to the pageant.

"Hey," Vaughn prompted. He squeezed my hand. "You still with me?"

"Yes, sorry. I was thinking about how much work there's going to be in the fabric store tomorrow."

"That reminds me, I have a surprise for you. Guaranteed to make your day better. But you have to wait until tomorrow morning to find out what it is."

"Then that's my cue to head home and get to sleep." I stood up and pulled Vaughn to his feet.

"I'll walk you home."

"I'll be fine."

"When are you going to accept that I just want to spend more time with you?"

I waited a few seconds, and then reached out for his hand. "I have an idea. Why don't you walk me home?"

"Sounds like a plan."

Vaughn's six-foot-plus height was a nice complement to my five-foot-nine stature, and we matched strides as we walked along Bonita. This time I didn't feel as though I had to pick up the pace between streetlamps. He kept my hand in his as we walked, and I didn't pull away. After we rounded the corner onto San Ladrón Avenue, I caught him looking at Charlie's shop across the street.

"Have you talked to my sister lately?" he asked.

"Yesterday. Why?"

"She's been avoiding me since the Midnight in Paris party. I think it has to do with that man we saw her with. I was hoping she'd confided in you."

"If she had, I wouldn't tell you," I said.

"And I respect that. But keep an eye on her, would you?"

"Sure, why not? I'm already keeping an eye on her for Sheriff Clark."

Vaughn stopped walking, even though we were still a few feet shy of the front door to Material Girl. "Sheriff Clark asked you to keep an eye on Charlie? Why? What does he suspect?"

So Vaughn *didn't* know the truth about Charlie and Clark.

"It's nothing like that. You know Clark. He feels like he's in charge of everybody in San Ladrón. Somebody acts a little different and all of a sudden, he has to start asking questions. Especially if there's a stranger involved."

I looked across the street. Charlie and the man with the white ponytail came out of her shop. "Come here," I said. I pulled Vaughn into the shadowy doorway to Tiki Tom's shop and put my arms around his neck.

"Hey, slow down," he said. He put his hands on my waist and leaned in to kiss me. I turned my head to the side and looked over his shoulder.

"There's that guy from the garden party," I said. Vaughn turned around. "This is the second time I saw him at her shop."

Charlie and the man hugged briefly. I pulled Vaughn closer to me in the shadows of Tiki Tom's storefront. The man got into her car and drove away. Charlie looked up and down the street, as if checking to see if she'd been spotted, and went back inside. A few seconds later, the lights went out.

Fourteen

The next morning I woke to kitty howling. Pins had migrated to my pillow sometime during the night and his fur was smushed into my cheek. Needles sat by the side of the bed meowing over and over like he hadn't been fed for a week. The clock read six thirty.

I turned off the kitty alarm by filling bowls with fresh food and water, emptied the litter box, and then showered and dressed in a black cotton boatneck and a pair of black capri pants. I slipped my feet into ballerina flats, swiped on tinted sunscreen, mascara, and lip gloss, and joined the kitties in the kitchen. While they circled around my ankles, sated by their meal of genuine animal by-products, I made a pot of Ceylon tea and heated up a frozen orange scone Genevieve had given me a few weeks ago. It wasn't nearly as good as a fresh one, but it was still better than anything you could buy in a grocery store.

I went downstairs to the fabric store around seven thirty.

After opening the register, I pulled the envelope of cash out from under the tray. There was a branch of my bank a few doors to the left of Material Girl, and if I hurried, I could make the deposit through the machine out front and be back before Giovanni showed up with a van filled with seamstresses. I pushed the bulging envelope into one pocket, pushed my ID and bank card into the other, and unlocked the front door. On the sidewalk in front of the gate stood a petite Asian woman with jet-black hair perfectly styled in a bouffant. She made a slight bow toward me.

"Good morning." She held a collapsible table under one arm and a sewing machine in the other. "Miss Polyester?" she asked. When I nodded, she replied, "I here for job."

"Are you with Giovanni?" I asked.

She looked to the left and to the right. "Who Giovanni? I here alone. For job."

"I think you might have the wrong store. I'm not hiring," I said. The fact that she was carrying a sewing machine made me think the confusion lay not with her location, but somehow with me.

"Mister Vaughn told me to come see you. He say you need seamstress for beauty pageant dresses."

"Yes, that's true. But it isn't a paying job. I'm afraid I can't hire you."

"Is okay. Mister Vaughn good customer. He say gold dress for you. Very pretty."

"You made the gold dress?" I asked. "My gold dress?"

"Your sketch very detailed. Easy to follow. Mister Vaughn knows I like making pretty things."

A car pulled up in front of Flowers in the Attic and Violet Garden got out of the passenger side. She held an assortment of wicker baskets. The top one overflowed with lace doilies, napkins, and place mats. The car pulled away from the curb and pulled around to the back. Violet looked at the woman with me, and then at me.

I stepped backward and held the door open. "Please come in, Ms. . . ." My voice trailed off while I waited for her to fill in the blank.

"Jun Wong." She crossed the threshold with steps dictated by both her short stature and her narrow skirt that matched her linen jacket. On her feet were round-toed pumps with sensible one-inch heels and thick leather soles. I didn't want to offend her by asking, but I suspected she had dressed for the opportunity of an interview.

"I have small dressmaking shop behind French tea café. I see what you do with fabrics for interior. Very pretty," she said, just as she'd said about my dress.

"Did you attend the Midnight in Paris party? I didn't see you there."

"Oh, I no party. I peek in windows at night. You know fabric," she said. She nodded as she said it, like I'd passed a test.

"My great-aunt and great-uncle used to own this store. In some ways I grew up here."

"Is good place for little girl. You learn important things. Like sewing."

"Where did you learn to sew?"

"In China. Many women learn sewing. It is good job. My grandmother learn first. I learn when I was ten."

"You started working when you were ten?" I asked with shock.

She laughed. "No. First job at thirteen. Until then I practice. I not get really good until I sixteen."

"And how do you know Vaughn?"

She paused when I said his name, and smiled a secret smile. "Mister Vaughn very good to me. He gave me loan to start my seamstress shop," she said. "But I getting older now. Not want to work as much. Loan paid back, but maybe time to retire soon." She looked around the store. "I set up now.

Store be busy soon." She set her sewing machine on the floor and unfolded the small table she had brought with her.

"You can use the sewing area that is already set up," I said.

"No, that for students. I bring my own supplies." She picked up her sewing machine and set it on top of the table. I watched her pull a power cord from a small cloth bag and connect it to the machine. Since she didn't seem to have brought a stool with her, too, I rolled a small cushioned chair from my desk to where she set up her workstation.

An air of determination surrounded Jun Wong. I recognized it from the attitude I'd seen so many times in the workroom at To the Nines back in Los Angeles. Sure, Giovanni was a cheapskate who would charge his own mother for a glass of tap water, but his employees were cut from a different kind of cloth. They took pride in what they did. Those ladies had adopted me when I took the job as senior concept designer, and they treated me with the same level of respect I gave them. Even though I'd just met Jun Wong, her presence was comforting.

Except that it thwarted my trip to the bank. I pulled the envelope from my pocket and put it back in the cash register.

"Jun, where did you park?"

"I no park. I walk."

"You carried your machine and table?"

"Table on wheels. Machine not heavy. I used to it." She set the top to her machine on the floor and unzipped the small bag that had hung over her shoulder. From inside she pulled a pincushion sewn onto a loop of elastic that she put on her wrist like a bracelet. She unpacked a seam ripper, two pair of scissors, and a yardstick, and then draped a tape measure around her neck.

"Have you had breakfast? Coffee? Tea?"

"Yes. I have nice breakfast before work." She patted her tiny stomach. "I eat well," she laughed. Her whole face lit up and her laughter rang through the store like charms on the bracelet Aunt Millie used to wear. For a split second, it was like my aunt was right there with us.

"You get ready for others. I okay by myself," she said.

"How do you know about the others?" I asked.

"I know more than you think," she said with a knowing smile. "About more than just fabric, too."

Before I could ask what she meant, there was a pounding on the back door. I crossed the room and unlocked it. Giovanni pushed past me. "You'd think you would have been ready for us," he said. "Where's the coffee? Where are the donuts?"

I ignored him and instead took the next several minutes to hug each of the ladies from the workroom at To the Nines. We shared a flurry of "Good to see you," "How've you been," and a couple "You wouldn't believe what Giovanni did last week." I ushered the six women inside and led them to the sewing stations.

"Ladies, this is Jun Wong. She's going to help with the dresses," I said. Giovanni stood by the front door, looking up and down the street.

"Mr. Giovanni was expecting food," one of the ladies said.

I excused myself while the ladies introduced themselves to Jun and chatted like giddy coeds who had been allowed out of their all-girls school for a mixer with boys. I joined Giovanni at the front door.

"Donuts or croissants?"

"Today, donuts."

"Coffee or tea?"

"Coffee."

"Can I trust you here while I go get it?"

"Don't insult me."

"Let me rephrase the question. The store is not open yet, but there is a chance that one or two or twenty young ladies who are pageant contestants will show up at any time. If I'm not here when they arrive, can you manage to keep things under control?"

He looked at his watch. "It'll take us about an hour to get the workstations set up. You get coffee and donuts and we'll be ready when the kids arrive." He pulled his wallet out of his pants and opened the billfold. What was this? Was Giovanni actually going to give me money for the donuts and coffee?

He peeled off a one-dollar bill. "Put this in the tip jar. Stores like that."

Cheapskate.

On a normal day, I would have walked the four blocks to Lopez Donuts, allowing internal negotiations to convince me that the walk would offset any baked goods I might eat once I arrived. Today I took my old yellow VW Bug. I knew I'd be too loaded down to make the walk back, and even though Maria or Big Joe would readily volunteer to help me, I didn't want to pull them away from their shop.

Business was better than it had been on Sunday, but they weren't breaking any records. Maria was behind the counter. I was third in line but the two people in front of me ordered a cruller and coffee each, so I advanced quickly.

"Hi, Maria, can I get three dozen glazed and two urns of coffee?"

"Now *that's* how you order in a donut shop," she said, looking at the man who was doctoring his coffee with half-and-half. "But I know you don't expect those pageant contestants to eat donuts. Whose army are these for?"

"My old boss's army." I told her about Giovanni bringing the workroom to San Ladrón to help me with the dresses.

"That sounds like a nice gesture. I thought you said that man was greedy?"

"You don't know Giovanni. He'll find a way to make this about him."

Maria went to the back to fill the pink boxes with donuts

fresh from the oven and returned a few minutes later. "Joe! Come out here and man the counter. I have to help Poly to her car," she said.

"I can handle it," I said.

"No you can't. I have to talk to you about something." She pulled the apron over her head and tossed it on the counter, grabbed a pink box, and pushed me ahead of her. When Joe came out to the front counter, he glared at me. I looked away and kept walking.

When we reached my car, Maria opened the door and got into the passenger side. She wrapped her arms around the pink bakery boxes on her lap. "Is everything okay?" I asked.

"No. I mean yes, probably. I mean, this is embarrassing."

I sat behind the wheel and started the engine. "What is it?"

"I'll tell you while you drive." She waited until I pulled away from the curb to continue. "I know you have a lot on your plate, and I wouldn't normally bring this up, but it's kind of important. And you're the only one who can help me."

"Maria, you're scaring me."

She sighed. "The last time I wore a formal dress was my wedding! That was"—she looked down at her body—"before the donut shop."

"A formal dress?"

"Nolene asked me to judge the pageant. That means I have to wear a formal gown. I don't have time to go gallivanting around San Ladrón trying on dresses like a lot of the other ladies around here. Between the cleaning business and the donut shop and the boys, it's a wonder my shoes match."

"Maria, you are one of the nicest people I've ever met, and your generosity made a huge difference to me when I first moved here. I'd be honored to make you a dress for the pageant."

"I don't want anything too fussy. I'm not a fussy type. And I can't handle a bunch of fittings, either. And nothing green. I heard nobody looks good in green. Oh, I shouldn't have asked."

"You *should* have asked and I'm glad you did. Come to the shop later today. We'll look at the fabric and you can pick out whatever you want."

"You pick out the fabric for me. Whatever you think will look good."

I waited for a car to pass before turning into the side street that led to my back parking lot. A small crowd had formed in front of the shop. Young women holding folders and sketch pads and portfolios that I assumed included drawings.

"Is that Charlie? Is she helping you, too?" Maria asked.

I hadn't expected to see Charlie that morning. She was with a tall, thin young woman with long, straight, brown hair. They crossed the street and stopped in front of Material Girl. The brunette said something to Charlie and then went inside. Like last night, Charlie looked up and down the street, then jogged back to her shop.

The plot thickened.

Fifteen

"Did you recognize that girl?" Maria asked as I made the turn and then turned into my parking lot.

"No, she's probably a customer."

Maria didn't look convinced. I parked next to the Dumpster and Maria got out and set the boxes on the passenger seat. "Do you want help carrying this inside?"

"No, I can take it from here. I'm afraid of what my boss is going to tell those young women. Especially since I've kept him waiting this long for his coffee."

I carried the two urns inside the store first and set them on the wrap stand. A group of contestants stood by the wall of silk. The seamstresses sat by their sewing machines, watching Giovanni, who had his arms crossed over his chest. He saw me with the coffee and came over.

"They won't listen to me. They say they've been instructed to talk to you only. I told them we could get started, but nobody made a move."

"There are three boxes of donuts in my car. Bring them inside and set up a station by the register. Until we're done with this, I doubt we'll have many customers, but if we do, offer them a donut."

"Wait a second. I'm not here to work for you. Your fabric store business is on your time."

"Do you want your donuts or not?" I said. He left out the back door.

I went to the front of the store where the young women stood. Yesterday, I'd been taken by the charge of enthusiasm that buzzed off them. Today, the giddy chitchat had been replaced with a solemn vibe. I imagined in the wake of their excitement over having made it this far, they realized they were competitors. A lot was at stake.

"Hello, ladies," I said. "We're lucky to have a talented staff of seamstresses with us today. I think the best thing to do is to get started. Why don't you form a line and I'll go over the sketches with you one by one?"

"But who goes first?" asked Tiffany. She wore a pink polo shirt, mint-green Bermuda shorts, and matching mint-green canvas sneakers. Already I sensed that she had appointed herself the fairness monitor.

"Alphabetically?" asked another.

"That's only good for you, Alison," I heard.

"Names in a bowl," I said quickly. I handed each contestant an index card and had her write her name on it. The folded cards went into an empty plastic bowl that I used for the cats' water when they were downstairs with me. I spun the papers around with my hand. As I called them out, the young women lined up. I'd expected someone to give me attitude, but I was pleasantly surprised. It seemed they each needed some direction and were eager to get started.

One by one I met with the contestants. While the tools they used to illustrate their concepts varied, they had all come prepared. One brought a computer with a stylus. When she turned on the power, her sketch was backlit. She seemed more eager to show off her technological skills than her interest in designing a dress, and twice I had to remind her that her consultation would last the same fifteen minutes as everyone else's. Another young woman held a piece of tracing paper that she'd used to copy the style of a dress she'd seen in a book on fairy tales. Most brought in a version of a sketch pad with an image drawn in the center. I was pleasantly surprised that they didn't all gravitate toward pink. For the three who did, we walked the wall of colors and found shades that worked for each of them.

After their consultation, each contestant carried her bolt of silk to Giovanni, who measured out her ten yards and took note of the color choice by her name in a master file. From Giovanni, the young women went to the seamstresses, who took measurements, studied the pictures, and started cutting patterns out of cheap muslin.

The plan was to break for lunch at one o'clock and return at two. I suspected Giovanni might not have arrived as early as he did if he'd known that was the plan, but judging from how he treated each contestant, I also suspected he kept his eyes on the prize of dressing the winner.

Many of the young women had packed lunches, but when given the offer of an hour of free time, they eagerly left the shop. Across the street and to the right, about half of the distance to Lopez Donuts, was a small area of covered tables and carefully cut lawn that would be perfect for an impromptu picnic. The young women walked to the edge of the block and crossed at the crosswalk, holding up traffic. Yet another way the pageant impacted the town.

Giovanni met me out front. "I don't suppose you made arrangements for our lunch, did you?"

I took the high road. "As a matter of fact, lunch is on me," I said. "Head up the street two blocks and turn in at Tea Totalers. I'll call Genevieve and tell her to expect you."

Giovanni raised an eyebrow. "You'll never turn a profit if you keep throwing money around like this," he said. He called to the ladies in the workroom and ordered them outside.

"Where's Jun?" I asked. "The lady who was here when you arrived?"

"She's inside. She said she brought her lunch. Do you want me to bring anything back for you?"

"I can handle my own lunch," I said.

I headed back inside and saw Jun picking at the contents of a plastic container with a pair of chopsticks.

"Jun, I'm treating for lunch at Tea Totalers. Do you want to go with the others?"

"I bring gyoza. Very yummy. Steamed dumplings. You like to try?"

"How did you steam them?"

"Over coffee burner. I bring pot and use water from sink. Tomorrow I bring enough for everybody."

"That's not necessary. I don't know if everybody will be here tomorrow."

"Then I bring for you. I bet you like."

"I bet I would." From the corner of my eye, I noticed a movement. When I turned, I saw the young woman who had been with Charlie standing on the steps that led to my apartment. I looked around for a moment and realized I hadn't seen her inside during the entire consultations.

"Hello?" I called. I walked over to the steps. "I haven't met you yet. I'm Poly Monroe."

"I'm Lucy."

"Are you a contestant?" She nodded. "But I didn't meet with you. Did you put your name in the bowl?"

"I got here after you started pulling names. It's okay. I don't mind going last."

It was a blatant lie, and I didn't know why she told it. I'd seen her enter the store when I was driving back from Lopez Donuts.

Lucy seemed skittish. I wanted to ask her about how she knew Charlie, or at least tell her I'd seen the two of them together, but I didn't want to spook her. She wore the name tag that the other young women wore, though considering she'd missed the check-in the previous day, I didn't know how she'd gotten it. In her hand, next to a bent manila folder, was the packet that I knew had been sent out to each of the young women who had made it through the screening process.

"What were you doing on the stairs this whole time?"

"Playing with the cat," she said. I looked down and saw Needles curled up on the stairs. He lifted his head off his paw and let out a polite little peep that was about half as loud as the one he'd bellowed that morning when he wanted food.

"Is there a Pins?"

"Yes, how'd you guess?"

"I read the tag on his collar."

"His tag says Needles."

"They're cats in a fabric store. I figured . . ." Her voice trailed off.

"You figured correctly." I bent down and scratched Needles's ears. His purr started up like a lawn mower engine. "Would you like to go over your sketch now? The rest of the contestants are going to be back by two and I think it would be best for you if you're caught up with them."

She followed me downstairs to the wrap stand and opened her worn manila folder. Inside was a piece of lined notebook paper with a drawing on it. It was a simple sketch that spent no time at all on the head, face, hands, or feet of the person wearing the dress. It showed a strapless dress, cut straight along the bustline, with a thin self belt. Instead of the full ballroom skirts that so many of the other young women had chosen for their dresses, Lucy's was a modest A-line style that fell to the floor. She'd colored it in with a shade of robin's-egg blue that I knew another one of the young women had already chosen.

"This is a beautiful dress," I said. "Where did you get the idea?" I had asked each young woman this question. Not because I suspected anyone of copying a design, but I thought it was important to understand their stylistic influences.

"Promise you won't laugh?"

"I promise."

"When I heard I had to design a dress, I went to the vintage store next door and saw pictures from an old newspaper. I have a pretty straight body so I thought this would look better on me than a sexy dress or a ball gown."

"Why would that make me laugh?"

She shrugged. "I know it's old-fashioned. That doesn't bother me, but I'll stick out like a sore thumb next to the others."

"Does *that* bother you?"

"No. Just the opportunity to spend time around others my age is great. At home, it's just me and my dad. He's the reason I'm here."

"Well, I think this is a beautiful dress and it'll look great on you. We will have to pick a different color because someone already selected the robin's-egg blue."

Her eyes darted toward the wall of fabric. "What about the one that looks green from one side and purple from the other?"

She was referring to a bolt of transfugitive silk. It was among the most beautiful that I had, only because the color changed so significantly based on how the light hit it. More than one of the contestants had grabbed at it when first given a chance to choose, only to put it back when they saw the way the color morphed under light.

"Are you sure you'd want that?" I asked.

"I think it's pretty," she said.

Not only was it pretty, but it would suit her perfectly. Her coloring was darker than some of the other young women, which gave her skin a natural glow that didn't require sun.

She had deep brown eyes and long, straight, dark brown hair, like an exotic princess in a Disney movie. It wouldn't matter what kind of light was used at the pageant. Both the shimmery olive and the iridescent purple of the fabric would complement her complexion.

"I'd like to see the sketch that inspired you. Jun, can you take Lucy's measurements while I pop next door?" I asked. Behind us, Jun looked up and nodded once.

I left the two of them and went to Flowers in the Attic. Lilly was behind the counter.

"Hi, Lilly, there was a young woman in here, long, straight brown hair, big brown eyes. She was looking at some pages from an old newspaper. Do you know where that might be?"

"Booth fifteen. I'll show you." She came out from behind the counter and led me past a display of vintage Bob's Big Boy collectibles on the left and a small vignette laid out with white leather gloves, a beige mink wrap, and an assortment of pillbox hats on stands to the right. To the rear of the store, we came upon a wire stand that displayed vintage rhinestone brooches and antique cuff links. On top of the case was a floral tray with newspaper clippings that had been preserved in clear plastic sleeves.

"Who was she?" Lilly asked.

"One of the contestants."

"Funny. I've never seen her around San Ladrón."

"I'm sure if she wasn't qualified, she wouldn't have the appropriate paperwork. From what I hear, the selection committee is very cautious because of some trouble in the past."

"Are you referring to my niece?" she asked.

I set the magazine pages down and put my hand on Lilly's arm. "Have you or Violet ever talked to anybody about Elizabeth leaving?" I asked gently. It worried me to think that either one of them had bottled up their emotions, letting them bubble to the surface once a year—or worse, creating a pressure cooker that threatened to explode.

"What good is talking going to do?"

"It might help you find an outlet for your anger."

"Violet finally found an outlet for her emotions and I don't blame her. It took her long enough but she finally did what she had to do to put this nightmare behind her."

Sixteen

Lilly's words sent a chill through me. "What did she do?"
I asked.

"Something she should have done a long time ago. Don't
underestimate the lengths a parent will go to for her children, even after her children have left." She wrote up a sales
slip, checked the tax on the calculator, and counted out my
money. I was short three cents so I took back all of the
change and gave her Giovanni's dollar bill.

"She must have taken it very hard when her daughter left.
I've heard people say there's a lot of pressure on these young
women. Does Violet blame herself?"

"Everybody knows there's only one person to blame for
what happened to Elizabeth."

"That must be why it's so hard for Violet. She's not willing to see the role she played in driving her daughter away.
And she can't get the forgiveness she so desperately needs
because Elizabeth cut all ties with her."

Lilly cut me off. "I'm not talking about Violet, I'm talking about Harvey Halliwell. He controlled every aspect of that pageant. Violet held her tongue for far too long. I'm just glad she had a chance to settle things over the weekend."

"She confronted Harvey on Saturday? At the Waverly House party?"

Lilly carefully rolled the magazine page and slid it into a small cardboard tube. "They had a meeting on Sunday morning."

"About what?"

"I believe that's none of your business," Lilly said. She held out the tube but pulled it away from me when I reached for it. "This is a painful time of year for Violet, and I'll not have you slander her. If I find out you're bringing up old wounds because you want to play detective, I'll be sure to expose what I know about the young woman Charlie brought to your shop today."

"Lucy? What do you know about her?"

"You're not the only one who keeps an eye on the neighbors," she said with a huff.

I took the cardboard tube and left Flowers in the Attic. Lucy was consulting with Jun, and I had about twenty minutes left before the young women were scheduled to return. Once the sewing machines started buzzing, there would be no time for breaks. A life-altering opportunity hung in the balance, and it was up to me to make sure each one of the young ladies in my shop got the attention she deserved.

Which meant I was going to need to find out what was going on with Charlie first.

I crossed the street and went into Charlie's Auto. Today, Van Halen had been replaced with Metallica. Charlie was under a car. The bottom half of her jutted out in a display of dirty blue coveralls and heavy black boots—even though it was summer. For all I knew, she wore her boots with her pajamas.

I squatted down next to her legs and put my hands up to

either side of my mouth. "Hey, you under there. It's Poly. Got a minute?"

"Not really," she said. "What's up?"

"I need to talk to you about Lucy."

Her legs bent and she stepped her feet along the concrete until she'd pulled herself out from under the car.

"I thought you weren't going to ask a bunch of annoying questions."

"Well, guess what? Surprise. I can't help myself."

"Fine," she said. "I know you won't go away until I tell you everything." She looked down at her hands. They were black with grease. "Wait for me in my office."

Within a few minutes, Charlie and I were sitting face to face in her office. She leaned back in her chair and gave me a direct stare. I recognized it as an act of intimidation that worked on a lot of other people in town, the people who tried to worm their way into Charlie's business. This time, Charlie's business overlapped with my business, and, aside from the fact that she was my friend, I needed to know what was going on. So, to keep things even, I stared back. After a few seconds, she smiled and tipped her chin down.

"You're a quick study, I'll give you that. What you need to know about Lucy? And this stays between us, got it?"

"It's not anything illegal, is it?"

She rolled her eyes. "If I were doing something illegal, Clark would be on me like white on rice. You think I don't know he's been watching me?"

"He's worried about you."

"He has bigger things to worry about." She chewed her lower lip for a second, took a drink from the mug on her desk, and looked at me again. "I don't know what I was thinking, getting involved with the town sheriff."

"You like danger?" I said.

"Clark's a pussycat."

"Okay, how about this: maybe after all the time you spent

running, you like the idea that there's somebody who could look after you? And not just because he wants to, but because it's part of his job?"

"You're skating on thin ice, Polyester." She turned away from me and jiggled the mouse to the computer but didn't do much more than stare at her screen. "Of course, I could say the same thing about you and Vaughn. You didn't have much money growing up and now you're dating a rich kid."

"It's not the same at all. I don't need somebody to pay my bills," I said. A touch of defiance had crept into my voice.

"And I don't need someone to make sure I get home safe at night. Doesn't change the fact that we're both drawn to the unfamiliar."

Behind Charlie, I saw the pageant contestants returning to the fabric shop. If the black-and-white cat clock that hung on the wall was right, I had three minutes left, not nearly enough time to finish our conversation.

"I don't have time to get into this right now. I have to get back to Material Girl." I stood abruptly and knocked the chair back a few feet. Charlie stayed seated and watched me leave. Traffic was steady enough that I had to hike to the intersection and wait for the signal to change. Charlie called out to me while I waited.

The light changed. "Yo, Polyester—don't you want to know why I sponsored Lucy to enter the pageant?"

I stepped back on the curb. "I thought only family could sponsor a contestant?"

"You thought right. Lucy is my sister."

Seventeen

Under any other circumstances, I would have canceled where I was going and gone back inside with Charlie to get the story. Today, I couldn't. Across the street the twenty contestants were filing into Material Girl. There was no way I was leaving my business in the hands of Giovanni.

"We need to talk about this. I'll come to your shop tonight. Don't make plans," I said.

"I already have plans. Don't expect me to be alone when you show up."

The walk signal changed to a countdown. I withheld the reaction Charlie had no doubt wanted and jogged across the street before the light changed again.

Giovanni met me at the door. "You didn't learn about long lunches from me," he said.

"Get out of my way."

The afternoon activities were simple. The seamstresses

mocked up versions of the dresses from the muslin and checked the fit. Once that step was complete, the contestant was free to go—if she wanted. The seamstresses would continue to work until Giovanni called it a day. Depending on how far we got, I'd have to call in my ace in the hole and get rooms at the Waverly House. I had a feeling we were going to need them.

After working things out with Adelaide, I leaned backward and spun the phone around, then started to dial again. I stopped before I finished and turned to Giovanni. "A little privacy, please?"

"Does this have to do with the pageant?"

"It has to do with business," I said. "What did you do at To the Nines while we were all working?"

"You'd be surprised." He walked to the wall of silk and rearranged a couple of colors.

I called the number. Beth Fields answered. "How's everything going today?" she asked.

"It's great. The girls are working with the seamstresses now."

"They're young ladies, not girls."

"I'm sorry. Nolene told me that but I keep forgetting. I didn't mean anything derogatory—"

"I know," she said. "It comes down from our legal department. We can't stop what the public says, but everybody attached to the pagent is to only refer to them as 'young women,' 'young ladies,' or 'contestants.' We don't want anybody saying that there's an impropriety attached to the competition."

I thought back to the first time Nolene had corrected me, and the story I'd heard about Violet's daughter. "I'll make more of an effort. I think we're going to be working well into tomorrow, so I made arrangements for the seamstresses to stay over at the Waverly House."

"That's a good idea. Send me the bill and we'll reimburse you. Or do you want a cashier's check? I can leave it with the security guard and you can pick it up tonight. How's that?"

"There's a security guard at Halliwell Industries? Until what time?"

"We keep a guard around the clock."

"Does anybody else work late?"

"Until the pageant is over, Nolene will be here most nights. The crew setting up for the pageant has been putting in extra hours, and there are a couple of people in the labs and the greenhouses, too. The rest of the offices empty out at six, six thirty. Why?"

"No reason," I lied.

"I'll leave the money at the security desk. You can pick it up any time."

I thanked Beth, and hung up.

The rest of the afternoon was a blur of colored silk, thread, and an assortment of languages. Most of Giovanni's seamstresses spoke English as their second language, and in the interest of making sure the dresses were exactly what each contestant wanted, there was a lot of overcommunication. By the time six o'clock rolled around, I was sure everyone in the workroom had picked up a few new words, whether they were Russian, Chinese, Korean, or Mexican. Giovanni, of course had defaulted to his usual Italian repertoire of "*Basta!*" and "*Piu veloce!*" which we'd all come to learn he used for "done" or "speed it up."

Even though I'd barely moved during the course of the day, by the time the young women left, I was exhausted and needed a shower. I wanted to get back to Charlie's to find out more about her relationship with Lucy, and I was more than a little curious about my trip to Halliwell Industries.

I scanned the workstation. The seamstresses showed no signs of stopping. "Quitting time is usually five o'clock. How long are they going to keep working?" I asked Giovanni.

"As long as it takes."

"I made arrangements for them to stay overnight at the

Waverly House. You can have dinner there, too. The whole thing's being paid for by the pageant, so you don't need to worry about the expense."

"They can knock these dresses out by"—he looked at his watch—"ten o'clock tonight."

"This isn't *Project Runway*. Someone could win or lose based on her dress. I don't want the women to spread themselves too thin and make a mistake that ends up costing someone the crown. The muslins are complete, and the young women have had their first fitting. They're not due back until noon tomorrow. We have all morning to get the dresses sewn. Why not let them enjoy themselves for an evening?"

"What's to enjoy?"

I looked back at the ladies in the workroom. Jun was comparing notes with Eiko, a Korean lady. They were about the same height—less than five feet tall—and were laughing like long-lost friends. Another lady pulled several plastic containers of candy out of her tote bag and passed them around. This wasn't just a job for them, this was a mini-vacation. A break from the workroom where they usually spent their Monday through Friday, a break from the families they tended to when they went home, a break from the cheap fabrics Giovanni expected them to use, and a break from the repetition of producing the same gown in a range of sizes.

"They seem so happy. What did you tell them before they came here?" I asked.

Giovanni grumbled something.

"Excuse me?"

"I told them we were coming to work with you for a few days." I couldn't have suppressed my smile if he'd paid me. "You don't have to be so happy about it," he said.

I left Giovanni with the women and went upstairs to freshen up. Throughout the course of the day, the seamstresses had come upstairs to use the powder room. I hadn't known it at the time, but many had left small presents for me. I found a container of freshly baked cookies on the kitchen counter and a Tupperware bowl of fresh tamales in the fridge. A jar of sun tea sat on the windowsill next to the Spritzdekor pitchers my aunt and uncle had collected in the thirties. And dear, sweet Eiko, who knew my real weakness, had brought a box of cream puffs from Beard Papa's. Good thing I'd already worn the champagne dress. When I finished eating their presents, it would never fit.

The dress had been hung on the valet stand next to the closet—I probably had my mom to thank for that. I ran my fingers over the delicate beadwork on the shoulders. I finally knew its history. Vaughn had taken my sketch to Jun to have the dress made.

"Mister Vaughn say you look very beautiful in the dress," said Jun. I hadn't heard her approach.

"You did a wonderful job interpreting my sketch. But how did you know it would fit me?"

"I watch you when you first come to San Ladrón. I like fabric and want to see inside of shop. When I see you, I understand Mister Vaughn's description."

I refused to take the bait. I remembered the woman who had been in Material Girl earlier in the week. "Do you have a lot of regular customers?"

"Ladies in San Ladrón bring me fabric to make dresses for their families. I happy you have pretty fabrics. I send many ladies to you."

"Did you send a woman and her little dog to me?

"Yes. Your shop good excuse for me to get her here."

An idea came to me, much like the idea of a happy hour that I'd had at Duke's. "Jun, earlier you said you might want to retire soon. If you did, would you consider coming here one day a week and being available for walk-in projects? I'd pay you, of course. I could advertise your services to people who didn't want to learn to sew themselves, and you could have your own space here so you wouldn't have to carry your table and sewing machine back and forth."

Jun smiled. "The ladies with the loud man say you will be nice to me. I like idea. I think about it."

"Thank you."

While Jun took her turn in the bathroom, I hunted through the apartment for the cats. I found them curled up on shelves in the hall closet. Pins was on the third shelf up and Needles was one above him. How they'd gotten to where they were, I'd never know.

After escorting Giovanni and company to the Waverly House, I showered and changed into a black hooded tunic, leggings, and black-and-white checkered sneakers. I hopped in my car and drove to Halliwell Industries. It was after eight. The sun was dropping and the temperature went with it. I was happy for the warmth of my hoodie. This time the lot was more empty than full. Most of the cars were parked by the edge of the lot closest to the path that led to the buildings. I eased into a vacant space.

A sidewalk ran down the center of the complex, with a building in front of me and one on either side. What I could see of each building's foyer was dark. If there was a security officer somewhere on the premises, he wasn't exactly visible. But it didn't make sense. Why would Beth have told me that it was fine to come tonight if it wasn't?

I stepped off the main path and crossed over the grass to the right of the building in front of me. In the distance, I spotted a greenhouse, and behind it were rows of orange chairs lined up facing a small platform stage. As I neared it, I noticed strands of white lights strung above the chairs in row after row. When plugged in, they would provide ample illumination for the pageant.

In contrast to the dark buildings, light spilled out of the glass panels that made up the greenhouse. As I grew closer, I saw the shadowy silhouette of a woman inside, moving along the length of the interior. She noticed me at the same time. She walked to the door and threw it open, and faced me, holding a large silver machete in her fist.

Eighteen

"Who are you?" she demanded. She wore a white surgical mask, and her words came out muffled. "What do you want?"

Moisture seeped out of the greenhouse. Combined with the drop in temperature, it left me feeling cold and sticky. I rubbed my hands over my arms to try to warm up. I was too close to turn around but too unsure of my situation to advance forward.

"I'm Poly Monroe. Beth Fields told me the security officer was holding money for me, but I don't know which building I'm supposed to go to."

The woman stood still for a few seconds, then turned away and set the machete on the edge of a wooden table in the middle of the greenhouse. She waved me forward. "It's gotten cold outside and I can't keep this door open for long."

I stepped into the greenhouse and she shut the door behind me. She reached up to her face and pulled the surgical mask down so it dangled around her neck.

"I'm Inez Platt," she said. "I work with the plants."

Giovanni had described Inez from when she was Miss Tangorli, and, aside from a series of scars on her cheeks, her beauty had not diminished with age. Her thick black hair was secured in a low ponytail and wide brown eyes were framed with long lashes and expertly shaped brows. She had an oval face with high cheekbones.

But the scars would have been hard to hide. A series of hash marks ran down the side of her cheeks. I didn't want to stare, but I couldn't imagine what had happened to leave the odd pattern burned into her flesh.

Inez walked in front of me toward a row of trees. She indicated the greenery that filled the interior of the greenhouse. "You haven't heard of me, have you?" she said.

"Only a little. I recognize your name, but to be fair, I'm not from San Ladrón. I've only moved here recently, and I've never seen you before."

"If you plan to spend any time in San Ladrón over the next week, you'll hear about me." She ran her fingers over the hash marks on her face, as if she needed to feel the scars to remind herself they were there.

"What happened?" I asked.

"An explosion at one of the factories in China. It was a publicity trip. Harvey and I were supposed to both be in the field but he asked me to stop off at the greenhouse to check on the plants. It was hot that day. The sun was so very bright. It was a freak thing, really. The scientists who had been working had left out a vat of acid to use to clean the grafting equipment. Nobody realized the heat lamps in the greenhouse were aimed at the acid. When I picked up a basket of Tangorli, the vat tipped and spilled on me. The acid ate through my skin and left me—like this."

"But the marks—they're like an imprint—"

"It was the texture of the towel I used to blot my skin.

The acid burned away my flesh. The grid from the weave left an impression on my face."

I winced as she told me the story, imagining the sensation of the acid eating through her skin.

"I was rushed to a hospital, but it was too late. They were able to do a few skin grafts to minimize the scarring, but we all knew I'd never have the face I had when I won the pageant."

"Were you angry?"

"At first I was—very. But imagine the irony. I wouldn't have been in that field if not for my face, and being in that field at that moment was what destroyed my face. It was almost poetic. I knew I had a chance to take my position and teach people that beauty is more than skin deep, which was why I entered the pageant in the first place. There was an insurance settlement, which I used for my education. I studied genetics and fruit splicing and Mr. Halliwell gave me a job in his laboratory."

"Do people know you work here?" At her confused expression, I clarified my question. "The pageant contestants? The media? Your story is so special."

"People know. The last time the media paid attention, they wrote a whole article about me. Do you want to know the title? 'The Tragedy of Inez Platt.'"

"Tragedy? But because of the contest, you became a botanist and now you work for the very company that sponsored the pageant. I would think you'd be an inspiration."

"People see different things when they look at me. I wanted to be an inspiration to women. I wanted to make a difference. Now I make my difference from behind the scenes."

I glanced down at Inez's hands. The scarring had marred the flesh on her hands as well as her face. A discoloration of pigmentation snaked up over her fingers, as if she'd dipped them in paint. She balled her fists up and stuffed them into the pockets of her lab coat.

"It took a long time, but I understand why people treat me the way they do. It's one of the reasons I work in the greenhouse. I'm one of the truly lucky people. I'm surrounded by natural beauty every day, and the trees don't mind that I have a few scars."

She walked to the wall and flipped a switch. I heard a series of sounds, like metal against metal, followed by the flush of water. Within seconds, a light mist filled the air.

"I hope you don't mind the moisture," she said. "It's warm in here, but the plants require water almost constantly."

"As long as it's warm, I'm okay," I said, remembering the chill to the air earlier.

While she tinkered around, adjusting the nozzles on the misters, I wandered the perimeter of the greenhouse. She was right; it was like a jungle. The dry chill from outside had been replaced by a tropical climate. Coupled with the view of the lush green trees that lined the walls of the greenhouse and the plants that hung from bamboo rods suspended across the interior, I felt like I'd left San Ladrón and arrived in South America.

"I don't want to disturb your work. It's getting late and you probably want to finish what you're doing and get home."

She laughed. "This is my home." When she saw my shocked expression, she laughed again. "I don't mean that I live here, I mean that working with these plants has become my life."

"How long have you been working here?"

"For Harvey? Since the accident." She gestured toward her face. "I know what you must think. Why would I want to work for the man who basically disfigured me?"

"I wasn't thinking that at all," I said.

"Why shouldn't you? Everybody else does. When I do head into town, I hear them. It gets worse during pageant time, so I mostly stay here. My name comes up in conversation, or in the occasional 'Where are they now?' feature in the newspaper. At least it did until Harvey made them stop. I never liked being the center of attention. Even before the accident."

Inez moved around the plants on the tables in the center of the room and adjusted branches and vines here and there. Wooden skewers sat on the end of the table, along with a black marker and a pile of index cards.

"Still, it's getting late. Can you tell me where I can find the security guard?" I asked.

She turned her back on the plant. "The security guard went home hours ago."

"But Beth told me there was security around the clock."

"There used to be. I don't know, maybe Beth thinks there still is. Six months ago I made arrangements with Mr. Halliwell to be alone at night while I conduct experiments for him. Since then, it's been just me and my staff. We keep an eye out on the place."

"Where's your staff? I didn't see anybody else here."

"The trees are my staff," she said with a laugh.

I was starting to wonder if Inez had lost more than her beauty-pageant looks during her accident. I backed away from her. "Can you tell me which building I'll want to go to for my check tomorrow?"

She pulled the surgical mask off from around her neck and set it on the table. "There's no need for you to come back. I'll take you there myself." She pulled a set of keys from a small box behind a bowl of small river rocks and tucked them into the pocket of her white lab coat. "Follow me." She went around the back of the greenhouse. A small golf cart was parked behind the building.

"This will be faster than walking," she said. She started up the cart and drove us to the building on the farthest side of the site. She parked on the grass next to the front door and let us inside.

In the foyer of the building was a large marble semicircle,

behind which was an empty black cushioned chair. A coffee mug sat on the desk. Inez moved around to the back of the desk, opening and closing drawers until she found one with a white envelope. "Polyester Monroe," she said. "Your full name is Polyester?"

"Yes," I said. "I was born in the fabric store, on a bed of polyester."

"It could have been worse," she said. "You could have been born on a bed of fleece."

She had a point.

I took the envelope and peeked at the contents. Inside was a cashier's check from Halliwell Industries made out for half of the sum we'd discussed. I folded the envelope and put it into my bag.

"Is that all you need?" she asked.

"Yes."

"Then you should go. I need to get back to the plants. Are you parked close?"

"In the lot out front. I can take it from here."

I said good-bye to Inez and left. She stayed behind. As I drove back to Material Girl, I wondered about her private access to the lab at night and how she'd arranged for the security guard to be gone. I wondered if she really was okay with having been scarred at a photo shoot. I wondered how hard it must be for her to see her pre-accident likeness used on the side of Tangorli juice containers all over the state.

And I also wondered about the mug of coffee on the desk of the absent security guard.

Nineteen

I backtracked over the winding roads, got lost in a small development of pink and blue houses with flat roofs, and found my way back on the road that met up with San Ladrón Avenue. It took ten minutes longer to get home than it took to get there, but I made it. I drove down Bonita, slowing as I passed Charlie's Auto. The bays were closed but the lights in the shop were still on. I parked the car next to the Dumpster behind Material Girl, then went in through the back door and back out the front. Seconds later, I was knocking on the door to Charlie's office.

She opened the door and pulled me inside. "What took you so long? We thought you'd be here hours ago."

I stumbled in, surprised to find Vaughn and Sheriff Clark already in the room.

"What's going on?" I asked.

"What's going on is that people are starting to talk and none of it's going to be pretty. The people in this room are the people who matter to me, so I want to set the record straight before the rumor mill takes over the town."

She opened the bottom drawer of her file cabinet and pulled out a bottle of red wine.

"Anybody interested?"

The rest of us nodded.

"Poly, go get some glasses from the top of the cabinet."

I left her in her office and retrieved four glasses from the fixture below the Eddie Van Halen poster. When I went back to her office, her feet were up on the desk and her hands were behind her thick, dreadlocked hair. "Who would have thought. Me sponsoring a beauty pageant contestant."

I glanced at Sheriff Clark. His face was serious, but not judgmental. He watched Charlie but didn't say a word.

Charlie poured a little wine into each of our glasses. She pushed one glass toward me and slid the second closer to her, but she didn't take a sip.

"Remember on Sunday how I told you about Ned?"

"Yes," I said. I didn't know how much of the story the men knew, but for now it seemed as though Charlie was getting me caught up with details.

"What I didn't tell you—what nobody knows—was that I wasn't eighteen. I was younger. And Ned legally adopted me. I'd been in and out of so many foster homes by then that nobody questioned the paperwork. So even though he treated me like a sister, legally, he was my guardian."

I looked at the faces of the men in the room. Vaughn stood still, his expression hard to read. I wondered what it was like for him to listen to Charlie talk about those days when he'd grown up here under the parental influence of the same people who had given her up for adoption.

Clark approached the back of Charlie's chair and put his hands on her shoulders. I expected her to fling them off but she didn't. She reached up and put her hands on top of his, where they rested.

"After Ned became my guardian, he wrote to each of my former foster parents to find out if they could tell us anything about my biological parents. Nobody wanted to talk to us. He left a letter with the adoption board saying if anybody wanted to get in touch with me—wanted to find me—that I was okay with it, and we left his address as my contact information. I remember feeling hopeful, like I was going to understand what happened, like there would be an explanation that I could accept. But there was nothing."

She let go of Clark's hands and took a drink from her glass of wine. "Ned filed a petition with the Los Angeles County District Two courts for a copy of my original birth certificate. The judge denied the request. It was like nobody wanted to help me know where I was from. At that point I stopped looking. If my birth parents didn't care that I was out there, why should I care about them?"

"Charlie," Vaughn started, but she held up her hand to cut him off.

"We grew up in different worlds, Vaughn. Don't pretend we didn't."

The room fell silent. If Charlie was done talking, I suspected we'd all stand there for hours anyway. Her story felt incomplete, and I couldn't picture any of us getting up and leaving after what she'd said.

"And then Ned got a letter from the adoption agency. They said my first foster parents had sent them my birth certificate. The city of birth was listed as San Ladrón. I told Ned I didn't care anymore. But when I turned eighteen, he gave me two thousand dollars and told me to put it toward a new start. So I came here. As good as any place, I guess."

My heart broke for the girl Charlie had been, the girl who had bounced around different families and went out on her own before she was legal. She could have fallen into so many bad situations, it was a testament to how strong she was that she didn't. Through all of that, she developed into a smart businesswoman who learned a trade and ran her own auto shop. And she'd accomplished it all with two thousand dollars of start-up cash. No Vanguard account, no loan cosigned by Mr. McMichael. Pride and belief in herself had gotten her far.

"After I left, Ned married his girlfriend and they started their own family. Man, that was ages ago. I showed up on his doorstep almost a year ago and that's when he told me I had a sister."

"Lucy?"

"Lucy." She picked up her glass of wine and held it up to the light, then set it back down. "A couple of months later Ned called me. He knew I lived in San Ladrón and he wanted to know if I'd sponsor Lucy for the pageant. The rules say you must either be a resident of the town or have a qualifying relative. 'Sister' is a qualifying relative. So here we are."

"Not so fast," Clark said. "You became her sponsor and she's living here. So why all the secrecy? Why have Ned drop her off in the middle of the night?"

"You know about that?" Charlie asked.

He leaned forward and put his hand on her knee. "Charlie, it's my job to know what's going on in the town. When I get a call about a stranger, I have to check it out."

"Somebody called you about Ned?"

He nodded.

"Who?"

"You know I can't tell you that."

She punched her fist down on the desk and the glasses rattled. "I knew this would happen. I try to lead a quiet life here and not get into anybody's business and the one time I do something nice for somebody, I'm grist for the rumor mill."

I watched Clark watch Charlie. He must have felt my stare, because his eyes shifted to me. I didn't smile. I knew if Clark really suspected Ned of something, he would have knocked on Charlie's door, made a friendly introduction as the local sheriff, and found out what Ned's business in town was. The fact that he didn't, but he knew about Ned's presence, told me an entirely different story. His job tipped him off that she had a strange man over at her shop late at night, but he wanted to respect her privacy. If those two were going to have any kind of a relationship, there were going to be problems.

"Charlie, why'd you keep it a secret?" Vaughn asked.

"You know why, Vaughn. If people go digging into my past, they'll find out that your parents are my parents. They'll wonder why you're the wonder boy who works with Old Man McMichael and what was so wrong with me that they gave me away. And then people will start rumors about Lucy. Why is she qualified to be in the pageant? Am I really her sister? And who's her father? A mechanic from Encino? She's a no-body from nowhere. They'll say she can't win a pageant. I wanted to shield her from that."

Charlie stood up and glared at us. Fire lit her eyes. She turned away and looked out the window. Whatever sense of camaraderie had existed in the room when I arrived had shifted to her against us. I was afraid she had changed her mind about confiding in us, or, worse, she'd back out of her sponsorship of Lucy.

"She can win the pageant," I said softly. "She's an amazing young woman. She's smart, kind, pretty, and gracious. Those are the qualities that win a pageant. It doesn't matter who her father is."

Vaughn stood up and went to Charlie. "You never told me about the different foster homes or about Ned. You never talked about your childhood. I didn't know anything about what it was like for you growing up."

"And you're not gonna find out any more about it." She turned around and gave him a gentle push away from her. "Thanks for bringing me dinner. I'll do your oil change tomorrow morning. Now get out of here so I can talk to your girlfriend."

I stared at Vaughn, who stared at Charlie. "Don't go

making Poly uncomfortable on my account, sis." He punched Clark lightly on the arm. "Come on, Sheriff, I think we've been dismissed."

The four of us left Charlie's office and walked into the open bay of her shop. The men left and Charlie and I stood next to her cabinet of tools.

"You're not going to distract me by calling me Vaughn's girlfriend," I said.

"I underestimated the impact of the G word," she said.

"Charlie, this is important. It's about you and Lucy. Where is she, anyway?"

"She's at my apartment. I told her I needed to run out for a while." She stood by the window, staring out at the street.

"Is there more to the story? More than you told Sheriff Clark and Vaughn?"

"There's always more, isn't there?" She sat back down, and for the first time since I'd met her, I saw pain in her face. "Somehow Ned found out I was Vic McMichael's daughter. He said it was time to collect the interest on his loan."

"The two thousand dollars was a loan?"

"Poly, I paid that money back years ago. Sent him a certified check. He never responded, never mentioned it. The check was never cashed."

"Did you ask him about that?"

"Once. He laughed it off and said not to worry. He said if he ever needed money, he'd come to collect. And then the postcard came, and he showed up. He helped me figure out where my parents lived, but I don't even know how he found out who they were."

"Tell me again how you found out that Vic was your father?"

"I didn't find out until after I moved here. Asked around, dug around. Spent a lot of time at the library going through old newspapers, looking for something. I almost missed it. 'Unnamed baby girl born to McMichael family.' The date and time matched what was listed on my birth certificate. After I found out who Adelaide was, I figured it out."

"You never told Ned?"

"I never told anybody but Vaughn." She turned away from me and punched her fist into the dingy gray heavy bag that hung next to the tool chest. It rocked back and forth, spinning slightly. The word *Everlast* moved to the left and then to the right. We both stared at it until it stopped moving.

"How did Ned find out? I mean, did he know I had a rich father when he gave me the two grand to start a new life? Or before that? Maybe he always planned to tap me for money."

"Have you asked him?"

"Why bother? He said now that Harvey Halliwell is out of the way, he wants me to pull some strings. I think the contest was just an excuse to get back in touch with me. He doesn't care about Lucy winning the pageant; what he really wants is a way to get to Old Man McMichael's money."

"Do you think Lucy knows he's using her?"

Before she could reply, there was a click behind me. Charlie heard it, too. We both raced to the back door in time to see a figure run past the small shed that sat behind Charlie's shop, dark brown hair flying behind her.

Lucy had heard every word we'd said.

Twenty

Charlie took off after her. I stood by the door. Seconds later an engine started up and a car jumped out of the darkness. It was the abandoned pickup that Charlie left in the yard behind her shop. The truck tore through the grass until it reached the sidewalk. It slowed to navigate over the curb, and then it took off into the night.

I waited by the back door until Charlie returned. She cursed. "I should have expected this," she said.

"You can't go through life expecting the worst of people. Ned did a very good thing for you when you lived with him, and there might be a valid explanation."

"I'm not talking about that, I'm talking about trusting the daughter of a mechanic with a rusted-out, broken-down car. To anybody else, that truck was a piece of junk. To a mechanic, it's a getaway car hiding in plain sight."

"Where do you think she'd go?"

"Who knows? The pageant rules say she's supposed to

reside with her relative. That's me. I doubt she'd go back to Ned, not after what she heard us talking about."

"What was she doing here? I thought you said she was in your apartment?"

"My apartment's not far from here. She could have followed me, or worse, maybe she planned to take the car before she heard us."

It was after midnight when I made it back to my apartment. So much had happened since this morning—Giovanni and the seamstresses arriving, Violet's angry outburst, Inez's story at Halliwell Industries, and Charlie's explanation of Lucy's relationship to her—that I couldn't believe it had only been a day. I took a quick shower, changed into a black cotton nightgown, and eased myself under the covers between Pins and Needles. Pins wrapped one of his gray paws over my leg and rested his chin on my kneecap. Seconds later we were all asleep.

The next morning, even the cats seemed to understand that I needed time to recharge. Neither of them was in the bed when I woke up. I pushed the covers back and walked through the apartment looking for them. They were in the kitchen, standing over their bowls, waiting patiently to be fed.

I opened a can of moist food for them and replaced yesterday's water with fresh from the tap, then raced through my morning routine. I expected Giovanni and company to arrive early and get started on the dresses. There was much work to be done, but I knew I couldn't expect them to stay over another night.

I emptied the residue from the coffee urns and refilled them with freshly brewed coffee from the modest Mr. Coffee in my kitchen. I'd place even money on the fact that Giovanni would have breakfast at the Waverly House and charge it to the pageant. So long as I kept him caffeinated during the day, we'd get along fine. I drank two cups before he and the seam-stresses arrived, leaving me jittery and anxious.

"What took you so long?" I asked when they showed up. "I've been expecting you for hours."

"It's eight o'clock. We have plenty of time to finish the dresses before the girls arrive at noon."

I saved the lecture on the "girls" versus "young ladies," as it would be wasted on Giovanni. "I trust you left some food at the Waverly House for the rest of the patrons?"

He thrust a take-out bag at me. "I even thought to bring something for you. Egg, Swiss, and prosciutto on a toasted rye bagel."

I peeked inside the bag. "I'm surprised you remembered what I liked for breakfast."

"I didn't. The girls told me. And before you say anything, you spend a night with them and tell me if they acted like girls or women."

I flashed back to the giddiness I'd seen yesterday when they left the store. "They're still women, Giovanni. Happy women who had a chance to step out of their lives for one night."

He shook his head at me.

The ladies took their spots at the sewing machines and started where they'd left off the previous day. I pulled my bagel sandwich from the bag, sniffed it, and savored the scent—melted cheese, caraway seeds on the bun, the saltiness of the prosciutto—before I bit into it. I hadn't had a bagel sandwich since moving from Los Angeles, but now that I knew the Waverly House made these, I had a feeling I'd be developing a new habit.

Jun Wong arrived shortly after Giovanni and company did. She hugged each of the other ladies one by one, then took her seat at her makeshift station. The sewing machines started buzzing, slowly mounting to a dull roar of stitches being sewn. As the clock approached noon, I grew more anxious. Would Lucy show up for her fitting? If not, where was she?

The answer wasn't the one I'd hoped for. A couple of young women arrived at eleven forty-five. I asked them to wait out front. At precisely twelve, I allowed them in. The early birds had been joined by the rest of their group—minus one. Lucy. I looked across the street and saw Charlie looking back at me. I shook my head and she went back inside.

I wasn't sure what to make of Lucy's disappearance. Was it embarrassment over her father having asked Charlie to sponsor her? Or was it guilt over expecting Charlie's familial connections to open doors for her? Lucy hadn't acted like she wanted preferential treatment. In fact, it was quite the contrary. She had waited on the stairs and let each of the other young women go first. She had chosen her fabric from what was left, taking the transfugitive silk that many others had rejected. She hadn't even shown up on that first day to check in. That was why Sheila, who'd stood in as the twentieth contestant that first day, had been able to go unnoticed.

In hindsight, Sheila's timing seemed odd. How had she known that Lucy wouldn't be at the store to check in? Surely she must have expected someone to at least take a head count. If we had come up with twenty-one young women instead of twenty, there would have been a roll call, which would have resulted in her being outed as the one person present but not expected. Wouldn't that have been more embarrassing than not showing up? So why risk it? Unless she knew Lucy wasn't going to show.

Sheila hadn't tried to hide her tears on Tuesday night. In fact, she was the one who had told me she needed to talk to someone. What if her tears were caused by something much worse than not getting into the pageant, like a confrontation with Harvey Halliwell that resulted in his murder? Would she invite me into her confidence in order to feed me a story that would send me off in a different direction?

"You're doing an excellent job of not getting involved," Giovanni said, jostling me out of my thoughts. It took me a couple of seconds to justify what he said with how I was feeling, considering I was pretty certain trying to figure out who killed Harvey would be considered "getting involved."

"You mean with the seamstresses and the fittings?"

"Of course. I expected you to be right in the thick of it."

"I don't think that would be fair. Part of this challenge is to allow them to come up with their concept and have it executed. We're here to advise, but that's it."

He studied me for a second. "You've grown up a bit since leaving my workroom. You're more confident. Your store just might make it after all."

Giovanni left me standing by the wrap stand, shocked into silence. He refilled his coffee and wandered the perimeter of the shop. He had told me a little about the beginning of his business. Had he started out like me: idealistic, loving fabric, viewing the world as my oyster? If so, when had he started catering to the disposable prom and pageant circuit? I could have joined him as he walked around and studied the fabrics that had survived the ten years when the store was closed, and those that I'd purchased more recently to round out my inventory, but I didn't. I sensed that he was having his own moment in time and I wanted to let him.

Try as I did, I couldn't shake my concerns over Lucy or my questions about Sheila, and the more I thought about each contestant, the more I tried to fabricate a connection between them. I wanted to know more about their pasts. But with Lucy missing in action, Sheila made the obvious choice of where to start. I needed an excuse to spend some time at the Waverly House. Too bad I hadn't thought of this when the ladies were staying there.

But there were other excuses for spending time there. I called Vaughn's office and asked his secretary to put me through.

"I'd like to make an appointment with you."

"I thought we'd bypassed the appointment phase of our

relationship. Should I reconnect you with my secretary? She has my schedule."

"I'm hoping she doesn't book your nighttime schedule. I'm calling to invite you to dinner."

"Hmmm, dinner. I seem to recall you inviting me to dinner a few months ago. So, Tea Totalers? What time?"

"Dinner at Tea Totalers has to wait. I want to take you to dinner at the Waverly House."

"Considering my mom runs the place and lets me eat for free, I think you might find a better place to spend your money," he said.

"No, it has to be the Waverly House. And it has to be tonight. If you're busy, I can make other plans."

"I'm not busy."

"So it's a date?"

"Is it?"

I considered the question. Was I asking Vaughn on a date? It seemed as though I was. Denying it wouldn't serve any particular purpose. Plus, I rather liked having taken charge like this.

"Yes, it's a date."

"Good to know. Are you going to pick me up?"

I stifled a giggle at the thought of me driving to wherever Vaughn lived just to drive him back to a restaurant that was two blocks from my house.

"How about we meet at the Waverly House at seven thirty?"

"Perfect." I hung up the phone and smiled to myself. Giovanni was right. I did have more confidence than I had in Los Angeles. Maybe there was something in the San Ladrón water.

When I turned around, the pageant contestants and the seamstresses were watching me. The machines had gone silent. As I looked back and forth among their faces, I realized they'd heard the majority of my conversation.

Jun Wong spoke up. "You make date with Mister Vaughn?"

I nodded. She clapped twice and the other women joined in. The young women looked around like they didn't know what it all meant. I flushed to a particularly hot temperature and fanned myself with my hand. Giovanni handed me a mug of coffee and clinked it with his own.

"You're the one who's always defending them," he said.

Nineteen dresses were completed by five thirty. Short of carrying them up to my closet, I didn't know where to hang them. I went next door to Flowers in the Attic to see if either Violet or Lilly had an extra fixture in storage that I could borrow for a few days.

Lilly Garden stood inside a large white metal birdcage that had been positioned at the front of the store. Tufted stools of varying heights were clustered together, each holding a metal tray filled with vintage jewelry. One held brightly colored flower pins from the sixties. Another held multifaceted rhinestone brooch and earring sets. A third held strands of wooden beads that had been threaded onto thin twine and tied into necklaces. Above the baskets of jewelry, she'd positioned a colorful toy parrot that had been wired to a swinging bar.

"Hi, Lilly," I said. "I haven't seen the birdcage before. Is it new?"

"It's been in storage. Violet thinks it's awful but I disagree."

"It's perfect for the jewelry display," I said. "Too bad the parrot doesn't talk."

She picked up a plastic remote from the counter and aimed it at the parrot. His swing started to move to and fro and his beak clacked mechanically. "Polly want a cracker," he said. Six times. Considering my name was Poly, I tired of it after one.

Lilly laughed. "Oh, he's going to be lots of fun. Just imagine how I can scare people when they're inside the cage rooting through the merchandise."

I thought about saying that maybe scaring off the customers wasn't a wise marketing strategy, but didn't. Instead, I moved into my request. "Speaking of fixtures in storage, that's why I'm here. Do you happen to have any extra rolling racks or merchandise grids?"

"I think so. Why?"

"The seamstresses have finished up with the dresses for the Miss Tangorli contestants and I don't have any place to hang them. If you have something you're not using, I thought maybe I could borrow it."

Her eyes grew wide and she gestured with her hand for me to keep my voice down. "I have a collapsible rolling rack that you can borrow, but you can't tell Violet. This pageant is hard enough for her."

I looked around. "Where *is* Violet?"

"She went out of town for a few days. Probably for the best."

On one hand, it made sense that Violet would go out of town to avoid the reminder of the catalyst for her daughter severing ties with her. On the other, if Violet had something to do with Harvey Halliwell's murder, it was awfully suspicious timing to take a vacation.

Twenty-one

"Does Violet make a habit of going out of town to avoid the pageant?" I asked.

"Oh, no," Lilly said. "This trip was very sudden. She didn't tell me where she was going or when she'd be back. That's why I wanted you to keep your voice down. I keep expecting her to walk through the front door."

The chime over the door rang. We both turned our heads at the sound, but it was Giovanni, not Violet, who walked in. "We need to get on the road soon if I'm going to get those women back to Los Angeles before midnight."

"I'll be right there," I said. I turned back to Lilly. "The rolling rack?" I prompted.

"Oh yes. Can you watch the counter? I'll be right back."

She disappeared through the back of the shop. Giovanni eyed the birdcage from top to bottom, then walked inside to look at the display. I clicked the remote at the plastic bird and it came to life. "Polly want a cracker! Polly want a cracker!"

it squawked. Giovanni jumped, and I doubled over in laughter. Maybe Lilly had something with the parrot after all.

Lilly returned with the rolling rack a few minutes later and I thanked her and rolled it to the fabric shop. In my absence, the seamstresses had sewn garment bags out of muslin. Each bag had an outside pocket made from the silk of the dress inside. Zippers had been inserted along the side seam. We placed each dress in its bag, zipped it shut, paper-clipped an index card with the contestant's name and her sketch to the top, and hung it on the rack. When we were done, twenty dresses hung on the rack. Lucy's had been completed but not fitted. I hoped for her sake that the measurements had been accurate. I refused to believe she wouldn't come back by the pageant.

I hugged each of the women from To the Nines good-bye and sent them on their way. They giggled, as if they shared a joke I hadn't been let in on. I walked them to the van in the parking lot and waved as Giovanni pulled out of the lot. As nice as it had been to be reunited with them, I was happy to have my store and my regular level of noise—as in mostly quiet—back.

Jun was packing up the last of her equipment when I went back inside. "I leave now, too, Miss Poly. Give you time to get ready for date with Mister Vaughn."

"Jun, about that date . . ."

"Is no secret Mister Vaughn likes you. You not like other women he date. Ladies tell me about man you date in Los Angeles. Sound like Mister Vaughn not like him, either."

"Just because we're different than each other doesn't mean anything."

"No, but it not *not* mean anything, either." She smiled. "Good night, Miss Poly. Enjoy surprise."

"What surprise?" I asked.

"You see." She rolled her sewing machine and table to the wall alongside the store, said good-bye to Pins and Needles, and left.

Without the craziness of seven sewers, nineteen pageant contestants, and Giovanni in the store, it felt like the day after Woodstock. I swept the floor around the sewing stations, collecting piles of fabric cuttings and threads and scooping them up in the dustpan. After the floor was clean, I made sure the sewing machines had been turned off and draped a cloth cover over each one so dust wouldn't get into the components and affect the performance. I rolled up the muslin and returned it to its shelf, collected the colorful tape measures that lay scattered across the tables, and carried the overflowing trash cans out back to the Dumpster. I had about an hour to get ready for my date with Vaughn, but before I spent any time wondering about what to wear, I needed a plan for what I wanted to accomplish while we were at the Waverly House.

First I called the restaurant. A man answered. I confirmed my reservations and then added, "I'd like a seat by the fireplace, if possible."

"We don't turn the fireplace on in the summer months."

"Yes, I know you use the gas log. I'm requesting it more for the ambiance than for heat," I explained.

"Are you looking for privacy? We have a nice table in the corner that looks out over the northern lawn," he said.

"No, thank you. The fireplace will be fine."

Yes, the fireplace was definitely where I wanted to sit. Because I still wasn't convinced that Sheila was innocent, and if she'd tried to burn what she'd received from the pageant committee and any parts of the documents were left behind, I wanted access to them. The real problem was going to be searching the fireplace without Vaughn knowing.

I changed into a black jersey dress with a scoop neckline in the front and back. The dress was fitted down to my thighs, where the fabric had been cut and seamed into long strips of fabric, about four inches wide, that fell to just above my ankle. Before I left, I measured several yards of black Spanish lace from a bolt that had a defect and cut it, then wrapped it around my shoulders like a stole.

I arrived at the Waverly House early, hoping to scope out the interior of the dining room before Vaughn and I were seated. Adelaide Brooks was in the lobby conversing with the maître d'. She saw me and excused herself.

"Poly, what a nice surprise. You look lovely. One of these days you're going to have to call ahead when you plan to visit so we can spend some time together. As it is, we're a little short-staffed tonight."

"How come?"

"Someone canceled the regular cleaning crew so the restaurant wasn't ready to open on time. And then Sheila called in sick, poor dear. I think she's coming down with something. She hasn't looked herself for the past few days."

Adelaide Brooks looked fresh in a sand-colored shift dress, with an ivory cardigan draped over her shoulders. On her wrist was a series of thin gold bracelets. Her glasses, which usually hung on a quartz-and-gold chain around her neck, were on her head. The chain draped down on each side of her face. The right-hand side was caught in a small gold hoop earring. She tipped her head to the side and tried to free it with her fingers. Wisps of her gray hair danced around her face.

I gave her a hug. "I don't want you to take it personally, but I'm not here to see you," I said.

"Oh?"

"I have dinner reservations."

"I see. You arrived alone?"

"I'm meeting my date here."

"Oh." Her face barely changed, and I silently gave her credit. If I weren't so tuned in to the subtleties of her speech,

I might not have noticed the difference between her first "oh" and her second.

"I'm a little early and there's something I wanted to ask you. Can you spare a couple of minutes?"

"Of course."

I stepped past the host's station and down the carpeted hallway that led to the building's southern entrance. It was kept locked except for special events, so I knew no one would interrupt us. The darkness of the hallway, magnified by the heavy cherrywood walls and thick burgundy oriental carpet under our feet, kept us from standing out too much.

"I haven't had a chance to talk to you since the garden party," I said. "It was a lovely event, even if it did end in tragedy."

"If I were being self-centered, I'd say we were fortunate that Harvey's body was discovered as late as it was. But I shan't allow myself to think that way. Harvey Halliwell was one of San Ladrón's most influential men and it's a shame to see him gone so soon."

"Did you know him well? I mean, were you and Mr. McMichael married when they were partners?"

"You do like to bring up my ex-husband, don't you?" She sighed. "Harvey and Vaughn's father were partners before we were married. They split a few years later. I did know Harvey, and I wish the two of them had been able to see past their differences and learn to work together. Harvey had several qualities that Vic lacked and vice versa."

"Like what?"

"Harvey was a humanitarian. Vic was a businessman. Harvey knew how to generate goodwill. Vic knew how to generate money." She put her hand on mine. "Don't get me wrong. We had a very nice life because of Vic's business sense. But there were aspects of our life together that were sacrificed because of that business drive. And ultimately, his love of his business was what drove us apart."

"I don't mean to bring up old wounds," I said. "I'm more interested in learning about Harvey than about Mr. McMichael."

She looked over my shoulder and her face froze. "Poly, I— Can you excuse me for a moment? I need to attend to someone at the front desk. I'll be right back." She put her hand on my arm and then hurried down the hall.

I checked the time on my phone. It was seven thirty. I didn't want to be late meeting Vaughn. I would explain to Adelaide later why I didn't wait for her to return. I turned my phone to silent and tucked it into my handbag. I was just about to turn the corner when Adelaide returned. "Crisis averted. Now, where were we?"

I looked into the hallway. Two couples were being led into the restaurant, and otherwise the lobby was empty. The front door opened and Vaughn walked in. He looked confused.

"Vaughn!" Adelaide said. "I think you'd be happier dining here tomorrow."

He approached his mother and kissed her on the cheek. "I think that would make things a little awkward for Poly, considering she asked me to join her for dinner tonight."

She looked at me. "Your date is with my son?"

I kissed Adelaide on the other cheek. "Thank you for keeping me company. Our reservation was for seven thirty, and I don't want to lose our table."

I led Vaughn to the host station, and the host led us to our table by the fireplace. Not only was there not a fire in the pit, but the fake fire was missing, too. Whoever was in charge of turning it on had either forgotten to, or chosen not to bother. Without the illumination I'd planned on having from the electric log, I couldn't see if there was anything in the fireplace interior. I took my seat on the side closer to the interior of the fireplace and draped my shawl over the back of my chair.

"I hope—" we both said at the same time.

"You didn't," we both said again, and laughed.

"Do I need to apologize for anything my mother said before I arrived?" Vaughn asked.

"Not unless I need to apologize for her telling you to leave. I told her I was having dinner here, but I didn't tell her who I was dining with."

"Embarrassed to be seen with me?"

"A little. It goes against everything I stand for."

"Dining out in public? Or being seen with one of the most eligible bachelors in San Ladrón?"

"Are you? I hadn't heard," I said.

"Maybe my status has changed. It's hard to keep up with these things," he said, waving his hand back and forth.

A waitress delivered a basket of freshly baked bread to our table. A thick blue sateen napkin had been wrapped around the bread, which was nestled in a small white basket. Steam, along with the scent of sourdough and rosemary, traveled from the basket into the air, tempting me to ignore the menu and indulge in a prison diet of bread and water.

"Shall I bring your champagne?"

I shot a look at Vaughn. He looked as confused as I was. I looked up at the waitress. "Our champagne?"

"Yes, a bottle of champagne was ordered for you this afternoon."

"By whom?"

She looked at a slip of paper in her hand. "Giovanni's girls," she said.

"Women," I corrected automatically.

"No, they specifically said to call them 'Giovanni's girls.'"

I hung my head and shook it from side to side. When I looked up at Vaughn, he grinned at me. "How about it? Would you like to start with champagne?"

"Why not?" I asked. Perhaps it would distract him when his date for the evening dropped down to her hands and knees and felt around the interior of the fireplace.

"Excellent." The waitress went to the bar and said something to the bartender. He was the same man who had been here when I'd visited with Sheila. He looked over at us, nodded, and bent down behind the bar. When he stood back up, he set two flutes on the counter next to a chilled bottle. As he popped the cork and filled our glasses, I turned my attention back to the fireplace and aimed the light from my cell phone at the interior. Behind the log, in the back corner, were a couple of balls of paper, just as I'd suspected. Sheila hadn't been out of her mind when she lit the fireplace. She'd been trying to destroy something.

The waitress returned with our glasses and a silver ice bucket that held the bottle. When prompted, Vaughn told her we needed a couple more minutes with the menu. She left and he reached across the table and took my hand.

"I'm glad you invited me here tonight," he said. "But judging from how you're studying the interior of the fireplace, I'm starting to think either you regret asking or you had something else in mind when you extended the invitation."

I was busted. The problem was, I needed to talk to someone. And maybe I wasn't so hot on the idea of scrounging around the interior of the fireplace after all.

"I'm about to ask you a favor that's going to test the limits of your understanding."

He raised his eyebrows.

"Can you create a distraction while I get something out of the fireplace?"

"I don't think there's a distraction big enough to hide a pretty woman crawling around on her hands and knees on the floor of a restaurant. Why?"

I slid my chair back. "See in the far corner? There are crumpled-up balls of paper. I need to look at them."

Vaughn stood and walked to the back of my chair. He reached around the side of the fireplace and clicked a small black switch. Within seconds, the fake log glowed orange.

He selected the broom from a circular stand of fireplace tools, reached it into the fireplace, and swept the crumpled balls of paper to the side of my foot. I bent down and scooped the balls of paper into my handbag. Vaughn put the broom back on the stand and took his seat.

"Shall we order?" he asked, as if nothing out of the ordinary had taken place.

I stared at him openmouthed as he studied the menu. It seemed I'd found an unlikely accomplice.

Twenty-two

The rest of our meal passed in a blur of filet mignon, lemon meringue pie, champagne, and small talk. Vaughn shared stories of his days at college in Virginia, and I told him about my early days working for Giovanni. The check came far too quickly and I swatted Vaughn's hand away. I opened the black leather folio to see the damage, calculated a tip, and filled the folio with money.

Vaughn held the front door of the Waverly House open for me and I exited into the cool night air. I wrapped my lace shawl around my shoulders.

"So, your place or mine?" he asked.

"Excuse me?"

"You didn't think I was going to let you off the hook that easily, did you?"

"It's getting late."

"I know. But we both know you won't even consider sleeping until you find out what's on those balls of paper from the fireplace. And considering my part in the retrieval process, I think it's only fair to let me see what you're up to."

The Waverly House, aside from being the oldest and most impressive building in San Ladrón, had a particularly disturbing view from the front lawn. It sat directly across the street from the sheriff's mobile unit. The lights to the mobile unit were out, and I suspected Clark had left for the day. I wondered if the officer who helped him when we found Harvey's body was still in San Ladrón or if he'd headed back to Los Angeles. I also wondered if Clark had turned up anything of interest regarding the murder investigation.

Vaughn had his hands in the pockets of his suit jacket and he nudged me with his elbow. "Is it really that hard a decision?"

"My place is closer," I said.

We walked along the sidewalk to the corner. It would have been shorter to cut down the alley and enter through the back door, but I preferred to enter through the front. Every time I walked through the entrance, I felt the pride of running a shop of my own. I pushed the gate to the side and unlocked the door. Dim light illuminated the store interior. I glanced around the shop and saw the rack of garment bags and sketches, grabbed Vaughn's hand, and pulled him up the stairs.

"You're a judge. You can't see what we've been working on in here," I said.

"Top secret, huh? Seems you've been bitten by the pageant bug, too."

"I don't know how I feel about the pageant, but these young women deserve equal chances to win and it wouldn't be fair if you got a sneak peek at their gowns before anybody else did."

"A level playing field," he said. "Just like Nolene said."

I unlocked the door to the apartment and shooed Pins and Needles away from the opening. Vaughn followed me inside and we headed toward the living room.

"Do you think there really can be a level playing field? As

much as Nolene talks about it, do you really think someone like Lucy has the same chance of winning as someone like Tiffany?" I asked.

"No, I don't." He lowered himself onto the sofa. "But not for the reason you think."

"Okay then, why?"

"Everybody has their own story. No one can change that. Lucy's story is different from Tiffany's, and they're both different from every one of the eighteen other young women who are competing. Add in their appearances. Lucy is exotic. Tiffany—and a lot of the others—are California girls. Blond, blue eyes, tan. Is it better to be the girl who looks different, or the girl who looks like everybody expects a California girl to look?"

"I know you have a point, but that's not what I was asking. I meant by trying to make things equal financially. Will that really make a difference?"

"I don't know that it should. Consider your judges. Duke: a local business owner who uses a wheelchair. Maria: another local entrepreneur who helps run two different businesses while she raises her family. And me: a rich kid who probably didn't have to work a day in his life."

"But you did. You do. I mean, you're more like Duke and Maria than a millionaire's son. You told me how you left San Ladrón to go to William and Mary when your father wanted you to go to *his* alma mater. You said he was mad so he cut you off and you paid for college yourself."

"That's all true, but did it change anything? In the end, I'm back here, working for him. Dad's in his seventies. He should have retired a long time ago, but the business is his life. Most likely I'll inherit it when he's ready to step down. Maria and Duke and Lucy and a lot of people have no idea what it's like to inherit a business."

"I do," I said quietly. I looked up at him. "And it's not as easy as it might seem."

I shifted my position on the sofa and my handbag fell from my lap to the floor. The clasp opened on contact and the balls of paper spilled out. Before I could scoop them up, Pins pounced. He swatted one into the hallway and chased after it.

"That's not a toy," I called after him. I stood to follow but couldn't move. I looked down and saw Vaughn's foot on the hem of my dress. I grabbed the carwash fringe and tugged at it. He moved his foot and Needles showed up and pounced on Vaughn's shoelace.

"You take Needles and I'll take Pins?" I asked.

"Deal."

I found Pins in the hallway. He had swatted the ball of paper under the armoire that held the towels and sheets and lay on his side, paws extended, trying to reach it. He turned his gray striped head toward me and mewed.

"That's what you get," I said. I squatted down and pulled the ball of paper out from behind one of the curved wooden legs. Pins jumped up and sniffed the paper. I pulled it away from him. "This isn't yours," I said.

"And it isn't yours, either," said Vaughn. "This is Sheila Bonham's background check." In his hand he held a very wrinkled piece of paper. "Does this have something to do with why she was so upset the other night?"

"My guess is yes."

"This is private information. We shouldn't even be looking at it."

I stepped forward and took Vaughn's hand in mine. "Sheila was working the drink station where Harvey Halliwell got the glass of Tangorli juice he drank before he passed out. She lied about when she was notified about the pageant. One of the other waitresses told me she received upsetting news by mail on Friday. That was before Harvey was murdered and before the finalists were to show up here. And she started a real fire in the fireplace even though they only run the gas log over the summer. I don't know how many pages she managed to burn, but these were left behind. It's not a straight line to murdering him, but it raises a lot of questions."

"Is this why you invited me to the Waverly House for dinner?"

"I invited you to dinner because I wanted to go to dinner with you. I invited you to the Waverly House because I wanted to snoop around the fireplace."

"Poly, I don't know how I feel about this."

"What if Sheila was so angry about not qualifying that she poisoned him on Saturday night and finished the job Sunday morning? She pretended to be one of the pageant contestants even though she knew she wasn't. The only reason nobody picked up on it was because Lucy didn't show, so we still had twenty." I paused for a moment. "I still don't know how Sheila knew that Lucy wasn't going to show." He remained unconvinced. "Vaughn, this isn't snooping. This is trying to find out what happened to Harvey."

He stared at me, his green eyes darkened by the lack of light. There was no smile to his face. He didn't drop my hand.

"If this is evidence, it should go to Clark," he said.

"We don't know if it's evidence or not. What I know is that this is information about Sheila. She asked me—begged me—not to tell your mom. And I didn't. But if she represents a threat to anybody—your mom and Charlie included—then we should look at these pages before we turn them over to anybody."

He turned around and walked toward the living room. When I didn't follow, he looked back at me. "Well? What are you waiting for?" he asked.

"The light in the kitchen is better."

We took seats opposite each other and worked at unballing the crumpled-up wads of paper. Two were badly singed, the information compromised by the fire. Vaughn turned the pages around and slid them across the table to me.

"I'd rather you look at them first. I've known Sheila for several years, and that's her personal business. If there's something there that disturbs you, tell me. Otherwise, I think it's best to keep her secrets secret."

I nodded and scanned the pages. It took a few minutes to figure out what I was looking at. Sheila's name and address were listed on the top of the piece of paper. The fields for date of birth and social security number were crossed out. A bold line had been drawn across the page, the indentation of the pen still present even though the pages had been crumpled into balls. There was one line of handwriting along the bottom of the page:

Entrant #47 does not pass background check.

Twenty-three

"Is it bad?" Vaughn asked.

I looked up at him. "I don't know. How long have you known Sheila?"

"Four years. That's when she started working at the Waverly House."

"Do you have any idea what kind of background check they run?"

"The usual. Credit, referrals, follow-up with former employers. Why?"

I put my hand over the document. "How easy would it be to fake that stuff?"

"You could probably fake the referrals and the former employees, but not the credit check. Why?"

"It says here that Sheila didn't pass the background check."

Vaughn reached for the pages and I pulled them away from him.

"You said you didn't want to see these."

"I changed my mind."

"Okay, fine. Help me understand what this means." I passed the page to him. While he looked over the info I'd already read, I moved on to the second page. It showed the overall results of Sheila's psychological profile. Comments below the scores cited concerns about her mental instability. Under general comments were the words: *We do not recommend entrant #47 be chosen to participate in the pageant.*

Entrant number 47. That's who Sheila was to the people who did the screening. But who would be able to connect those numbers to the names of the test takers?

"Do you think Harvey had access to this information?"

"I don't know. Why?"

"It says something here about mental instability. That's not something she would want to get out. What if she confronted Harvey at the garden party about this? What if she snapped when she didn't get in?"

"Sheila is thin. Harvey was a pretty sizeable man. It wouldn't exactly be a fair fight."

"Harvey was stabbed. You don't have to be strong to stab someone. You just need the element of surprise."

"Do you really believe Sheila is the killer?" he asked.

"Do you really believe she couldn't be?"

"It's hard to think that someone I've known for years could do something like this," he said.

"I think the bigger question is: What's stressing her out so much that she's on the verge of losing it?"

It was after eleven when Vaughn and I reached Material Girl. Any sense of romance that had lingered from our date had left in light of the information about Sheila. We said good night, and he headed back to the Waverly House, where he'd left his car.

After a sleepless night filled with questions upon questions, I got up at five thirty, fed the cats, and considered what I'd discovered in the past few days.

I'd learned the truth about Charlie and the story of her sister Lucy. And then there was Ned, Lucy's father. He'd been talking to Harvey Halliwell at the garden party. I was still certain that I'd seen him take something from inside Harvey's jacket. Knowing that Charlie herself suspected Ned of wanting to capitalize on her connection with the McMichael family only made my suspicions worse. Charlie owed Ned a lot for giving her a home after the years she'd spent bouncing around foster homes, and for giving her the money to start her own life. I imagined those four years were the only time Charlie had let down her guard when she was growing up. But Ned had put her in a difficult position. He had asked her to make amends with her biological father in order to help her sister. That was bound to change any fond feelings Charlie had for Ned.

Then there was Sheila. She'd lied about her application and had been rejected over a background check. Was whatever she was hiding big enough that she'd kill to keep it quiet?

And Violet Garden. She blamed Harvey for losing her daughter. She said she was going to put a stop to the pageant once and for all. Had that threat included murder of the pageant's founder?

But Harvey had been paranoid. What had he said when I tried to help him? *They're all out to get me. Me and my money.* So who would have the best chance of getting his money? One of his employees. And I knew three of them: Inez Platt, Beth Fields, and Nolene Kelly.

First, there was Inez. Once the face of the Tangorli advertising campaign, she now spent her days in a greenhouse with plants she referred to as her friends. Was she really the faithful employee of Halliwell Industries, happy to move from the limelight to the privacy of the Halliwell laboratories, or had she held a grudge all these years—one that she finally acted on?

Beth and Nolene worked in the corporate side of Halliwell Industries. But why would either woman kill her employer? Nolene had admitted to having financial control over Harvey's accounts. He was worth more to her alive than dead. And Beth was so distraught over Harvey's murder that she could barely keep the phone lines straight at the front desk.

It was all so confusing, I should have stayed in bed.

But I didn't. I took a quickie shower, slapped on minimal makeup, and dressed in a black T-shirt and cargo pants. As soon as I saw Charlie raise the hinged doors in front of the bays of her garage, I ran across the street and joined her in her office.

On any given day, Charlie had a rolled-out-of-bed appearance that was equal parts out-all-night and don't-mess-with-me. When she made an effort, there was a dash of hot rod pinup girl in the mix. Today her thick dreadlocked hair had been pulled back in a low ponytail. Dark circles under her eyes, caused from lack of sleep, not leftover eyeliner, gave her a weary look. A black bandana was tied around her forehead and worn low like the host of *Pimp My Ride*. She already wore her standard blue coveralls and her black leather motorcycle boots.

"Any word from Lucy?" I asked.

"Nada. When she wasn't back by midnight, I went out looking for her. I think I got five minutes of sleep."

"What about Ned?"

"What about him? He went home and left Lucy in my care. What could I possibly tell him? Lucy's eighteen. She's the same age I was when Ned told me to go start a life of my own. I understand that. If she felt like she had to leave, then I'm not going to be the one to stop her."

"Lucy isn't reliving your life. She grew up with parents.

She's had one home, one family. It isn't like when Ned encouraged you to start your own life."

"She doesn't know that. Did you think at all about what we were in the middle of when she overheard us? I said I thought her father was using her to help me get to McMichael's money. I practically accused him of it. If she heard that, she'd think she was a burden. Or that she didn't have any chance of winning the contest on her own. Or worse. Maybe she never wanted to be a part of this contest. Maybe her father pushed her into it because he's hoping she gets a big payoff."

"Have you told anybody else that she's missing?"

"Like who?"

"Anybody. Big Joe, Duke, Vaughn, Genevieve—"

"No. Maybe I should. She doesn't know anybody here. She doesn't know where anything is. She already got lost once. I can't imagine where she'd go."

"She does know somebody. She knows Nolene." I reached for Charlie's phone.

She put her hand on top of the receiver. "If you let Nolene know Lucy hasn't been staying with me, she'll be disqualified."

"I have an idea. Trust me." I kept my hand on the phone and stared down Charlie until she moved her hand away. I called Halliwell Industries and asked to speak to Nolene's assistant, Beth.

"Hi, Poly. Is everything fine with the dresses?"

"Yes. They're all complete and hanging on a rolling rack at my shop. That's why I'm calling. Can we coordinate a time and place for me to hand them over to the young women?"

"I thought they would have taken them when they were done. Hmmm." I heard a clicking sound from the other end of the phone, and imagined her fruit earrings clacking against the receiver. "What are your store hours?"

"Ten to six daily. Twelve to six on Sunday. The thing is, it's just me at the store, and I need to concentrate on regular business. If we can set up a window of time for them to pick up their dresses, it would be less disruptive than if they trickle in one at a time. Plus, well, it seems more fair that way, too."

"It does, doesn't it?" The clacking stopped and I heard papers rustling. "How about Sunday afternoon? The salons across the street are closed so the young ladies can finalize hair and makeup choices. I'll add to their agenda that they need to visit with you when they're done."

I didn't want to have to wait until the end of the day tomorrow. "Can you send me a copy of their agenda? Maybe I can figure something out."

"Poly, this pageant runs on a very tight schedule. Details are kept confidential so there can be no accusations of favoritism."

I sighed. "What about Sunday afternoon? Can they come to me before they do hair and makeup?"

"What do you expect them to do with their gowns? Hang them in the beauty salon where they can absorb the smell of hair spray and processing fluid? No. Sunday afternoon. I'll make sure they know."

I set the receiver back on the cradle and turned to Charlie. "Do you know Beth Fields?"

"No. Who's she?"

"She's Nolene's assistant. She's the one who's going to call the contestants and tell them to come see me tomorrow night. Which means she's the one who's going to know if one of the young women is missing."

"So I have until Sunday afternoon to find out where Lucy went."

Twenty-four

I headed back to the fabric store, no smarter than I'd been when I left. Lilly was out front with Tiki Tom. They stared at Tom's new window display. Inside the narrow window was a large movie poster for *Blue Hawaii*. The image showed Elvis, his guitar, and several island girls. Tom had wedged a small wooden table into the window and covered it with hula girl collectibles: ceramic salt and pepper shakers, ashtrays, lamps, and wood carvings. On the floor were instructional DVDs on how to hula dance.

Tom stroked his pointy gray beard. "Something's missing," he said. "I can't put my finger on it."

"Ask Poly. She likes to get involved with things that have nothing to do with her." Lilly stepped backward, gave me a tight-lipped smile, and went to her shop.

"Did I miss something?" I asked.

"Never mind those Garden sisters. They don't like that you're involved in the pageant."

"My involvement is almost over. The dresses are done and the young women are going to pick them up on Sunday afternoon. With that one exception, it's back to business as usual for me."

"Still, I'd be careful if I were you. Violet gets a little irrational this time of year, and Lilly gets overprotective. Probably for the best that anybody connected to the pageant steers clear of them."

"Maybe I can convince them to close the shop early on Sunday," I said. "Now, about this window, I know exactly what's missing. Wait here."

I unlocked the door to Material Girl and found a rack of brightly colored, tropical printed bolts of cotton. There were six. I carried the stack of them to the cutting station and measured off two yards of the top one, a leafy green print with bright red hibiscus flowers printed by the border. Small yellow and white flowers filled the center of the fabric and added to the image, conjuring up the lush gardens of Polynesia. I folded the cutting over itself, selvage edge to selvage edge, and carried it to a nude bust form. With care, I wrapped the fabric, fold side up, around the back of the headless and armless mannequin, crossed the fabric in front, and knotted it at the back of the neck. It took a little effort to adjust the fabric over the bust and ensure modesty, but when I was done, I had a no-sew tropical dress that had taken five minutes to assemble.

I rolled the bust form out the front door and onto the sidewalk. Tom whistled.

"You just happened to have that lying around?" he asked.

"I made it just for you."

"Well, she's just what this window needs. How much you want me to charge for the dress?"

"The dress isn't for sale," I said. "But there is one thing you could do for me if you want."

I outlined the idea that I'd gotten the other night at The Broadside. Genevieve had said that for women, going to a bar was a social event, and that was what I was going to give them. Their very own happy hour at the fabric store. Women could come to the store, order fabric like they would order drinks, and spend the next hour learning how to make the fabric into something wearable. I'd start with a no-sew project like a pareo that could be tied a hundred different ways.

"Tell you what," Tiki Tom said. "Since you're lending me your mannequin, I'll lend you a portable tiki bar. You can take the orders from there. Give me a flyer and I'll promote your thing from inside my store and send out an e-mail blast for you. Maybe you can talk up my merchandise and we could get a nice crossover of business. It's just the beginning of summer. Definitely perfect for luau season."

"It's a deal." I thanked Tom and headed back to Material Girl to work out the details of my plan.

Several hours and four customers later, I realized I hadn't eaten all day. I called The Broadside. "Do you have anything healthy on your lunch menu?" I asked Duke when he answered.

"Define healthy. Our burgers are one hundred percent pure beef. If you want, I'll toss in an order of onion rings so you can get your vegetables." He chuckled.

"If only Earl of Sandwich delivered, I wouldn't have to put up with this."

"Why do you need delivery?"

"I'm trapped at the store. No help today. If I want to eat, it's you or pizza."

"So, what'll it be?"

I sighed. "I'll take a burger. Just make sure there's lettuce and tomato on it."

Twenty minutes later, Duke rolled his wheelchair into my shop. A white plastic take-out bag dangled from one of the handles of the chair. He spun himself around and backed up. "Door-to-door delivery. How do you like that?"

"I like it a lot. Thanks." I fished in my wallet for a ten.

Duke's lunchtime special was the five-dollar burger. When he pulled his own wallet out to make change, I stopped him. "Keep the change."

"It's not often I get a hundred percent tip," he said.

"It's not often I get a marketing idea from hanging around a bar," I said back.

"You really were stealing my ideas?" He narrowed his eyes but I could tell he was being playful.

"Yep. And Tiki Tom is in on it, so you better watch out."

"I don't have to worry about that guy. He's as loopy as the nets he has hanging from his ceiling."

"I wouldn't be too sure of that." I untied the bag and pulled out the burger. Juices were pressed against the inside of the parchment paper that it had been wrapped in. I tore off the top of the paper and took a bite, careful to keep my hands from getting soiled.

Duke felt around the pocket on the outside of his chair and came up with a bottle of water. "Figured you'd want something to drink with it."

"You figured right." I uncapped the bottle and took a long drink.

"So what's this all about?" he asked.

I told him about my idea to have people come to the store between four and six for a fabric happy hour. "Tom's going to lend me a tiki bar so people can actually order. And the first project won't require any sewing. Only the purchase of two yards of fabric."

"What are you going to have them make?"

"A pareo. Go next door and look in the window."

Duke rolled himself out of the shop and returned a couple of minutes later. "Not bad," he said. "You said you got this idea when you were at my place?"

"Sort of. Genevieve was the one who triggered it. We were talking about your clientele." I stopped talking. I didn't want to insult Duke's regulars. They were the people who paid his bills, not me and my lousy once-a-month burger habit.

"It's okay. I know my crowd is a little rough around the edges. I've tried to do something about it but nothing seems to work. Is that why you and your friend don't come more often?"

"A little. Genevieve's the one who said that for women, drinking is social. That's what connected the idea of a social event with a happy hour."

"I like it. Tell you what. I'll add a couple of island drinks to the happy hour menu. If your customers are already in a social mood, maybe they'll come over when they're done. If I can get enough of a different crowd to start showing up, that'll change the mix."

"Duke, that's a great idea. I'll make sure to let my customers know. Assuming anybody shows up," I said.

"When are you planning on starting this?"

"I don't know."

"Why not tonight? Do a trial run. You've got a couple of hours before four o'clock, right? And you're open until six?"

"Yes, but can I really get the word out in a couple of hours?"

"There's one way to find out," he said. He backed his wheelchair away, spun in a half circle, and left.

As it turned out, I could. First I sent an e-mail blast to my growing list of customers. After that I called Genevieve, Maria Lopez, and every other person I knew in San Ladrón and asked them to help spread the word. Then I went next door and helped Tom carry the portable tiki bar to my shop. He moved the sewing area to the far wall and positioned the bar on a diagonal inside the entrance. I emptied a round fixture that held a dozen bolts of fabric, put the tropical prints on every other spoke, and filled in the spaces between them with luxurious sateens that conjured up the colors of blue sky, sand beaches, teal oceans, and fern-green leaves. Tom moved the mannequin from inside his window to the sidewalk between our two stores and pinned on a sign that said, *Learn to dress like an island girl! Free hula lessons with purchase.*

I downloaded four Martin Denny CDs from iTunes and played them over the fabric store's sound system, then called Vaughn and asked if he was interested in cutting out of work early for the rest of the day. I rolled the rack of pageant dresses to the back of the fabric store, into a small section that had been partitioned off years ago. I didn't like spending time back there and planned to one day tear the wall down and expand the shop.

The event was successful. Genevieve arrived with three of her new regulars, and two of Maria's sisters who helped her run Neato came with friends, too. Many of the ladies who had stopped in the shop for one thing or another—a yard of fabric here, a spool of thread there—left with a re-newed interest in the possibilities that the fabric store held. Even Betty, the no-sew tablecloth customer, had gotten my e-mail and showed up with her faithful companion, Archie.

After a demonstration on the mannequin, I handed out an instruction card with twenty ways to tie a pareo and a link to a page on my website where I promised to post even more.

"Are you going to run sewing classes?" asked one lady.

"How about teaching us to make curtains?"

"I want to make an apron."

"I could make pajamas for my husband."

"I could make pajamas for my dog!"

But the question that kept coming up over and over was, "Will you do this again next Friday?"

I answered yes without hesitation. For an impromptu event, I considered it a success beyond my wildest expectations.

One by one the women left. Betty and Archie lingered

behind. "So, what do you think?" I asked her. "Maybe you'll pick out fabric for yourself instead of your furniture."

She held up a bag. "I already did," she said. "I need a dress for a special occasion, and I think I'm going to dust off my sewing machine and see if I can make it myself."

"That's terrific," I said. "A special dress to celebrate a special occasion. Who wouldn't want that?"

Her eyes clouded. "I don't know if it's going to be much of a celebration, but it's something I've put off for a long time."

I didn't like that her happiness had been replaced by seriousness so quickly. I put my hand on her arm to console her. "Betty, is there something you want to talk about?"

"I— No. It's just"—she looked up at me—"there's something I have to do here in San Ladrón. I just wish it weren't going to be so hard."

"Sometimes the hardest things to do are the most rewarding," I said.

"I'm not looking for a reward. I'm looking for closure."

I didn't need to look around at the fabric shop to know the place needed some TLC, but that could wait. I went to the coffee station and poured two cups of hot water, then placed tea bags into each. "I don't know about you, but I need to sit down. Can you join me?"

Betty looked hesitant at first but then seemed to decide to stay. She took one of the disposable cups from me and sat down in one of the vacant chairs. I turned another empty chair to face her and sat down, resting my foot on the seat behind her. Archie stood on the exposed concrete floors. He strained the length of his leash trying to get to the foot of the stairs. I looked up and saw Needles's orange furry head poking around the side, staring back at him. Archie yipped twice, then looked at Betty and me to see if we saw Needles, too. He turned back and barked again. Betty kept the loop of the leash wrapped around her wrist.

"You never did tell me what brings you to San Ladrón," I said.

She took a sip of tea. "I write articles for an online magazine. A bunch of them, actually. It doesn't pay much, but every once in a while one gets syndicated and I get wide exposure. I thought—this pageant might make for an interesting story."

The way she hesitated while talking made me suspect that she was choosing her words carefully. Not lying, but piecing together a safe answer for me while keeping her real agenda to herself. Like the first day she'd walked into Material Girl, she seemed unsure of herself.

"Do you know much about the background of the pageant? Or are you learning as you go?" I asked.

She glanced up at me and then back down into her cup. "I knew somebody who was a contestant once, but I thought maybe things had changed. I came here to get some background information, local color, and then maybe track down some previous contestants to find out how it impacted their lives."

"A human interest piece. So how is that related to your search for closure?"

"What?" She looked up at me, confused.

"Earlier, you said you came here for closure. I'm curious about how that relates to the article." Something dawned on me. "Your friend, the one who was in the pageant—what's her name?"

"She asked me not to say," she said. She stood up and carried her cup to the wrap stand. "I should be going before it gets too late." She tugged Archie's leash in the direction of the front doors and they left.

I spent the next forty-five minutes putting the store back together. Fabrics were rewound on their bolts, scissors were collected and stashed in cylindrical cups on the cutting table, yardsticks and tape measures were returned to their bins by the wrap stand. I threw out all of the empty paper cups and swept the floor. Eventually, I ran out of energy and collapsed into a plastic chair. I closed my eyes and tipped my head back, inhaling and exhaling deeply.

After several breaths, someone in front of me cleared his throat. I opened my eyes and saw the silhouette of a man in an expensive business suit standing next to the mannequin draped in a luau print.

Vic McMichael was paying me a visit.

I jumped up from my chair and smoothed out the creases in my cargo pants. Threads from the cuttings of tropical printed fabrics clung to my T-shirt. I brushed at them but there were too many to wipe away.

"I imagine that's a side effect of running a fabric store," Mr. McMichael said.

"When it comes to work attire, I can't win. At the dress shop in L.A. it was grease stains and glue guns. Now it's thread from frayed fabric."

"Which is perfectly acceptable for the job you have."

"I always heard I should dress for the job I want. I guess I am."

"Ms. Monroe, it was my understanding that your business day ended at six. If you don't have any pressing engagements, there's something I'd like to discuss with you."

"Does this have to do with the loan on my fabric store? The first payment isn't due until September."

"No, this doesn't have anything to do with that. I'm here to talk to you about Lucy Rains . . . and about my daughter, Charlie."

Twenty-five

If there had been one thing I didn't expect Mr. McMichael to say, that would have been it. I stood, speechless, staring at him. He stepped closer and held his hand out until it touched my sleeve.

"Ms. Monroe?" he said.

"Poly. Call me Poly."

"Fine, Poly." He didn't ask me to call him Vic, which was probably for the best, as I wasn't sure I could do it if he did.

"Mr. McMichael, can you give me a few minutes to finish closing the store? I think we would both prefer not to be interrupted during our conversation."

He nodded once, slowly, and closed his eyes in a long blink. I held out an open palm and gestured toward the chair. He stepped closer to it but didn't sit down.

As intimidating as Mr. McMichael could be, I refused to let him know his visit shook me up. I walked to the front door at a normal pace, turned the *Open* sign to *Closed*, and pulled the hinged green gate across the opening and secured it. When I turned back toward Mr. McMichael, I saw Needles on the wrap stand behind him, one paw out, swatting at his sleeve.

"Needles!" I said.

Mr. McMichael's eyes went wide. "Excuse me?"

"Needles is behind you." I crossed the room and scooped the orange kitty up from where he stood and set him on the ground. He meowed at me.

"Are these the kittens from the Dumpster? My son told me about them."

"Yes, this is Needles. There's a gray one around here somewhere. His name is Pins."

"Cats in a fabric store. I imagine it's great fun for them. Have they caused you any trouble?"

"Not after I moved the chiffon and netting to the top shelf," I said. He smiled. "I may not know everything there is to know about running a fabric store, but I'm a quick study."

He glanced at the display of tropical fabrics and the tiki bar at the front entrance of the store. "I can see that."

"Mr. McMichael, you didn't come here to find out what kind of promotions I'm running. I don't really have much of an office down here in the store. Would you like to follow me upstairs? We can talk in my living room."

A troubled expression came over his face. I knew that once upon a time, when he had been married to Adelaide, he had been friends with my great-aunt and great-uncle. A falling-out over money had resulted in the loss of friendship and from there had eroded into the belief that Mr. McMichael had something to do with my great-aunt's murder. It had been a long time since anyone invited him to ascend those stairs and relax in that living room.

But this whole move to San Ladrón had been about new beginnings for me. I'd left my boyfriend, my job, and my post-college friends so I could reopen the fabric store. I made a new set of friends with Genevieve and Charlie and Vaughn and the Lopezes, and more people than I could list. Maybe in the spirit of new beginnings, Mr. McMichael deserved one, too.

I powered off the cash register and then pulled a heavy canvas cover over it. On a normal day I'd finish up by sweeping, but that could wait. Mr. McMichael followed me to the stairs. Halfway up Needles bolted past me, then sat by the front door waiting for me to catch up. The door was open a crack. I pushed it farther, trying to remember the last time I'd cleaned.

A quilt lay in a pile on the sofa with Pins in the middle of it. His head was on his paw. He opened one eye and looked at us. I gave him a gentle wake-up nudge and tugged on the quilt. He stood up, stretched, and hopped from the sofa to the coffee table. I tucked the quilt on the bottom shelf of the maple end table next to the sofa and turned back around to face Mr. McMichael.

He stood, formally, by the front of the room, framed by the wood molding that surrounded the door. His eyes scanned the interior of the room. I hadn't done much in the way of decorating since moving in, so I knew what he saw was what my Uncle Marius had left behind when he passed away. And knowing that Uncle Marius had mourned my Aunt Millie's murder for the last ten years of his life, I suspected he hadn't spent much of his alone time decorating.

"Can I offer you anything? Tea? Coffee?"

"No, thank you." He looked at the lace curtains that barely contained the sunlight that spilled in from outside, then scanned the rest of the room. "It's been a long time since I've been in this room," he said.

"Mr. McMichael, why don't you have a seat?"

He moved to an overstuffed chair that was covered in a floral pattern, set his briefcase down next to it, and sat. I took a seat on the sofa but didn't relax. For a couple of awkward seconds we both stared at Pins, who had decided to clean his face. When he was finished, he sat for a second and then lifted his leg and started cleaning down below. No!

Mr. McMichael cleared his throat. "Poly, last night a young woman came to visit me. Her name is Lucy Rains. Do you know her?"

"She came to you? Why?"

"It seems she is related to my daughter through adoption. She overheard a conversation between you and Charlie, and it upset her very much. I'd like to know what that conversation was about."

"With all due respect, that was a private conversation. It would be a violation of Charlie's trust to tell you."

"My dear, you're dating my son. And you provided a solution to my ex-wife's fund-raising problems while avoiding the almost unavoidable war with me. You made no secret of your suspicions of me when you moved to San Ladrón, and I assume you were not happy when I cosigned the loan for your fabric store. Yet when I told you I wanted to talk to you about Charlie, you let me into your home. You have somehow managed to befriend my estranged daughter and even inspire her trust. I respect that friendship. But after talking to Lucy, I have reason to believe that Charlie might be in danger, and I can't take that chance."

"What else did Lucy tell you?"

"Her dad has known for a long time that I am Charlie's biological father. He knew when Charlie lived with him. He contacted me for money on more than one occasion."

"You paid him off to keep your identity secret?"

"No. Had Charlie wanted to know my identity, she would have found out. The paper trail was not sealed."

"That's not what Ned told her."

"I'm starting to see that." Mr. McMichael studied me. "I'm afraid my ex-wife and I had moved into a place where we wanted little to do with each other. The one thing we agreed on was that our baby would have a better life with a family who wanted to be together than with two people who wanted to be apart. We gave her up for adoption in the hopes that she would grow up in a home more stable than the one we could provide."

I looked down at my hands for a moment and rubbed my thumb against the rough calluses that had developed from sewing. "When did you find out about the foster homes?"

"Not right away. I knew very little about Charlie's childhood. I felt I didn't have the right to interfere. Vaughn was young, and I didn't want him to feel the repercussions of the divorce, either. I spent most of my time at work, establishing the business so he would have something to inherit."

I stared off to the side of the chair for a few seconds. "Charlie tried to find you. She left a letter with the adoption agency, filed a petition for her records, and contacted each of her foster parents. Or she thought she did. The only piece of information that ever reached her was from her first foster parents. They sent her birth certificate and that brought her to San Ladrón. If nothing else she did ever reached you, then how did you find out?"

"I received a letter from a Mr. Ned Rains in Encino. I don't know how he found out the truth, but I know he didn't learn it from Charlie. He described her, sent pictures of some personal things that we had given her when we took her to the agency—her baby blanket and a stuffed animal. I didn't want to believe that he was talking about her. I contacted the adoption agency and asked them where she was. They confirmed that she'd been in and out of several foster homes and that her whereabouts were currently unknown. Everything matched what Mr. Rains told me in the letter."

"What did you do?"

"I was devastated. I'd wanted her to connect with a family and instead she had gone through most of her life alone. And all the while, I'd worked on building up an empire to leave to my son. The guilt was almost overwhelming."

I studied Mr. McMichael. His voice was strong and steady, and he maintained the appearance of control that I'd come to associate with him. Yet his words spoke of great emotional wounds. Had he come to disassociate himself from what had happened to his only daughter in order to accept his role in her life?

"Soon after I confirmed the truth with the adoption agency, I received another letter from Mr. Rains. Charlie had practically raised herself at this point, but he said he would give her a place to live and teach her a trade. From then on, I received postcards every few months telling me about her skills as a mechanic, her aptitude with cars, her tenacity. He didn't ask me for money until she turned eighteen."

"The two thousand dollars," I said quietly. It seemed like such a small amount to ask a man of Mr. McMichael's means.

"Two thousand dollars?" he repeated.

"Charlie told me when she turned eighteen, Ned gave her two thousand dollars and told her it was time for her to move on, to start her own life. That's the money she used to come to San Ladrón."

He stood up suddenly and turned his back on me. He pushed the lace curtains aside and stared out the window in the direction of Charlie's Auto. He didn't turn around when he spoke.

"No, it wasn't two thousand dollars. It was fifty thousand dollars in a trust fund. I didn't want it to be traceable back to me so I called in a favor from a friend."

I could think of only one friend of Mr. McMichael who would be willing to do a fifty-thousand-dollar favor.

"Harvey Halliwell?"

He turned back toward me. "Yes. I wrote him a check and he set up an account for Charlie under Halliwell Industries."

Twenty-six

"So Ned thought the money came from Harvey?" I asked.

"That was the intent. When I set up the trust, I told Harvey I was not to know the details of the account."

"Meaning what?"

"It was far too late for me to try to get involved in Charlie's life. The money was there. She could take it out in a lump sum, or refuse to take any of it. I didn't want to know."

"Does Adelaide know anything about this?"

"Adelaide knows nothing about this. I handled the details of the adoption. Our divorce was not what you'd call amiable, and I felt no need to inform her of the terrible mistake we'd made."

"And now it seems like Ned never told Charlie about the account."

"Yes, it seems like that's a possibility. Please understand. For me to expect anything from Charlie would have been wrong. I had given up my rights to be a father to her. Ned Rains offered her a home and that's what I wanted for her. But I felt it was not my place to interfere in her life, not at this point. I don't know what became of the money, but it was given with no strings attached."

"Mr. McMichael, if you set up an account with fifty thousand dollars and Ned only gave Charlie two, what happened to the rest of the money?" I asked.

"At this point I have to assume he kept the money for himself. Even more troubling is, after speaking to his daughter Lucy, I suspect she did not benefit from the windfall. She came to me because she thinks her father confronted Harvey Halliwell over money the night before he was murdered."

"He was there," I confirmed. "They argued. Harvey collapsed on the ground and Ned took something from his jacket."

"You are sure of this?"

"I saw it with my own eyes. Vaughn was with me but he didn't. I've played that night over and over in my mind and I can't figure out if I'm missing something. What I don't understand is that Harvey regained consciousness within about a minute. He left before we could call the police."

"And he was found murdered the next morning."

"Was Harvey prone to fainting? Did he have a preexisting medical condition?"

"Quite the contrary. When I suffered my heart attack, Harvey was the picture of health. Almost overnight I became dependent on medication to regulate my pulse while Harvey charged around China like a youngster. Nothing makes a man feel old like the knowledge that he can no longer keep up with his friends. Harvey claimed it was the Tangorli juice he drank all of the time." He chuckled to himself. "He sent me cases when I was recovering."

I flashed back to the night Harvey had passed out and remembered him drinking something orange. Was it possible that Ned had put something in the juice that made Harvey faint?

"Did he arrange for there to be juice at the Waverly House garden party?"

"I imagine so. He arranged for all of the social events to stock pitchers of Tangorli juice for him. Most of the time he donated cases for free publicity."

My mind started buzzing. Ned had been at the party, but so had Sheila. As an employee of the Waverly House, she would have had access to the food and beverage.

"I think we need to talk to Sheriff Clark and tell him what you told me," I said.

"Sheriff Clark has been privy to everything I've told you today."

"So he knows about Charlie?" I caught myself.

"Yes. I asked him to keep it confidential, but in the interest of protecting both her and Lucy, I wasn't willing to keep a secret that could possibly save a life."

"Where is Lucy now?" I asked.

"She spent the night in my guest room."

I thanked Mr. McMichael for confiding in me and walked him to the front door. During our conversation, the sun had started its descent, creating long shadows behind the cars parked by the curb and alongside the streetlamps and benches that lined the road. I looked left and right for the silver BMW I expected to see. It wasn't there.

"Where's your car?" I asked.

"In light of circumstances, I suspected you would not want my car to be parked in front of your store." He waved his hand at the yellow taxi idling by the curb across the street. "My car is parked in my space in front of my office."

The taxi pulled around to the front of my building. Mr. McMichael shook my hand. "My son is a very good judge of character," he said. "Thank you for inviting me into your home."

We shook hands. "Thank you for confiding in me," I replied.

He shut the door behind him and the taxi sped off down the street.

I stole a peek at Charlie's shop. The bays were closed and the lights were off. If Lucy had returned that morning, the two of them had a lot to talk about. I went inside the fabric store and swept half of the interior before taking a break to think over what Mr. McMichael had told me.

Charlie believed that Ned Rains had put a roof over her head and put food on her table. She thought of him as the skilled mechanic who taught her how to work on cars, the generous man who gave her the money she used to start a life of her own when she turned eighteen. But she was starting to doubt all of that, with good reason.

According to Mr. McMichael, Ned had known about Charlie's real past. He established contact and communicated about Charlie's life with some degree of regularity. For four years. And then, when the money arrived, it was in a trust marked Halliwell Industries. That trust linked Mr. McMichael's wealth to Harvey Halliwell's company.

Soon after Charlie left, Ned and his girlfriend married and had a daughter: Lucy. Had Ned planned all along to tap Mr. McMichael for more money? Or more probable, had he used up the trust fund that had been established and gone back to the well—not the McMichael well, but the Halliwell well?

I followed my train of thought. Harvey had been instructed to keep Mr. McMichael in the dark about the activities of the account. What if Ned had continued to go to Harvey for money? What if Harvey never learned that Charlie had left? As a goodwill gesture on behalf of his friend, he might have continued to make payments. If that was the case, there had to be a record of those payments.

The only question was how would I gain access to Harvey's accounts? And then I remembered one person who would know: Nolene.

Considering I'd had suspicions about Nolene before I knew about Ned, I wanted the element of surprise when I talked to her. It was after eight and she told me she was at the office until nine most nights.

I headed to Halliwell Industries. Traffic had thinned to only a few drivers, and I pulled into the parking lot about ten minutes later. Unlike the last time I was here, I counted seven cars in the lot. One of them was a blue convertible. I parked under a lamp and headed toward the path that led to the main building. A golf cart chugged its way around the back and the driver waved. Even though the driver's face was covered in a surgical mask, I recognized Inez's long black hair and tanned skin. I waved back and she stopped the cart.

"You coming to see me?" she asked.

"Not tonight. I'm hoping to catch Nolene," I said, and pointed up to the main building.

"She's been burning the midnight oil since Harvey died." She pulled a lanyard from around her neck and handed it to me. "Security's pretty sparse at night. Take my pass key and go to the ninth floor. She's the first office on the left."

"Don't you need this?"

"In the past thirty years I've lost half a dozen key cards. Harvey never considered me a security threat since I spend most of my time in the greenhouse. He had extras made for me." She reached inside her white lab coat and pulled out another orange lanyard like the one she'd handed me. "I think he wanted me to be available whenever he wanted a glass of fresh Tangorli juice."

"He called you for that?"

"Why not? The greenhouse is next to the field of trees. What could be fresher than a pitcher of juice made from freshly picked fruit?"

Inez drove the cart away. I turned the key card over in my hands. It was a white rectangle with a hole along one end. An orange cord had been clipped to the hole. "Halliwell Industries" was printed on the front of the card. On the back was a magnetic strip. I approached the building and tugged on the front door. When it didn't open, I looked around until I found a freestanding box with a small slot. I fed the card into the slot, "ACCESS" appeared on the screen in green digital type, and the door released with a quiet *click*.

Inez had been right about the security booth being vacant. I activated the elevators with the key card and rode to the ninth floor. Locked glass doors with the words "Halliwell Industries Corporate Offices" met me when the elevator doors opened. Once again, the key card gave me access. After a few steps down the carpeted hallway, I was outside an office with Nolene's name out front. The door was open but Nolene wasn't there.

I turned around and scanned the rest of the floor. Closed doors painted in citrus shades lined the perimeter of the floor. Cubicles sat in the center of the space.

"Nolene? Are you here?" I called. No answer. I stepped inside her office, put my hand in my sleeve, and tapped her keyboard through the fabric. The screen remained dark. A peek at the tower told me the computer had been powered off. Had she left for the night? I rolled her desk chair back and found her handbag on the floor by the foot of her chair.

She was still here, somewhere. I stepped back out front and called her name again. No response. It appeared that for now, I was alone in the executive offices. There was no telling how much time I had. I used the flashlight app on my phone to illuminate the shelves in Nolene's office and zeroed in on a shelf of notebooks marked "Financial Records."

Bingo.

The spines of the notebooks were each labeled with a range of years. On the third shelf up the dates corresponded to the years Charlie lived with Ned. I wedged my phone under the bottom of a binder on the second shelf and aimed the light down at the pages. It was slow going, first figuring out how the notebook was organized. I was halfway through the third notebook when I heard a sound in the hallway.

Twenty-seven

The binder fell from the shelf and landed on the carpet. I bent down for it and tried to put it back on the shelf. The surrounding notebooks had tipped, leaving no space. In a panic, I shoved the notebook into my messenger bag and left Nolene's office. Inez stood on the other side of the glass doors. She fed a key card into the slot and the doors clicked open.

She stepped inside the offices and looked back and forth in the dark. "Did you find Nolene?" she asked.

"No. I called her name but she didn't answer."

"Maybe she left."

"Her handbag is still in her office."

"That's odd." Inez clicked on the overhead lights and went to Nolene's office. "Were you in here all this time?" she asked.

"When she didn't answer me, I thought maybe she was in the ladies' room. I was kind of hoping she'd come back and tell me where it was," I said, shifting from one foot to the other to make a convincing show of my lie.

Inez brushed her long black hair off of her shoulders. "Come with me. I'll show you where it is."

I followed her out of the offices and down the hall to the restrooms. "I'll wait out here for you. I hope you don't mind, but I'm calling it a night and I don't feel right leaving you alone in the offices."

"Sure, I understand. I'll be out in a second." I went into the ladies' room, locked myself into a stall, and shoved the financial records into the bottom of my bag. I didn't feel great about stealing information from Halliwell Industries, but after talking to Mr. McMichael, I had a feeling Harvey's murder had something to do with money. I flushed the toilet for good show and then washed my hands. The paper towel fixture was empty so I dried them on my T-shirt. Inez stood in the hallway waiting for me.

"How are the pageant dresses coming?" she asked.

"They're all done. The young women are picking them up on Sunday afternoon."

"Isn't that pushing it a little close, with the pageant being on Sunday night?"

"Nolene's timetable, not mine."

Inez pushed the down button by the elevator wells. "Nolene is the master of scheduling," she said. "She probably ran downstairs to check on the event setup."

The elevator doors opened and we got inside. I looked around for a slot for the key card and Inez waved me off. "What goes up must come down," she said. "You only need the card to activate the up elevators." She held out her palm and I set the card in it.

We reached the front doors. Inez exited first and held the door open for me. "If I see Nolene, do you want me to have her call you?"

I became self-conscious about the fact that if Nolene discovered the missing binder, Inez could very easily finger me as a thief.

"No, I'd actually prefer if you didn't mention that I was here. This whole pageant, well, I'm afraid I've made a nuisance of myself with questions. That's why I didn't bother to call first. Would you mind not saying anything?"

Inez smiled. "If the trees won't tell, neither will I."

It would have taken me approximately ten minutes to get home from Halliwell Industries if I hadn't driven right past the intersection of San Ladrón and Bonita Avenue and ended up near Vaughn's place of business. Maybe my subconscious was trying to tell me something. Too bad it was well outside the range of normal business hours. But as long as I was in the neighborhood . . .

I called Vaughn, secretly hoping he wasn't asleep or on a date.

"Hello?" he said.

"Vaughn, it's Poly."

"Good. That means my Caller ID hasn't been compromised."

"I didn't call too late, did I? If I did, I'm sorry. I— We— Can you—"

"This isn't a purely social call, is it?"

"I need to talk to someone I can trust."

"Where are you?"

"The parking lot in front of McMichael Investments."

"How late do you think I work?"

Despite my growing concerns about what I'd learned that evening, I laughed. "You know how you keep telling me you bought a fixer-upper around here? If I promise not to mention the circular saw in the living room, can I come over?"

"Sure. You're about five minutes away."

He gave me directions, which I repeated three times to make sure I had them straight. He was right about the time, and about five minutes later (six and a half), I pulled up in front of a six-story apartment building. Vaughn stood out front, talking to the doorman. He jogged to the car and opened the door before I had a chance to double-check my reflection.

"If I'd known your building had a doorman I probably wouldn't have invited myself over."

"What doorman?"

I pointed to the man in the uniform and Vaughn laughed.

"That's Rubio. He lives in the apartment below me. He wants to pay off his mortgage in five years so he moonlights as a chauffeur."

I might have been mistaken about the doorman, but when we got into the old elevator and Vaughn pushed the button labeled PH, I knew there were a few things I had assumed that would turn out to be right.

The elevator had black-and-white marble on the floor and the walls. Dim lighting filtered down from behind decorative metal scrollwork that I suspected hid the means of escape should the whole contraption malfunction. We reached the penthouse floor and Vaughn led the way around a ten-foot-tall ficus tree that sat below a skylight to a large black door. A silver doorknocker hung above the peephole, and to the right of the door was a tarnished nameplate that said *V. McMichael*.

Vaughn rubbed his fingers over the nameplate. "Hand-me-down from my father. It pays to share his initials, at least when it comes to monograms." He unlocked the door and I followed him inside.

The interior smelled faintly of garlic and basil. A colander of pasta stood on a counter in the kitchen and an empty skillet, still shiny from olive oil, sat on the stove. I leaned over the counter and inhaled deeply. Vaughn stepped behind me and closed the door.

"Welcome to my abode," he said. "It's nowhere near finished, and so far the only people who have seen it, aside from family, have been here to deliver something."

"I guess that means I'm special," I said.

Vaughn put his arms around me. "I guess it does," he whispered.

I leaned back into him and looked around the room. The flat ceiling had been decorated with a mural that radiated out from the center to the corners in metallic colors. Gold, silver, bronze, and copper. The shapes had no hard edges like a decal or a design that had been taped off, but instead floated against the creamy white of the ceiling.

"It's a late deco design, isn't it?"

"The whole apartment is. The last owner hid the beauty of the space. I'm trying to undo what he did to cover it up."

The floor was wood parquet, assembled in a chevron pattern of alternating shades of pine and cherry. The walls were painted a creamy white in alternating stripes of matte and gloss. The room was anchored by a dark gray velvet sofa and two matching chairs around a glass coffee table. All of the furniture exhibited the tubular influence of the art deco era. A vacuum sat off to the side of the room, and in the center of the coffee table, as if it were a Marcel Duchamp readymade piece of art, sat a circular saw.

"I didn't want to disappoint you," he said. He slid his fingers up my arms and gently turned me around. "But you didn't come here to see my circular saw," he added.

"No, I didn't." I took his hand and led him to the sofa. "In the past couple of days, I've learned things about people that I don't think they'd want me to know. One of those people is your sister."

"Charlie's a private person. I don't blame her for that. I admit I was hurt the other night when she told us what it was like for her when she grew up, but that was a selfish reaction. It's hard to accept that I had opportunities she didn't, but I can't change the past."

I leaned forward and ran my hands over my head. How was I going to ask for Vaughn's help without telling him what his father had told me? Could I violate his dad's trust in order to help his sister? Or to help Lucy? Even if it meant learning that her father—Charlie's guardian—turned out to be Harvey Halliwell's killer?

"Hey, hey, what's wrong?" Vaughn asked. He reached forward and brushed a tear off my cheek. Until that moment I hadn't realized I'd started to cry.

"I know too many secrets. I have to violate someone else's trust in order to confide in you and that's not an easy thing for me."

"Can you tell me anything without using names?"

"You'll know who I'm talking about."

"Try me."

I inhaled through my nose and blew it out of my mouth, the way the doctor tells you to breathe when he's listening to your lungs with a stethoscope. "Ned Rains knew your father was Charlie's father almost the entire time she was staying with him. When Charlie turned eighteen, Ned asked your dad for money."

"How do you know that?"

"I can't tell you."

"There are only two people who could verify that story. Ned Rains and my father."

"I'll let you draw your own conclusion."

"So Dad gave Ned the two thousand dollars that he gave Charlie?"

"No. Your dad arranged for a trust of *fifty* thousand dollars for Charlie. But he didn't want it to be traced back to him. He asked Harvey Halliwell to set up the account and handle any correspondence. His instructions to Harvey were to manage the situation with the utmost discretion. He didn't even want to know details. He felt he had given up the right to be involved in Charlie's life, and he didn't want to cause her any more pain by trying to assuage his own guilt over how she grew up."

"How do you know this?"

"I can't tell you," I said again.

"But you're sure it's true?"

"Beyond the shadow of a doubt."

"Then that means Ned kept forty-eight thousand dollars for himself."

"It might mean that. It might also mean that he continued to ask Harvey for money. He's the one who asked Charlie to leave. What if he never told Harvey that Charlie moved out? Harvey might have continued to give him money when he asked and nobody would know."

"Why would Harvey keep making payments?"

"I don't know. I keep remembering what your dad said about them understanding each other. But that's a lot of money. Is that how the rich operate?"

"Not my dad," Vaughn said. "But if Harvey ever stopped sending money, Ned might show up in San Ladrón and confront him face to face," Vaughn said. "You said you saw Ned take something from Harvey when he passed out."

"But you didn't."

"I wish I had. I would like nothing better than to back you up on this."

We sat next to each other in silence. Vaughn leaned against the back of the sofa.

"There's one other thing that bothers me," I said.

"Only one? I can think of half a dozen."

"Nolene told me she handled Harvey's accounts. What if she knew about this? Either she did and she approved the money, or she didn't at first and cut it off when she found out that Charlie left."

"She could have been the catalyst for Ned confronting Harvey at the party."

I glanced up at Vaughn. "If you were to see the financial records of Halliwell Industries for the years after Charlie moved to San Ladrón, could you tell if there were withdrawals that stood out?"

"Poly, I don't know that I like what you're asking me."

I leaned forward and put my hand on his thigh. "Vaughn, someone killed Harvey. If I'm right, and he was murdered over this money, then your father, your sister, and Lucy are all wrapped up in it and a killer is on the loose. Those people are important to both of us."

"What are you asking me to do?"

I pulled the notebook out of my messenger bag and set it on the table. "I borrowed this from Nolene Kelly's office."

His eyes were trained on the leather cover of the notebook. "Borrowed," he repeated.

"I'll get it back to the shelf where I took it as soon as I know what it means."

He opened the notebook and flipped through the first few pages. I didn't interrupt him. The only sound in the room was the ticking of the grandfather clock in the hallway. Several pages in, he sat up a little straighter and flipped backward to an earlier page. His finger traced down the row of numbers and he flipped forward again. Finally he sat back against the sofa and shut the notebook.

"You were right. Harvey's been making deposits into an account every year for the past eighteen years."

"For how much?"

"Fifty thousand dollars."

"That's a lot of money," I said. "Close to a million dollars. Why would Harvey pay that kind of money to someone he hadn't met?"

"That's what we have to find out next."

Twenty-eight

The amount of money that we were discussing was stag-
gering. Two thousand dollars might not have seemed like
much of a motive, but a million dollars sure was. Someone
had been moving that money out of the Halliwell accounts
for eighteen years.

"How do we find out if that account is Ned's?" I asked.

Vaughn set the notebook on the table. "Your guess is as
good as mine. Probably better, since you found out this
much. Tell me what you're thinking."

"I can go two ways with it." I pulled my feet up under me
Indian style and ticked the first point off on my index finger.
"Ned has been lying to Harvey and collecting the money all
this time. Harvey finds out and cuts him off. Ned comes to
San Ladrón on a night when he knows he has a good chance
he'll run into Harvey—it was the social event of the year,
right?—and confronts him. Ned gets angry with whatever

Harvey says, but we show up and he has to leave. The next day he goes back and kills Harvey."

Vaughn shook his head. "There are too many holes. Why would Ned kill Harvey if Harvey is the goose that laid the golden egg? And if it was the heat of the moment, wouldn't the murder have happened when we saw the confrontation? Coming back makes the whole thing seem premeditated, which sounds even worse for Ned."

"I also can't justify why he'd risk killing. He knew we saw him. Remember? I called out to him when he took something from Harvey's jacket."

"Okay, what's your second theory?" Vaughn asked. He moved a pillow from behind him to the top of the sofa. I moved it behind my head and looked up at the ceiling.

"Nolene had access to Harvey's money. She told me so herself. What if she saw the money going into the account all those years and started asking questions? Or worse, what if she started taking the money for herself? Ned might have confronted Harvey at the party, but if Nolene figured out the connection between Ned and Harvey, she would have known that sooner or later they'd find out she'd been diverting the deposits to herself. Maybe Harvey found out and Nolene freaked."

"Any other theories?" Vaughn asked.

"A couple. There's Violet, Sheila, Inez, Beth . . ."

Vaughn stifled a yawn. It was contagious, and I yawned next. "Violet's been making threats about shutting down the competition. She left town a few days ago and hasn't been back. Her store is next to mine, and she could have very easily murdered Harvey and taken the shortcut from the Waverly House to her shop without anybody noticing. She had opportunity. And Sheila maybe has a motive, depending on the results of her background check. Inez might be holding a grudge for the lab accident that scarred her. And Beth could just as easily have discovered the money since she works for Nolene."

"Have you told Sheriff Clark any of these theories?"

"What's there to tell? It's all guesswork. Clark is going to be extra careful with this case, and that means I need evidence." We both glanced at the notebook on the table. "Evidence that I can explain how I came to be in possession of without acknowledging that I've committed a crime myself."

"You have to return this to Halliwell Industries. Do you know how you're going to do that?"

"Not really."

"We need a game plan, and as much as I like having you here, I think we both need some sleep before we can focus." He yawned again. "You're welcome to stay over if you want."

"Excuse me?" I asked, instantly wide-awake.

"On the sofa. Or you can sleep in the bed and I'll take the sofa."

"I'm not staying over!" I stood up. Vaughn stood, too, and grabbed his keys. "Where are you going?" I asked.

"I'll drive you home."

"No you won't. I'm perfectly capable of driving myself. Go to sleep, and meet me at Lopez Donuts tomorrow morning at seven."

His eyes were drowsy, but his brows went up. "Seven?"

"Okay, seven thirty. Don't be late."

After all of my righteousness about showing up on time, I slept through my own alarm and woke to the insistent sound of my ringing phone. I knocked it to the floor while trying to answer it.

"Hello?" I said.

"Where are you?" Vaughn asked.

"What time is it?"

"Eight fifteen."

It couldn't be. I threw the covers off the bed, startled Pins and Needles, and ran to the kitchen. The clock on the microwave confirmed what Vaughn said. "Where are you?" I asked.

"On a bench in front of Lopez Donuts. I thought you left without me."

"I'll be there in ten minutes." I flung the phone to the kitchen table and raced to the bedroom to change back into yesterday's clothes. I stuck my head under the sink faucet, brushed my teeth, and raked my hair away from my face with my fingers. I shoved my feet into black canvas sneakers, grabbed my bag, and left.

Vaughn met me on the sidewalk with a large cup of coffee. "You look like you need this."

"I can't believe I gave you a hard time about oversleeping last night. Let's go."

"Where are we going?" he asked.

"Charlie's. She's been worried sick about Lucy. I need to tell her that Lucy's safe."

"I think you're going to have to revise your opening lines."

"Why?"

He pointed to the auto shop. "Because Charlie has company."

Ned stood inside the first bay talking to Charlie. His back was to the street, but I recognized him by his white ponytail and black leather jacket. Charlie noticed us first and put her hand on Ned's arm. She said something to him and he turned around. I stiffened. Any excuses we'd fabricated about why we were visiting went out the window.

"Act normal," Vaughn said. "You don't want him to know you suspect him of anything."

I reached down with the hand not holding the coffee cup and threaded my fingers through Vaughn's. He looked at me, surprised. "You said to act normal, right?"

He squeezed my hand. "Right."

There was very little normal about strolling up to Charlie's auto shop hand in hand with Vaughn, but I hadn't seen Charlie for a few days, and I figured why not give *her* something to think about?

"Hey," Charlie said. "You guys just wandering the streets of San Ladrón, or did you come here for a reason?"

"Nice to see you, too, sis," Vaughn said. "Is everything okay here?" he asked, looking back and forth between Ned and Charlie's faces.

"Why wouldn't it be?" Ned asked.

Charlie put her hand on Ned's arm. "Maybe they can help," she said.

He put his hands up in front of him in the universal sign for "I want no part of this" and turned around. Charlie reached out and caught him by his elbow. I wouldn't want to be on the receiving end of the look she gave him.

"The more people who know, the worse off things are going to be for me," Ned said.

"What exactly is going on here?" I asked.

Charlie looked at Ned. "If you won't tell them, I will. There aren't a lot of other options."

Ned yanked his arm from Charlie and stormed away from us, past the dingy car in the first bay, to the workbench at the back of the auto shop. His shoulders sagged and the tough guy demeanor was replaced with an air of dejection.

"Charlie, what's going on?" I asked when I thought he was out of earshot. "Where's Lucy, and what is Ned doing here?"

"Lucy's still missing. Ned came back to ask me to help find her."

"Lucy is safe," I said. I looked at Vaughn, who nodded his encouragement.

"Where is she?" Ned said, racing forward.

I thought about how desperate Lucy must have been to

go to Mr. McMichael, and how it wasn't my place to give away her secret.

"I'm not telling you where she is," I said. "She's scared of you. She thinks you might have killed Harvey Halliwell, and I'm starting to believe maybe you did."

Charlie's face flushed red and her hands balled into fists. Two thick chunks of hair came loose from her ponytail and swung alongside her cheekbone.

"Ned was at the Waverly House party. He was arguing with Harvey. We still don't know what he took from Harvey's jacket."

Ned stepped forward and held his hands up. "I didn't take anything." He glared at me for a few seconds and stuffed his hands into the pockets of his leather jacket. He shook his head, like he couldn't believe what was happening. "You saw me put something back."

Twenty-nine

"You put something in Harvey's jacket after he passed out?" Charlie asked.

Ned nodded. "I didn't think you saw that. I thought you'd assume I was making sure he was okay."

"I don't believe you," I said. "Whatever you put there would have been found."

"I'm sure it was, but nobody would think anything of it. I put back his heart pills."

"But Harvey didn't have heart problems," I said. But before I continued, I thought about how I knew that.

It was something Mr. McMichael had said during our visit. He had been talking about his own heart attack, and he commented on how old it had made him feel to see Harvey running about China while he was recovering. Big Joe had mentioned it, too.

So was Ned bluffing? I needed to find out.

I knew Vaughn had moved back to San Ladrón from Virginia, where he'd established himself with a reputable financial firm, when his father had the heart attack. I just didn't know when that had been. And I hardly thought it was a question I could ask in front of Charlie and Ned, considering nobody else was supposed to know Mr. McMichael and I had visited to begin with.

Only there was no way for me to proceed until I knew more, and there was only one person in the room I could ask.

"Vaughn, I need to talk to you. Alone. Outside."

"No," Charlie said.

"Yes," I said back. She looked as surprised as I felt. "I'm trying to help. You know that. So when I say I need to talk to Vaughn alone, you should know I mean I need to talk to Vaughn alone."

She put her hand on Ned's bicep. "Come with me," she said, and pulled him away from us. "Poly won't let anything happen to Lucy. When you asked me for help, I said you'd have to trust me. That means trusting my friends."

Ned glanced back at me, but this time went with Charlie. I rushed Vaughn outside to the bench on the sidewalk. After looking around to make sure nobody could hear us, I took his hands in mine and looked him straight in the face.

"When did your father have his heart attack?" I asked.

"My father? What does he have to do with this?"

"Please, just think. How long ago was that?"

He tipped his head back while he thought. "Nine years ago?"

"You're sure?"

He nodded. "I interned at the firm in Virginia for a year before they hired me. I got the news of Dad's heart attack at the party where we were celebrating my first full year on the job."

For the first time since I'd met Vaughn, I saw a trace of

his regret that he'd left that life behind. Now wasn't the time to ask him about that. "You didn't want to come back to San Ladrón, did you?"

He looked down at our hands. "He's my only father, Poly. What would it say about me if I didn't come back when he needed me?"

"But you did come back." I squeezed his hands. "And because of that, we can help Charlie."

"How?"

"Come back inside with me." I stood up and led him back to the auto shop. Charlie and Ned sat in Charlie's office. They both looked up. Charlie's eyes moved to Vaughn, who was staring at me, too. Turns out having all eyes on you isn't such a comfortable feeling.

"Ned, why did you have Harvey's pills at the Waverly House party?"

"I came here from Encino to talk to Harvey Halliwell, and even though I was pretty sure I knew which one was him, I checked with the bartender. She pointed to the guy with the glass of OJ. I started to follow him and one of the hostesses stopped me. She handed me a pill vial and asked if I'd make sure he got it."

I felt like I'd been hit by a bug zapper. "One of the Waverly House hostesses gave them to you? Can you describe her?"

"Sure. She was pretty. Red hair, early twenties, fair skin. Why?"

I was pretty sure Charlie, Vaughn, and I were thinking the same thing. We hadn't heard the last of Sheila. But aside from this new information, I knew there was something up with Ned's visit, something he wasn't telling us. "Ned, why was it so important that you talked to Harvey that night? Why'd you come here from Encino to talk to him?"

He dropped his head down in shame. "I'm not proud of my behavior. Harvey Halliwell was involved in a—a business deal of mine a few years back. I never knew if he knew who he had invested in, and I was afraid somebody might find out and think Lucy had an unfair advantage in the pageant because of my connection with Halliwell Industries."

"Harvey invested in your auto shop?" Charlie asked. I could tell from her expression that she was surprised.

"You wouldn't know anything about it," he said slowly. "It was right about the time you left."

"Sounds like fishy timing to me," she said. She stood up and walked to the side of the office where Vaughn and I sat. Her emotions were more locked down than a seized transmission. She stood behind our chairs and crossed her arms over her chest. I almost felt sorry for Ned, because Charlie had just let him know it was three against one.

Almost.

He stared at her, and then shifted his eyes to me. "I can't talk about that. Not now."

"Did you kill Harvey Halliwell?" Charlie asked Ned.

"No! All I wanted was to make sure there wouldn't be a problem with Lucy entering the pageant. When I told him who I was and mentioned the—the business deal—he got all red in the face. At first he said he didn't know what I was talking about, and then he said I wasn't to ever talk about that again. I know it was stupid not to walk away, but I wasn't sure. So I stood there, trying to figure out if my being here made him more mad. He turned away from me and drank his glass of orange juice and a few seconds later he collapsed."

"And that's when you put the pills back into his jacket," I said.

"Yes."

I closed my eyes and tried to picture what I'd seen that night. And I couldn't be sure if Ned had taken something or had left something. The way I had seen things, it could have gone either way.

"Harvey didn't have a heart condition." I said. "What

would happen if someone who doesn't have a heart condition took nitroglycerine?"

Vaughn was the one who answered. "Nitroglycerine causes the blood vessels to dilate almost instantly."

"Would it harm him?" I asked.

"The pill probably wouldn't, but if it was followed up with a large dose of sugar, it might make him light-headed enough to faint."

"A large dose of sugar," I said slowly. "Like a glass of Tangorli juice?"

Thirty

Harvey Halliwell had been known to give his Tangorli juice credit for his good health. When he went to events around town, he arranged for there to be a supply just for him. And according to Ned's story, Harvey had been at the bar getting a glass of juice before he headed outside. How difficult would it have been for a person with access to nitroglycerine tablets to dissolve one in Harvey's drink?

Not very difficult if that person worked as a hostess at the very location where Harvey ordered his drink.

So Sheila had opportunity. And it seemed she might have had means. Now more than ever I needed to find her and ask her a few pointed questions.

I glanced at the cat clock on the wall of Charlie's office. The eyes moved side to side, counting off the seconds. It was quarter after nine. I had forty-five minutes before it was time to open the fabric store for business, and at least part of that time needed to be used for a shower and change of clothes. That didn't leave time for much else.

"Ned, I know I can't tell you what to do, but I think you should talk to Sheriff Clark and tell him what you told us," I said.

"Why? So he can pin a murder on me? I'm not going anywhere or talking to anybody until I know Lucy is safe. She's the only reason I'm still in San Ladrón."

I could tell from the way Charlie stared at me that she wanted me to tell her where Lucy was. I shook my head. *No way, José.* If Charlie found out her sister went to Mr. McMichael for help, there would be all kinds of trouble. Nope, that information was going to have to stay with me.

"I have to go open the fabric store," I said. "I'll be there until six." I looked at each of their faces. Nine hours seemed like a really long time. I wasn't even sure if Ned would still be in San Ladrón by the time I got off work. I stood up.

Vaughn stood, too. "I'll walk you there." He headed out of the office and I followed him.

Behind us, I heard Charlie say to Ned, "How about you help me out for the day? Saturdays are always busy and it might be nice to boss you around for a change."

"Sure. It'll give me a chance to see if you're taking any shortcuts on your oil changes."

I stopped by the exit and turned around. Ned followed Charlie to the back of the auto shop. She removed two sets of coveralls from a row of hooks on the wall and tossed one to him. They both stepped into them in the same manner: flop the coveralls on the ground in front of them, step into the left leg, step into the right leg, pull them up to the waist, and then shrug the sleeves over their arms at the same time. The circumstances of Charlie's upbringing and subsequent adoption might have been unconventional, and I strongly suspected that Ned had taken advantage of Charlie's background, but at the moment, the bond between them was stronger than onetime boss and employee.

"Hey," I called out to Charlie. "I need an oil change. Here's my key. Come get the car when you get a chance." I pulled my VW key off my key ring and tossed it to her. She snagged it out of the air with one fist.

"You got it," she said.

Vaughn stood by the traffic light at the intersection when I left Charlie's. The walk signal was counting down. If he was in any kind of hurry, he'd just missed his window. It wasn't hard to figure out that he'd been waiting for me.

"A part of me wants to tell you that you owe me an explanation," he said.

"A part of me wants to tell you to mind your own business."

"Is that the same part of you that came to my apartment last night and asked for my help?"

I considered his point. "Probably not."

"So where does that leave us?"

"On a street corner in San Ladrón, waiting for the light to change."

"That's not all that far from where we started."

The light shifted to green and we crossed. Usually when Vaughn and I walked side by side I matched his stride and we fell into a comfortable rhythm.

Not today. Across the street, Violet Garden laced a chain through the door handles of Flowers in the Attic.

"I'm not used to having people walk faster than me," he said.

"Look," I said. I pointed at Violet. He picked up the pace.

I miscalculated my step onto the sidewalk and fell forward. Tripping and falling down wasn't as big a deal to me as you might think, largely because I'd gotten used to being clumsy for most of my life. Tall person, small feet. I liked to think of it as my own genetic curveball.

Vaughn pulled me back up to my feet. I dusted myself off and looked at Violet. She was staring at us. She looked back at the doors to her shop and tugged hard on the metal chain that was threaded through the handles. She'd miscalculated the length of chain that she'd need to lock the door, and unless the heavy metal links changed their physical properties and stretched like elastic, the ends weren't going to get close enough to be secured by a padlock.

Good thing there was neighborly me to come to the rescue, at least now that I was back on my feet.

"Hi, Violet. Do you need help with that?" I called out to her.

She scowled at me and yanked on the chains again. I passed Tiki Tom's store. He stood by the register, bouncing along to the music pumping through his headphones.

Violet put a hand out and stopped me in my tracks. "You've caused trouble ever since you moved here. First that homicide, then the sign in front of your store that broke the sidewalk, and now this pageant. It's a wonder I waited this long to close the store."

"You're closing? For today?"

"For good. There are more important things in life than selling old trinkets."

"What about Lilly?"

"It's not all her choice. There are two of us running this store and I have just as much say in when we should close our doors as she does."

"Violet, don't be rash."

"Rash? You don't know the first thing about rash decisions. I made a rash decision eighteen years ago when I listened to Harvey Halliwell and entered my daughter in that pageant. I don't know if I'll ever see her again." She choked on her words. "But I still have a daughter out there somewhere. And she deserves for me to honor her. I've spent the last eighteen years placing a value on the memories of strangers when I haven't done anything to value my own."

Her hands were shaking. She held the chains, and they rattled like a ghost in the attic of a haunted house. Instinctively, I stepped closer to her and put my hands on her shoulders. She didn't shrug me off. Tears streamed down her cheeks and dripped onto her pastel-pink blouse. She tucked her chin and I gently turned her toward me and hugged her. She held her arms up in front of her chest, as if protecting her heart from a sudden blow. I suspected that blow had come when her daughter went to live with her ex-husband and that the annual pageant had become an unwelcome reminder of the void left in her life.

Out of the corner of my eye, I caught Jun Wong heading toward us. I tipped my head toward the doors to Material Girl and let go of Violet for a moment to feel around inside my bag for the keys. The petite Chinese woman took them and unlocked the gate and then unlocked the door.

"Violet, let's go inside the fabric store. I don't think you want to be out here on the street."

She acquiesced. I kept an arm on her shoulders and guided her inside. Jun set her equipment down and pushed a rolling chair over to where we stood. I lowered Violet into the chair and got her a box of tissues.

"I miss her so much," she said. "So much, Poly. I never meant to push her into something she wasn't ready to do. Why won't she answer my letters? Why won't she return my calls?"

Jun pushed a second chair behind me, and I sat down across from Violet. "I can't answer that."

Violet pulled two tissues from the box and made an effort to get her sobbing under control. In time, the only evidence of her emotional breakdown was the redness around her nose and eyes and the irregular rise and fall of her chest when she breathed. She reached her shaking hands into her handbag and plunged into the sea of tissue and loose dollar bills. "They're not here. Why aren't they here?"

"What are you looking for?"

She sat up and placed her hand over her heart and closed her eyes. Her chest rose and fell twice, but even though her hand was pressed against the floral fabric of her dress, it continued to shake.

"Violet, are you okay?" I asked.

She opened her eyes and held out her open handbag. "My heart is racing. I need to calm down. Look inside and find my nitroglycerine tablets, would you?"

Thirty-one

"Violet, when did you last have your pills?" I asked.

"The garden party. I was looking for money for the tip jar. I set them on the drink station outside."

I looked at Vaughn. "Go get the sheriff," I said.

"No need to get me. I heard everything," Clark said.

Clark came into the fabric store and walked over to Violet. She looked confused by his presence. "Sheriff Clark, what are you doing here?" she asked.

"Ms. Garden, I think you should come with me. I have a couple of questions to ask you about the murder of Harvey Halliwell."

Violet jumped up from the chair where she sat. Her eyes went wide and she stepped backward, knocking the chair a few feet away. "You think— What— No!" she proclaimed. "You can't possibly think that I killed him."

"Ms. Garden, we have reason to believe that Harvey Halliwell was poisoned the night of the party, and you just admitted to having access to his drink. Your anger toward him raises questions."

"Harvey was killed on Sunday," she said.

"Can you tell me your whereabouts on Sunday?"

Violet looked up at me. I knew she'd gone to the Waverly House. She'd told me as much when she caught me talking to Nolene. There was no use denying it.

"I had a meeting with Harvey on Sunday."

"We've been over Mr. Halliwell's calendar and there's no record of a meeting."

"That's because I asked him to be discreet. I didn't want his assistant to know. All that Nolene Kelly thinks about is that pageant. She doesn't see what it does to the women who enter." She dropped her voice to a whisper and looked down at the ground. "She doesn't think about what it did to my family."

"I'm sorry, Ms. Garden, but you're going to have to come with me," Clark said.

"But all I wanted to do was something good."

"Why were you meeting with Harvey?" I asked.

Clark shot me a look that told me to stay out of it, but it was too late. Violet was looking for someone to listen to her and I'd given her a platform.

"I had a proposal for him. A scholarship in Elizabeth's name. Available to any girl who fit certain criteria: a decent GPA, a desire to pursue an advanced degree, a plan for her future. The Miss Tangorli pageant has become outdated. Harvey's money could do far more good if it was spread around than if he put it all into the pageant. It was time he made a change. The pageant couldn't continue forever."

I stole a glance at Vaughn, who caught my eyes but then looked back at Violet.

"What did he think?" I asked.

"He agreed. I drew up the paperwork and volunteered to administer the scholarship until he set up a nonprofit to take over. I wanted to give him the paperwork from the IRS to prove that we'd met their requirements."

"What did Harvey think about your idea?" I asked.

"He loved it. He knew he was too old to travel to China every year. He had no children, no one to leave the company to. He recognized that the scholarship would establish his legacy in a way the pageant couldn't sustain, especially after he passed away."

She was right. Once Harvey Halliwell passed away—even if it had been in the future and at the hands of natural causes—the pageant would have become less important. *He* was at the heart of the event, not the young women, not the setting, not Nolene Kelly, not the Tangorli fruit. It was him. He had done such a good job of branding himself as Mr. Tangorli that without him, the exotic fruit was just another version of an orange, and the pageant was just one in a number of events that rewarded the combination of beauty and brains.

"Sheriff Clark, there is nothing worse for my plans than for Harvey Halliwell to have been murdered. You must see that. But he and I had a productive meeting. This fund would give *all* young women a chance at money for their education, providing they wanted it. That's all I ever wanted for my daughter."

"You did that for me?" asked a soft voice behind us. We turned around and saw Betty standing in the doorway, holding Archie to her chest. He squirmed a bit, but then relaxed against her.

"For you?" I asked. But as I stood there staring at the nervous woman who'd been making repeated visits to our stretch of Bonita since talk of the pageant had taken over San Ladrón, I realized that Betty was no out-of-town stranger. "Betty—that's a nickname, isn't it? Short for Elizabeth. You're Violet's daughter."

She looked at me and nodded, and then looked back at Violet.

"Elizabeth?" Violet said. She stood slowly and set the used tissue on the cutting table next to her.

"I—I'm sorry it's taken so long—"

Violet ran forward and threw her arms around Betty. Little Archie got squished in the hug, and he yipped a couple of times to make sure we all knew he was there. Violet released Betty and stood back and looked at her, then hugged her again.

"You came back," Violet said. The hysteria had left her voice, and tears of happiness streamed down her face. "After eighteen years, you came back," she said again.

When their hug ended, Betty seemed to pull herself together. She looked at me and Vaughn, at Clark for a brief second, and then back to me. "My editor says my articles are fine but they don't connect on an emotional level. He told me to find a subject that I related to and write about that. So I came here to see—to put the past behind me and—to—"

"To get closure," I said.

She smiled. "Yes." She turned back to Violet. "Mom, did you mean what you said? That you met with Harvey Halliwell to establish a scholarship in my name?"

Violet relaxed her embrace and stepped back, keeping her hands on Betty's shoulders. "Yes. I couldn't let my anger over the pageant control me any longer. I couldn't let other daughters feel what you felt."

I thought back to what Tiki Tom had told me about Violet. Before opening the antiques shop next door, she had been an accountant. She would know how to handle money and how to set up the scholarship. She would have been able to advise Harvey on how to accomplish her suggestion. He wasn't here to tell us if he had said yes or no, but listening to her, I had a strong sense that he had probably said yes.

"Ms. Garden, do you have any proof of this meeting with Harvey? Anything at all?" Sheriff Clark asked.

She looked at him as if for the first time noticing that he was in the room with us. "What kind of proof do you need?"

"Anything," I said.

"I met Harvey in the parking lot next to the Waverly House. I wanted to see the gardens one last time, so I walked behind the mansion. Harvey was waiting for me in the lot. I didn't see his orange car, and when I asked about it, he said he had asked one of his employees to give him a ride in her convertible."

I turned to Clark. "Are there cameras in the parking lot?"

"Yes. They were installed a few years ago when someone thought it would be funny to toilet paper the trees."

Vaughn cleared his throat. "The cameras haven't been operational for at least six months. With the budget cuts, the staff decided to keep the cameras in place as a deterrent but not tell anybody that they weren't working." He looked at me. "That's what happens when your operating budget is at risk."

Violet reached into her handbag and pulled out a sheaf of folded papers. "Sheriff, would these do? These are the documents I had drawn up for my meeting with Harvey. As we talked, he made notes, and then he asked me to make the changes and e-mail him a fresh copy." She held the papers out and Clark took them. Upside down I could see orange hand-written notes in the margins of an official-looking document.

"That's his handwriting, for sure. But all this tells me is that you met with him. It doesn't tell me what condition you left him in."

I closed my eyes and tried to remember finding Harvey's body. "What about the Waverly House employees? Did any of them see you?"

"They were busy breaking down the serving stations."

"What about the garden gnome?" I asked.

"Ms. Monroe," Clark said, "I know you're not asking me to question a garden gnome."

"When I found Harvey's body under the weeping willow tree, I knew it was important that nobody else got close before you arrived. I made a circle around him with Xavier's tools."

"Xavier?"

"The head landscaper. They were fixing up the garden after the party. I grabbed the rake, the shovel, and a garden gnome, and laid them all end to end to create a barrier. It was the best I could do on short notice. But if Violet met with Harvey in the parking lot, and Harvey was found dead under the weeping willow tree, then wouldn't the gardeners have had to see him walk past again?"

"Not necessarily. Ms. Garden, how did you leave your meeting with Harvey?"

"I went inside the Waverly House for brunch and Harvey excused himself to make a phone call. That was the last I saw of him."

All four of us—Jun Wong, Vaughn, Clark, and I—stared at Violet. I wasn't sure if Jun even knew what was going on, since she hadn't been a part of so many of the earlier conversations, but she knew that Violet had said something important.

Jun looked at Vaughn. "Mister Vaughn, if the lady was inside the Waverly House, how could she be outside with Mister Halliwell?"

Vaughn looked at the sheriff. "I think that's a very good question."

Sheriff Clark looked at Violet. "You wouldn't happen to have any proof that you were inside, would you?"

"Would my receipt work? I kept it for tax purposes. After all, we *were* having a business meeting," she said, her familiar defensive tone sneaking back into her voice.

Clark pulled off his hat and wiped the back of his bare arm across his forehead. "Ms. Garden, I'm sorry for the trouble. I'm going to need to see that receipt."

She nodded, and then looked at Betty again. I had a feeling a family reunion would take place before Clark got his receipt.

I gave up any hopes of a shower and change of clothes and opened the store. It was well beyond my normal hours, and in a way we'd been lucky not to be interrupted by a customer. In a different way—one that spoke to my potential profits as a fabric store—I was not so lucky.

"I have to stay here until six," I said. "I think you should go to the Waverly House and see if you can find out anything—about Sheila, or about the Tangorli juice that Harvey drank, or about anything."

Vaughn looked uncomfortable. "There's a good chance that someone took Violet's nitro tablets at the party and slipped one into Harvey's drink. The fact that her pills are missing says something."

"I can't figure those pills out. Ned says he put them in Harvey's coat after someone fitting Sheila's description gave them to him. Where did Sheila get them? Did she steal them from Violet, or did she find them on the drink station? And did she think they actually were Harvey's, or did she know she was setting up Violet? I found them on the ground. I gave them back to Harvey, but Sheriff Clark didn't find them. So did somebody take them?"

"What did Harvey do when you gave them to him?"

"He studied the label and put them away." I realized why the pills bothered me so much. "The one person who would know that those pills didn't belong to Harvey Halliwell was Harvey Halliwell. So why would he take them from me? Why not just say they aren't his and move on?"

Vaughn shrugged. "I guess we'll never know."

I put my hand on his arm. "That's just it. Harvey must have recognized the pills. He knew who slipped him one. When he left my shop the day after the party, he was on his way to confront the killer."

"But who is that?"

"I don't know. We're right back where we started," I said.

"Not really. We're not on a street corner anymore."

I looked at Vaughn like he had two heads before I remembered our conversation less than an hour ago. "I can't keep up with much more than I already have in my brain. For the next eight hours, my mind is on fabric."

"Okay. I'll be back at six."

Vaughn walked out the door, and I turned to Jun. She stood with her hand on the top of her sewing machine. "Miss Poly, is good thing that happened with Miss Violet and Miss Betty."

"Yes, it is a good thing." And if I hadn't been so distracted by the murder and the running of the store, I might have figured it out sooner. The first day Betty was in the store she hadn't given her name, and the second time she said she'd been headed for the antiques shop until my mom all but hijacked her. Had my mom revealed her relationship to me then, would Betty have told us the truth? Maybe. Or maybe she'd been so nervous about seeing her own mother for the first time in eighteen years that she would have taken any excuse to postpone the inevitable.

That was why she said I helped her more than I'd know. My store gave her a reason to keep coming to our stretch of Bonita Avenue.

Jun cleared her throat. "Miss Poly, I know you no ask me to come here today. I think about your offer and I think I try. Is okay with you if I give trial run like your happy hour?"

I wanted to hug her. "Jun, it's more than okay. You can set yourself up wherever you want. I'm going to work on a display of silks. Now that the pageant dresses are done we might get some interest in them. If you need anything, you let me know."

"I be okay." She nodded slightly and turned away. Again I marveled at how efficient she was. She flipped the latch on a plastic carrying case and sixteen clear plastic drawers tipped out toward her. One held tape measures. One held her pincushion. One held needles, a few held thread. I'd never seen such a thing.

"Where did you get the case?"

"My husband buy for me at hardware store. He say I need easier way to carry everything.

"I didn't know you were married," I said.

"He passed away many years ago. I support myself now," she said proudly.

"You're an inspiration to the women of San Ladrón," I said.

While Jun organized her sewing supplies, I maneuvered the fixture of silk to the front of the store and moved the floral display to the space now left vacant. Unlike the raffia bust form that I'd draped in floral cotton at the beginning of the week, the satins were stiff and serious. To unroll a bolt and drape it over a bust form would create creases that would take far too long to steam out, especially since I knew how important it was to keep water from coming into contact with the silk satin. Spots from water would discolor the fabric and even change the texture. It was one of the reasons silk satin was so expensive, but its luxury couldn't be matched by any other fabric in the store.

The pageant contestants had chosen from the colorful bolts, each wanting a color that showed off her skin tone to the best advantage. Their relative youth led them to the pink, purple, and blue palette. One had chosen black. Lucy had selected the green that turned purple in certain lights. But not one of them had chosen the silver or the gold. I fingered the material, letting the smooth, heavy weight of it slide through my fingers. It was a shame the beautiful metallic fabric wouldn't be represented at the pageant. To my eye, these were the prettiest bolts of the lot. They reminded me of the thirties, when dresses were incandescent; when glamour was paramount.

And then I remembered there was still one dress to be made for the pageant. Maria Lopez's.

I slid the silver and the gold fabric from the fixture and, with a bolt under each arm, carried them toward the bust form by the front sewing area. Three flips of a bolt of fabric roughly equaled a yard of fabric. I counted out enough flips to equal four yards and draped the unfolded fabric over the shoulder of the bust form. After securing the fabric to the shoulder of the mannequin, I repeated the same thing with the gold on the other shoulder.

Without being asked, Jun joined me. She matched the fabric at the front of the form and pinned down the length of it with tiny silver pins, and then repeated the same process down the back. The neckline had a deep V, as did the back of the dress. Jun pinned the side seams under the armhole while I retrieved a length of wide ivory grosgrain ribbon from the wall of trim. When Jun stepped back, I wound the ribbon around the waist of the dress and tied it in a bow in the back, letting the ends trail down to the floor.

"You have someone special in mind for this dress, Miss Poly?" she asked.

"Maria Lopez. She's one of the judges of the pageant," I said. "She wanted a dress to wear tomorrow night."

Jun smiled. "This will be nice dress for nice lady. I see her go to houses to clean and take care of boys. She deserve pretty dress like this."

I moved to the other side of the dress and pinned down the length of the fabric.

"Do you think there will be another pageant after this one?" Jun asked.

"Why wouldn't there be?"

"If Miss Violet gets her wish, the pageant money will go into the scholarship fund. Maybe someone not like that."

I considered it. "You think someone knew Harvey was going to end the pageant after this year and didn't like that decision," I said slowly.

"If pageant money goes away, lot of people lose job," she said. "Losing job is bad thing to happen to a person."

"Yes, it is." And even though I had questions about Sheila and Ned and Beth and Inez, I knew that the person who was at the middle of the pageant, who controlled the money, was Nolene Kelly. And if she lost access to the pageant, she might lose everything.

Thirty-two

I left Jun with the pins and made a phone call to Halliwell Industries. A man answered. I asked to speak to Nolene and he put me on hold. A few seconds later, he returned.

"She's not answering her phone. Can I take a message?"

I chewed my lower lip. "Did she come in today?" I asked.

"She's been in and out of here all morning. Would you like to leave a message or not?"

Considering the operator already had my name, there didn't seem to be much of a point in acting covert now. "Sure. Tell her to call Poly Monroe at the fabric store. I have to talk to her about the pageant dresses."

"Hey, you're that Polyester girl. Were you really born in that store?"

"Sure was," I said. "On a bed of polyester. That's where I got my name."

"You ever wish it were something different?"

About a hundred times a day when I was in grade school.

Only now, I didn't mind so much. My name meant more to me than if it had been picked out of the phone book or if I'd been named after a celebrity who was popular that year. "Maybe once or twice," I said.

"Good for you," he said. "Okay, Polyester Monroe, I'll give Nolene the message. Is it urgent?"

"A little. If I don't hear back from her in the next couple of hours, I'll call again."

"Good deal," he said, and hung up.

I tapped my finger on the receiver and thought about what he'd said. What was in a name? For me, a whole bunch. For Charlie, who pretended not to acknowledge her birth parents, not much at all. Vaughn's name opened doors. Even Genevieve had the French name that inspired her to become a Francophile and eventually model her tea shop like a Parisian café.

I thought about Lucy Rains. How her name connected her to Ned Rains, who had approached Vic McMichael all those many years ago. And I thought about Violet and Lilly Garden, my neighbors, how their names were obviously selected to be a play on words, and how Violet wanted to create a scholarship in her daughter's name.

Jun had removed the pinned dress from the bust form and moved it to her sewing machine. She threaded the machine with a sparkly gold thread and turned the dress inside out so she could stitch the side seam. I walked past her to the front door and looked outside for customers. Any customers.

Where were the customers?

Tiki Tom was on the sidewalk with his scorpion mug. "It's getting to you, too, isn't it?"

"What?"

"The pageant. Look across the street and tell me what you see."

I had always wondered about the string of beauty salons that lined Bonita Avenue. How could it be possible that a town as small as ours needed so many? But today, there were lines out the doors. Women and daughters sat on benches out front, smocks over their clothes and caps on their heads. The scent of perm solution and fake nails hung in the air and triggered a cough.

"This is because of the pageant?" I asked.

"Yep. Started like birds in that Hitchcock movie. First it was one girl, then two. Then a couple of mothers showed up. I turned away for a couple of minutes and the next time I looked outside, there were lines coming out the front of every salon on the street. Fat chance of either of us doing any kind of business today. The Garden sisters are the smart ones. They didn't even bother to open."

I told Tiki Tom about Violet and Betty. "You missed the reunion," I said.

"Whoa," he said. "That's been a long time coming." He drank from his mug. "Next year I'm going to host Polynesian Week leading right up to the pageant. Maybe I can get some of the fathers to drop off their girls and come in for Hawaiian ribs and island drinks."

"And who's going to drive them home?"

"Ah, didn't think about that part. So let's see. I'll need a shuttle service, maybe some live entertainment . . ." He went back into his store and started taking notes on a pad of paper by the register. Whatever Tiki Tom came up with for the following year would cost him far more than he'd make. I suspected he didn't really care all that much as long as it brought people he could talk to about tiki mugs and hula girls into his shop.

When I went back into the fabric store, Jun was pulling the dress over the top of the bust form. She'd used a simple straight stitch over each shoulder and gently pulled on the thread to create gathers that cascaded down. The silver and the gold fabric met in the middle and had been stitched together at the bottom of a modest V-neck. The two metallic fabrics complemented each other in a way that bold brights or muted pastels could not, and I knew, next to Maria's naturally glowing Latina skin, the dress would be a showstopper. Better than almost any of the other dresses that had been completed this past week.

Between the remerchandising of the silk display, the construction of the dress, and the conversation with Tiki Tom, I'd lost track of the hours. Not only had lunchtime come and gone, we were closing in on happy hour.

"Jun, did you have lunch?"

"Yes, I eat while you talk to Mister Tom."

"The dress looks lovely. I'm going to see if Maria can come over and try it on. We need to pin the hem for her, and it might be best if it's entirely done and picked up before the contestants arrive tomorrow to pick up their own dresses."

Jun nodded while trimming a few threads. I called Lopez Donuts and Big Joe answered.

"Hi, Big Joe, can I speak to Maria?"

"She's working a Neato job today. Anything I can do for you?"

"No, this is definitely a Maria question."

He grunted. "You women think you can solve everything by yourselves. I know my wife does. Now she's rubbing off on you. Give me a shot. I bet I can help you with your problem, whatever it is."

I giggled. "I need to pin the hem on Maria's gown for the pageant and I need her to try it on for me. Unless you think you can put it on and stand at the exact same height as her?"

"She didn't tell me she ordered a brand-new dress for this thing."

"Big Joe, you hush up. Maria is going to be practically the center of attention up there between Duke and Vaughn. Besides, I'm not charging her."

"Oh no, you don't. She ordered a dress, she better pay for it."

"First you criticize her for asking me to make her a new

dress, and then you criticize me for making it free. Men," I said.

"Speaking of men, didn't Vaughn have your dress made for you? How'd he know it would fit?"

"I don't know." The question had bothered me before, and I had yet to get a satisfactory answer. I didn't like the idea that he'd been that accurate with my measurements from the time I fell on top of him.

"I know where her head comes when we slow dance," he said slowly. "Would that help you?"

"Why don't you just tell her to come see me when she gets off work?"

"Because maybe I want to do something nice for my wife. You ever think of that?"

"Okay, sure. Come over whenever you can."

"I'm just closing the place down now. I'll be there in fifteen minutes."

"Do me a favor? Bring me something to eat?" I asked.

"Women," he said, and hung up.

It didn't take him fifteen minutes to arrive and I had a feeling that even the donut shop had been affected by the flurry of salon activity along Bonita Avenue. Big Joe handed me a waxy white bag and a cup of coffee. "Coffee's strong. Been sitting on the heater since this morning. I brought you a regular glazed and a chocolate glazed."

"This is your idea of a meal?"

"You didn't say you wanted a meal. You said 'something,' and I figured you knew you were talking to a donut store. Besides, can't have you turning into skin and bones," he added.

I took the bag and inhaled the sweet sugary scent. "This'll do." I pulled the chocolate glazed out and bit off half.

"Now where's this dress?"

Jun was taken aback at Big Joe's presence in the fabric

store, but I explained that he was going to help us figure out the hem and then surprise Maria with the dress. She stood back as he approached the bust form and put his arm around the waist as if he were going to dance with it.

"Can you lower this thing?" he asked.

"Hold her so she doesn't drop on my head," I instructed. I dropped to my hands and knees and reached up under the fabric. After loosening the tension knob, I called up, "Lower her to the right height."

He gently lowered the form, pulled it back up a couple of inches, and then lowered it again. In the background, the phone rang. I was stuck under the dress. "Jun? Can you answer the phone? Tell them I'll call them back," I said. The shadow of the seamstress hurried past me while I held the form in place.

"Hello, this Poly's store," she said. "She busy under fabric. Can I take message? She call you back."

Busy under fabric? I wondered what kind of picture that painted to whoever was on the other end of the phone, and then felt a *thunk* on my shoulder.

"That's it," Big Joe said.

I pushed my hand up under the torso of the form and turned the knob to tighten it into place. When I was done, I slowly backed out from underneath. Big Joe put his arms on the waist of the form again and pulled it close. "That's my Maria," he said.

"You're sure?"

"Sure I'm sure. I dance with my wife every night after we put the boys to bed."

I couldn't help myself. I threw my arms around him in a giant bear hug. "Maria is lucky to have found you," I said.

"And I'm lucky to have found her. Sometimes people get lucky and find the person who fits them the best."

I waited for him to make a comment about Vaughn, but

he didn't. He tipped his head to the side and looked at me funny. "Nobody's going to push you in a direction you don't want to go, Poly. But if you *are* thinking about going in a particular direction, you might not want to wait too long."

My face felt hot. I turned away from Big Joe and looked at Jun. "Who was that on the phone?"

"Miss Nolene."

Figured that was the phone call I'd miss.

"Did she leave a message?"

"She say she be in office for all night, very busy. She say you can stop by any time up to nine."

I looked at the clock. It was closing on six. Nobody would have noticed if I'd closed the store early today, but it was a matter of principle.

"Mister Joe and I finish dress for Mrs. Joe," Jun said. "I close up shop after we're done. The whole street closed except for beauty shops. Even Mister Duke closed for night."

"He did?" I looked out front. The easel that usually sat in front of The Broadside advertising happy hour specials was nowhere to be seen.

"Go on, get out of here. I'll help her close up the shop," Big Joe said.

"Thank you, both of you," I said. I threw my phone into my messenger bag and raced out the back door. If I hadn't tripped over the doorjamb, I would have made really good time.

Charlie had left my VW Bug parked in the space on the corner of the lot. The driver's-side door was unlocked and the keys were in the ignition. If I'd owned something fancier than a late-eighties model Bug, I might have been more concerned about anti-theft measures, but for the moment, that was the least of my concerns.

Inside the car, on the passenger-side seat, was a paper floor mat with the black logo for Charlie's shop printed in the middle. Across the right-hand side of the image of a pickup truck was her messy handwriting.

Yo Polyester. Find anything out about Sheila?

I folded the floor mat and then folded it again. The Waverly House was just around the corner. I double-checked my watch. I had time to make a quick stop and still catch Nolene by nine.

Even though the Waverly House was within walking distance, I pulled the car out of my spot, exited the lot, and turned right, circling the block until I pulled into one of the spaces by the restored Victorian mansion. I got out of the car and stood on the corner, staring at the majestic building. It fairly glowed thanks to tiny white lights that had been inset under the eaves and window casings. As the sun continued to drop, the illusion would deepen.

A small silver BMW pulled into the parking lot next to my VW Bug and Vaughn got out.

"Fancy meeting you here," he said. "Mind if I join you?"

"I don't want to be rude, but I'm not going to the Waverly House to see your mother," I said.

"I didn't think that you were."

"But there's a good chance that if she sees me, she'll want to chat, and I don't want to be rude about that, either."

"Okay, how about we divide and conquer? After the way I left her two nights ago, I figure she's itching to ask me about our date."

"What are you going to tell her?"

He looked down at me, his green-and-gold-flecked eyes sparkling with the sunlight. The afternoon breeze blew his sandy-colored hair across his forehead. He didn't say anything at first, and the longer we stood there facing each other on the sidewalk by the Waverly House, the more self-conscious I became.

"I'm not sure what I'm going to say. I'm not even sure I'd call it a date."

"There was dinner and champagne," I said, "and we were dressed up. That should count for something."

"In the big picture of looking like we're on a date while we're investigating one of my mother's employees, it counts for a lot. Only I don't think it's that great an idea to bring that up to her, either."

"I see your point. How about this? Tell her I didn't feel well so we left early."

"It's her restaurant. She'll blame the chef."

"Tell her you forgot you had another date," I said with a smile.

"I'm not that big a playboy," he said.

"Okay, fine, tell her it was a wonderful evening and we both can't wait to do it again."

"Is that the truth?"

I made a big show of looking over my shoulder in both directions, then turned back to him. I put my hands on his cheeks and made him stare me directly in the eyes. "It's our best bet for not blowing our cover," I said. I rose to the balls of my feet and gently kissed him on the mouth.

I turned around and walked toward the entrance. Vaughn caught up to me on the short flight of stairs in front of the building and turned to face me. "I'll distract Mum, see, and you get the goods," he said in a low voice. His eyes looked out over the top of my head, across the street and at a family idling in the parking lot. He winked and opened the door. My playful attitude vanished when I spotted Sheila behind the hostess station. I sobered quickly and looked to Vaughn, making no secret of why I'd come in the first place. He had turned the opposite direction into the dark wooden vestibule, where he stood, studying one of the photos hanging on the wall. I was on my own.

"Hi, Sheila," I said. "Do you have a minute to talk?"

Her lips pressed together into a flat line. "You need to leave me alone," she hissed in a low voice. "I need this job."

I lowered my voice, too. "I already know that you lied about your pageant results. If you want me to leave you alone, you're going to have to tell me the truth."

"Fine." She grabbed my elbow and pulled me down the hall. Vaughn looked as shocked as I felt when Sheila pulled me into the men's room.

"I don't think we're supposed to be in here," I said.

She locked the door from the inside and then turned around. "Why won't you just leave me alone?"

"Because a man is dead and you've been acting very suspicious."

"You think I killed Harvey?" she said. Her eyes grew wide and all of the color drained her face. "Why me?"

She wasn't acting like a guilty person, but that didn't mean anything. I had one chance to confront her with what I knew and this was it. "Someone slipped nitroglycerine into Harvey's drink at the Garden Party. I found out later that you gave a vial of pills to someone to give to him."

"Because when I found them on the drink station, somebody told me they were his."

"Who told you that?"

"I don't remember. It was dark and there were a lot of people in front of me. I don't usually work the beverage station. I was just trying to keep up with the drink orders." She looked confused. "The pills weren't his? And that made him pass out?"

"They might have killed him that night," I said. I had no reason to think that was true, but then again, I didn't have a medical background so what did I really know? "You were lying the other day when you told me you thought you were a contestant. You already knew you weren't. How did you know only nineteen young women would show up at Material Girl?

If Lucy had been there, we all would have known that you didn't belong."

Sheila deflated before my eyes. She leaned back against the wall between the metal fixture that blew out hot air to dry freshly washed hands and the edge of the sink. Even though I was intent on what she had to say, I hadn't forgotten where we were and what was mounted along the wall behind me. It wasn't my first time in a men's restroom thanks to the years I'd spent living in downtown Los Angeles, but it was an experience I hadn't been itching to repeat.

I could tell that Sheila wanted to get out of there, but her body language wasn't that of a caged animal, ready to strike, or a scheming psychopath calculating her next move. It was of a lost little girl in the body of a twenty-two-year-old.

"What's going on, Sheila? What are you trying to hide?"

She stared down at the floor and pushed the toe of her shoe back and forth over the ceramic tiles. "I have really bad credit," she said. "When I graduated from high school, I applied for student loans, but I cashed the checks and spent them on an apartment and clothes and a car. I dropped out of school and kept charging things until they wouldn't let me charge anymore."

"That would have shown up on a background check," I said.

"When I got this job, I was going to make a change. I wanted to put all of that behind me and earn my own way. But then I heard from my family back in Illinois. My dad got laid off and then got sick. My mom hasn't worked in years. What kind of a job could she get? Her biggest talent is reading *People* magazine the day it comes out. They needed my help so I started sending money to them."

"Why did you enter the pageant?"

"I thought, if I had a chance to win, I could make them proud of me. Instead of seeing me as a college dropout with a hundred grand of debt, I would be famous. My mom likes famous people."

"But the background check disqualified you from the pageant," I said.

"I should have let it go and moved on, but then that Lucy stopped me while I was walking to work and she asked me for directions. She said she was a finalist but that she didn't really care about it. That's not fair, you know? Why should she get to participate when she doesn't even want to, and I can't? So I told her she was in the wrong area of San Ladrón. I told her to get back on the highway and take the third exit, and then turn left. If she followed my directions, she'd be gone for over an hour. I just wanted to be a part of it for a little while, just feel like somebody."

I stepped toward her and put my hand on her arm. "You *are* somebody," I said. "Adelaide Brooks counts on you to help run the Waverly House. And your parents probably don't say it enough, but I'm sure they love you for the person you are."

There was a knock on the door, and then it rattled against the lock. Sheila and I both looked at the door. The knocking persisted, and then came Vaughn's voice. "Poly? I saw you go in there with Sheila. I—um—there are people waiting to use the facilities."

I'd gotten what I came for. I unlocked the door and pulled it open. Vaughn faced me. "Excuse me," I said. I led Sheila out of the men's room as if we'd had every right to be there, but I stopped a few feet short of the hostess station and turned back to face her. "You owe it to Adelaide to tell her the truth," I said. "She's going to find out one way or the other. If you're honest with her, she might let you keep your job."

It took a lot longer to reach Halliwell Industries while battling traffic than it had the other times I'd gone. I hadn't waited for Vaughn when I left the Waverly House. Nolene was expecting me and the clock was ticking. If there was a way for me to blame the traffic on the pageant, I would have.

Sure, my shop was benefiting from the involvement in the pageant, but I was beginning to think that anybody who aligned themselves with Miss Tangorli was in for a streak of bad luck by association.

I pulled into Halliwell Industries around quarter after seven. The lot was half full. I parked in a space marked *Visitor* by the back and walked down the sidewalk between the two buildings that faced each other. At the end of the sidewalk, I turned left and approached the security desk. A bald Mexican man dressed in a navy blue blazer over a white shirt and orange tie sat behind the desk. He looked vaguely familiar, but I couldn't place him.

"Hi, I'm Poly Monroe. Have we met before?"

"I'm Xavier. You probably saw me at the Waverly House."

"That's right," I said. "You were working on the gardens for the Midnight in Paris party."

"I work part time covering the front desk here. Second job. Can I help you with something?"

"I don't know," I said. His presence behind the desk threw me off. "I called earlier. Did I talk to you?"

"Nope. We've had musical chairs at the desk today. Half of the regular staff is out sick. My shift started at six."

"Oh. Well, Nolene said I could stop by any time."

"She's up there?" he asked. "That woman covers more territory in a day than most people do in a month. My fiancée wears one of them Fitbits—you know, the thing that tracks how far you walk?—and I bet she still doesn't clock half the mileage of Nolene."

Xavier opened up a visitor log and placed it in front of me with a pen. "Sign in at the next available space and I'll give you a pass."

I wrote my name and set the pen down. "Is this a new procedure? The other night I came here with Inez and I didn't have to sign in."

"After hours?" he asked. I nodded. "Yeah, things get a

little more relaxed at night. You gotta be with someone who can give you access, though. Key cards track everybody so we can tell who went where. If you don't have a key card, you can't get in."

I silently thanked Inez for lending me her key card the other night. If she hadn't trusted me with it, I would never have found the paper trail of money that went right through Nolene's office. And almost immediately, I felt guilty. Inez had trusted me with her key card and what had I done? I committed a crime while I was there and stole information that shed a less-than-flattering light on her former boss. If anyone ever discovered what I'd done, how would it have looked that Inez had been the one who gave me access?

Xavier spun the visitor log around to face him and set it on the desk blotter. He bent down to a drawer on his right and pushed a bunch of white plastic tags around inside a drawer until his fingers landed on one he wanted. "Easier for me if it's not coded already." He fed the key card into a small box and pressed a couple of numbers on a keypad.

"Why do you keep coded key cards?"

"New employees, interns, what have you. Mr. Halliwell used to have lots of tour groups coming in and out. He loved showing the place off. We'd go through a hundred cards in a month," he said.

"What would happen if someone didn't turn theirs in when the tour was over?"

"If they ever tried to use it to get back in, I'd know. I know everywhere everybody goes, thanks to those cards. Every staff card is programmed with their employee numbers."

"What about at night when you're not here?"

"The locks track the activity and I review it when I get in." He shook his head. "Nolene sure has been putting in a lot of hours since Mr. Halliwell was murdered. When I came in this morning, the key card activity from last night was all in her office."

But Nolene hadn't been in her office. I had. Which meant somebody had duplicated Nolene's key card, and why do that? To make it look like she'd been in the building. So someone could have the run of Halliwell Industries without ever being detected.

Thirty-three

"Don't worry, you're not asking anything the cops didn't. I take pride in my job. Never lost a visitor pass yet," he said proudly. He pulled the white card out of the small box and handed it to me. I clipped it onto the strap of my messenger bag and thanked him. I was halfway to the elevators when Xavier caught up with me and pressed the call button on the elevators.

"Ninth floor. You'll need the card to activate the elevator once you're inside and then again to open the doors to Nolene's floor. Her office is the first one on the left."

I pretended all of this was new information and thanked him. What was I going to say to Nolene when I arrived? Would she already have noticed the missing notebook, or could I get it back into the bookcase without her noticing?

The ninth floor was dark. I used the key card to open the offices and followed the carpeted path to Nolene's office. Her door was shut and locked. Unfortunately for me, it required an actual key, not a rectangle of plastic with a magnetic strip.

Xavier had said she was here, so I called out to her. "Nolene? It's Poly Monroe. Are you here?"

No answer.

The longer I stood in the dark sea of cubicles, the more I realized that I'd been tricked.

We'd all been tricked.

Nolene wasn't here. She hadn't been here earlier, and she probably hadn't been in the office for days. Xavier said he could track the employees by the use of their key cards. What a perfectly marvelous way to make him think someone had been there who hadn't.

I sank into a black office chair and thought through what I was starting to suspect. Xavier had told me that Nolene was putting in long hours, but he hadn't even seen her. He'd only seen activity from her key card. He had even talked about last night—the night that I'd been in the offices—and specifically mentioned Nolene. I knew for a fact that she hadn't been in the offices that night, because I'd been here.

Maybe Nolene hadn't been here, but her key card told a much different story.

Every move I'd made required the use of that card. What if the card that Inez had lent me wasn't coded with her employee information but with Nolene's instead?

I pulled out my cell phone and called Vaughn. The call dropped due to poor reception. I spun the desk chair around and searched the surface for the desk phone. When I found it, I pressed zero, hoping to be connected with Xavier at the security desk. The phone rang eight times before I hung up.

Xavier could have gone to the restroom. He could have gotten up to buy a coffee. He could be on another call. He could have been distracted from his post. And who could have distracted him? Someone he already trusted with the front desk.

A bell in the hallway announced the arrival of the elevator. The red neon of the *Exit* sign cast a glow across Beth's cropped gray hair as she advanced from the elevators to the glass doors. I dropped to my hands and knees behind the cubicle and wrapped my arms around my legs. I couldn't see her, but she couldn't see me, either.

Beth had been the person to first throw suspicion onto Nolene. And Beth said she had a medical condition. Was it related to her heart? If so, Harvey would know about it. He might have recognized the pills. Enough that he would have arranged a confrontation with her the day after the party—the day that he was killed.

Beth had means. She had opportunity. And she certainly could have seen what went on in Harvey's accounts.

The locks by the glass doors clinked as if they'd been opened. Moments later the particular grating sound of a key being threaded into a lock told me where Beth had gone. I crawled out from under the desk and looked up at Nolene's office. The door was open. The back of a white lab coat filled the doorway, until Beth moved out of my range of vision to the wall of financial notebooks. She laughed the low rumble of a woman who has discovered that the trap she laid was successful. The laughter grew louder and she walked out of the office. I ducked back down and lost sight of her. Her feet were silent on the carpet, but there was no denying the sound of the glass doors closing and locking behind her. I crawled to the edge of the cubicles and peered around the edge, watching her stand by the elevator. The doors opened, she got on, and they closed.

I had to get help.

Out in the hallway, I ran to the fire extinguisher. As predicted, a building map indicated the stairs. I ran to the end of the hall, pushed the door open, and started down the eight flights. I tripped once, between the sixth and fifth floors, but scrambled back to my feet and kept going.

The exit opened onto the greens behind the building. It took me a second to get my bearings, but when I did I headed to the greenhouse. I kept close to the building so the large lights that illuminated the grounds wouldn't draw attention to me.

The greenhouse was lit from the inside. Orange heat lamps cast a glow over rows of trees that were being spliced and seeded. A mist clung to the inside of the glass walls, making it hard to make out much more than the silhouette of a person moving about inside. I crept as close as I could, dropped onto my knees into the damp soil, and pressed my face up against the glass. The bottom corner had escaped the film of moisture thanks to the leaves of a large tree that sat in front of me. What I could make out between the leaves wasn't much. But it was enough to see that Beth wasn't alone.

Nolene Kelly was on the floor, her hands and feet bound with green tape. A smear of something dark was caked to the side of her face.

Blood.

Nolene's head moved up and down, as if she'd been asked a yes or no question that needed to be answered. Her eyes were only half open. I fished my phone out from my pocket and called 911.

"What is your emergency?" a female voice asked.

"Someone's being held at Halliwell Industries. Send the police as soon as you can," I whispered.

The operator continued. "Hello? Can you speak up? I can barely hear you."

"Halliwell Industries. Send the police to the greenhouse. Hurry," I said.

"Tell me what's happening," she said.

I turned to look back inside the greenhouse and froze. Nolene was still tied up on the floor, but Beth was gone. I turned my back on the greenhouse and shrank down behind the overgrown foliage that lined the perimeter of the glass structure.

The voice of the 911 operator was audible through the phone in my hand. "Hold one moment," I whispered. I put the phone on speaker and turned up the volume. I threw it as far as I could.

The operator spoke again, this time loud enough to sound as though she were there. I peered around the side of the building and watched Beth raise her head at the sound of the voice. She moved in that direction. I moved to the opposite side of the building, staying out of Beth's vision.

"What the—?" she muttered, and then, seconds later, she cursed. Bent over, I ran around the rest of the greenhouse until I reached the door and ducked inside.

Nolene's eyes widened when she saw me. I raised my finger to my lips and pointed behind me. "Beth will be back soon. We have to get you out of here."

She shook her head back and forth quickly. I reached around the back of her head and untied the strip of fabric that had gagged her. As soon as it was loose, I cut through her wrist and ankle bindings with an oversized pair of gardening shears.

"Poly, you have to get us out of here. You don't understand."

"As soon as I untie you, we have to run."

The door to the greenhouse shut behind me. I turned, expecting to see Beth. Instead, I saw her distorted silhouette on the other side of the glass. Her hands fumbled with something by the door. She turned and disappeared into the dark night.

I raced to the door and pushed. The doors bowed out slightly but snapped back when they met with resistance. She'd threaded a thick length of pipe through the greenhouse handles, trapping us inside. Moisture broke out on my forehead and under my arms. The greenhouse was hot—hotter than it had been the previous night when I'd been there. I wiped my forehead with the back of my arm and looked around for another exit.

That was when I saw that the glowing orange lamps were aimed at a large rubber balloon that was suspended from the ceiling.

"What is that?"

"I don't know. I don't know how long I've been here. Beth keeps saying it's poetic. Over and over—'It's poetic.'"

As I moved closer to the lamps, the heat became almost unbearable. It was like a tropical rain forest inside the glass enclosure: hot, wet, and itchy, as if I'd been bitten by a thousand mosquitoes and then rubbed down with salt. I waved my hand in front of the lamp and felt a scorching heat.

"What's in the balloon?" I asked.

"I don't know. I don't know anything." Nolene leaned forward and sobbed openly.

With one arm, I swept dozens of small seedlings onto the ground and then climbed onto the table in the middle of the room. The rubber on the outside of the large balloon had started to blister. Under the balloon was a large metal funnel connected to a series of black soaker hoses that were draped, like a string of Chinese lanterns, to the far corners of the room.

Droplets of orange liquid oozed out of a tear in the balloon, followed by a trickle, and then a stream. Once the rubber tore, the liquid gushed out into the metal funnel. It bubbled and hissed. Soon the black soaker hoses jumped with the contact of whatever it was that was filling them.

Beads of orange liquid pulsed out of the hoses and dripped onto the plants. The first to come into contact with the liquid wilted immediately. The green plastic of the pot melted.

Acid, I guessed. I glanced up at the other hoses and realized if we waited any longer, we'd be unable to escape the shower. The plants would die. The future of Halliwell Industries would be demolished.

Poetic.

I put my hands under Nolene's arms and hoisted her to her feet. "We have to get out of here now," I said.

"We can't. She locked us in," she said.

I ran to the doors and shook them again. The spray of acid hit my hands and burned like bee stings. I pulled a thick black plastic tarp from under a table of seedlings and held it over Nolene's and my head. Why had I used my phone to create a diversion?

I searched for a way out. The acid fell from two hoses, killing the plants below them on contact. To my left was a large oxidized tin watering can. I grabbed the handle and swung it against the wall of the greenhouse. The glass cracked.

I pulled back and swung again, this time with both hands. The glass cracked more, and then it broke. I kicked at the broken panes until the opening was big enough for us to fit through. I pushed Nolene first, then bent down and crawled through.

"Go to the main building and call for help," I said to Nolene. "Hurry." I gave her a push.

Nolene took off across the greens. I swiped at the skin that had been exposed to the hot acid, brushing away imaginary irritants. Too late, I saw Beth alongside the greenhouse, weaving in and out of the pageant seating.

"You have no connection to Halliwell Industries. But still, you had to play the hero." She held a lit torch. The dancing flames illuminated her twisted expression. "Do you know what the funny thing is about heroes?"

"What?" I said. I looked back and forth between her face and the torch. The weather had been dry—scarily so. I didn't know what the open flame would do to the acid-soaked trees inside the greenhouse, but I knew the Tangorli fields would go up like a match set to a scarecrow if she got close.

She stepped away from the greenhouse and thrust the torch at me like the Wicked Witch of the West in a face-off against

Dorothy. "Heroes make excellent victims. People try to rescue you. And if you die, they'll celebrate you all the same."

"Why are you doing this?"

"There's a million dollars in a bank account with my name on it." She staggered a moment and put her hand to her chest. "I paid my dues with this company. I'm not going to live forever and it's time to make my move."

"Your medical condition—it's your heart, isn't it?"

She dropped her hand from her chest and pointed at me. "You should have minded your own business. Nobody would have known if you didn't go snooping around."

"Harvey knew," I said. "He figured out that the fifty-thousand-dollar deposits were to you," I said.

"You know about them? That's too bad. Too bad for you," she said. She put both hands on the torch and waved it in my face. I stepped back but didn't say a word. "Congenital heart defect. That's what I have. Harvey wanted people to think this juice could make people live a long life. Not me. No amount of Tangorli juice is going to change the condition I was born with. When I started working for him, it was my job to audit the financial records. You know what I found, don't you? A fifty-thousand-dollar deposit sent to a nobody from Encino. The payment happened right in the middle of the pageant planning and nobody ever questioned it. That's when I first got the idea."

"You've been stealing from Halliwell Industries ever since."

"I opened an account and wrote threatening letters to Harvey every year, demanding payment."

"Harvey wouldn't have paid them off. He wasn't trying to bury a secret."

"Harvey never saw the letters. I wrote them, filed them, and sent the money to the account. If anybody looked into it, there was a paper trail in place to point to a mechanic in Encino who was extorting money all these years. And the beauty of the plan was that I never got greedy. Fifty thousand every year for twenty years. A million dollars, with interest. And nobody questioned it."

"So why kill Harvey now?"

"I saw the application for that Lucy girl. The address was the same as the one where Harvey sent the original money. I didn't know the relationship between that family and Harvey, but I couldn't chance it. I sent a letter—a real one—saying that I knew about the girl in Encino. I didn't know why he'd paid them off all those years ago, but there had to be a reason."

"There was. He was doing a favor for a friend. And you killed him because of it."

"I killed him because he found out about the rest of the deposits. He found the letters. He sent a reply to the address on file saying that there would be no more payments."

"So you confronted him at the garden party."

"He needed to be scared. I slipped a nitroglycerine tablet into his Tangorli juice so he'd pass out. I didn't plan to kill him, not at first. I wanted to scare him into thinking that I had some kind of power over him."

"But Sheila found the pills and thought they were his. And when Harvey saw the vial, he knew who was behind everything. He knew it was you."

"I knew he had that meeting with Violet Garden. It was on his calendar for two months. I confronted him in the gardens on Sunday. He said he was going to turn me in to the authorities. I had to kill him to get away. And then I came back here and replaced his calendar with a new one. No appointment with Violet Gardens meant she'd look like she was lying.

"But now I'm free. I can finally have a life that doesn't belong to Halliwell Industries. And after tonight, there's going to be nothing left of Halliwell Industries."

She reached out with the hand not holding the torch and pushed me. I stumbled backward several steps and tripped over a chair. Behind me, the Tangorli fields loomed. Beth touched her flame to a branch. The fire spread quickly. Weeks of dry temperature without the break of rain had left the field in poor condition. And what an easy way to get me out of the picture.

In the distance, sirens called out their approach. The scent of burned oranges filled the air as tree after tree went up in flames. If I didn't get out of the field soon, I'd be a human tiki torch. Adrenaline, anger, and courage came together and I charged her.

I knocked her to the ground. The torch fell from her hand. Flames licked my pant leg. I grabbed onto Beth and rolled us away from the fire, over and over each other, until we were up against the back of the greenhouse. I climbed off her and grabbed at a metal spigot, spinning it so hard it came off in my hand. Water spit out of a green hose that had been coiled on the ground. Beth got up and ran away. I aimed the hose in her direction and pulled the nozzle, shooting a stream of cool water in an arc that caught her between her shoulder blades.

She fell forward. I ran with the hose and showered her with water, pinning her to the ground with the spray. When I caught up, her short, spiky gray hair was plastered to her face and water dripped from the plastic fruit cluster earrings that hung from her ears. She gave up the fight.

Thirty-four

The rain that we'd so sorely needed in San Ladrón came that night, helping to put out the fire. I was ushered from Halliwell Industries to the hospital, where I was checked for everything from smoke inhalation to bruised ribs. Sheriff Clark showed up and I told him what happened. After getting a clean bill of health, I went home. I used half a bottle of moisturizing shower gel on the parts of my skin that had been exposed to the acid, fell into bed sometime after midnight, and slept straight through to Sunday afternoon.

When I woke, both cats were nestled on my pillow, leaving me only a corner for my own head. I ran my hand over Pins first, and then Needles. "Hey, you two," I said. "You almost lost me last night."

Needles stood up and walked straight at my face. He bumped his cold pink nose against my own and then turned his head and ran the top of it over my cheek. Pins stretched his gray paws out in front of him, the left paw landing on top of my fingers. They had come to depend on me over the past several months, and I wasn't ready to let them down.

I took another shower, this time mostly to tame the hair that I'd slept on while wet, and dressed in a long black jersey dress that ended just above my ankles. I slipped on a pair of gold sandals and added a long gold chain around my neck. A little mascara and lipstick and I started to feel human. Having lost my phone at Halliwell Industries last night, I didn't know if anybody had tried to reach me. What I did know was that secrets—the secrets everyone was trying to keep from everybody else—had made me suspect people who should have been above suspicion.

The Miss Tangorli pageant had made everyone crazy, only not in the way I'd been warned. Maybe I'd bought into the warning too much and had let the buzz about the pageant go to my head. But now, after my showdown with Beth, bits and pieces of information had come together in an entirely unexpected way. There were answers to questions I hadn't wanted to see, and questions that I didn't deserve to know the answers to. It was time everybody put aside their own concerns and learned to work together.

I went downstairs to the shop and made a couple of phone calls from the fabric store phone, then headed out to Charlie's Auto.

Charlie stood over the workbench where her tools were scattered. Her thick dark hair was pulled into two loose ponytails on either side of her head. A red bandana was tied around her forehead, catching stray hairs that had come loose. Her normally dark lips were uncolored, showing their natural red shade. The dark circles under her eyes had only grown deeper.

"Lucy's still not back. I don't know how to reach her."

"It hurts, doesn't it?"

"What?" she asked, her head snapping up to focus on me.

"Knowing you want to say something to someone in your family but not knowing where she is or whether she'll listen."

"Don't make this about me, Polyester. Lucy's life was nothing like mine."

"Charlie, you think you know everything, but can you stop talking for five seconds?" Her eyes went wide. "Ned found out who your father was when you lived with him. He contacted Vic before your eighteenth birthday."

"No, he didn't."

"Yes, he did. Ned told Vic about you—your life in Encino, your skills as a mechanic. Vic McMichael wanted to set up a trust for you but he didn't know if you would be receptive to him reaching out. He asked Harvey Halliwell to set it up. He didn't want it to be traced back to him. It was supposed to be a onetime thing so you wouldn't have to worry about money."

"There was no trust."

"Yes, there was," said Mr. McMichael from the doorway.

We both turned to face him. He stood outside the shop. Today he wore a tan suit and tie and looked as if he was prepared to take a meeting, even though it was Sunday. He held a brown leather briefcase in one hand. I stepped back and held my arms open in a gesture that welcomed him into the conversation.

"Mr. McMichael, I think the money's still sitting in a bank account somewhere." I turned to Charlie. "It was in confidence. You have to accept that."

Charlie looked back and forth between our faces.

"I sneaked into Halliwell Industries Friday night and looked at the financial records. There was a fifty-thousand-dollar withdrawal every year for the past eighteen years."

"That's almost a million dollars," Mr. McMichael said.

"Plus interest. I thought Nolene was guilty of skimming money at first, but it didn't make sense that she'd kill her golden ticket. But Beth Fields audited the books when she first started working at Halliwell Industries. She saw the original fifty-thousand-dollar payment to Charlie's account and traced it back to the letter from Ned. That's when she got the idea. She faked letters demanding more money and filed them. If anybody discovered the payments, they'd assume someone in Encino was extorting money from Harvey. She set the whole thing up to look like Harvey was paying someone off."

"Harvey discovered the missing money," Mr. McMichael said. "He knew someone was stealing from him. That's when he confided in me. He told Nolene she had to take her unused vacation time. He wanted her out of the way so he could see if it was her."

"That's why she bought all that luggage," I said. "But she returned it after he was murdered. She's really one of those people who loves her job so much she doesn't want to take time off." I turned my attention back to Mr. McMichael. "Sorry to interrupt. That luggage was bothering me."

He smiled, and then continued. "Harvey sent a letter to the address on file saying he wouldn't make any further payments and that he was opening an investigation leading to blackmail charges. If he'd found out Beth's identity, she would have lost everything."

Charlie spoke up. "Why didn't she just leave then? If your math is right, she had a million dollars in a bank account. She could have disappeared."

"Not without Harvey finding her. She would have had to clean out the bank account, close it, and hide all evidence that she was the one who opened it. But if Harvey died, then nobody would go looking into old financial records. Beth had a heart condition. She slipped one of her nitro tablets into Harvey's drink at the garden party. She knew what it would do to him. Only she must have dropped the vial. Sheila found it and thought it belonged to Harvey. She gave it to Ned, who put it in Harvey's jacket after he passed out."

I thought back to that night. Vaughn and I standing under

the privacy of the weeping willow tree branches. Until Harvey collapsed, he and Ned hadn't known we were there. By chasing Ned away, I gave up our secret presence. If Beth had been watching, she would have seen me ask Vaughn to go get help. That might have changed her plans.

"When Harvey saw the pills, he knew they weren't his. He knew about Beth's health. He told her the Tangorli juice was what kept him healthy. She was bitter about it. She managed her condition with medication. It must have been curious enough—the pills, him passing out, the demands for money. When she confronted him on Sunday, he figured out exactly what she was up to. So she killed him."

"She had so many opportunities to disappear. I still don't know why she stuck around."

"The pageant was right around the corner, and that gave her a unique opportunity to make it look like *that's* why he was killed. Think about it. This whole time we thought his death had to do with the pageant. From her post at Halliwell Industries, she was able to keep an eye on everybody. She needed the pageant to continue to create enough of a distraction for her to plan to leave. If the pageant had taken place, I bet that's exactly when she would have left."

"When Harvey first suspected something, he asked my firm to look over his accounts. We would have found her."

"But how long would it have taken?" I asked. "She made one withdrawal every year. Even if you started with the current books, you would have had eleven months to go through before you found it, and there are so many expenses attached to the pageant that you might have assumed it was related to that."

"But you discovered it in a week," Mr. McMichael said.

I looked away. Yes, I'd discovered the truth, but I'd broken the law in doing so. It wasn't a proud moment.

"I'm glad you found all these answers, but we still don't know where Lucy is," Charlie said.

I interrupted her before she could continue. "Charlie, when Lucy ran away, she went to Mr. McMichael. She knew he was your father. She overheard your concerns about Ned and she didn't know where else to go. Everybody she's met since she got here is connected to you. Except for him," I said, indicating the businessman with my thumb. "But since he's your father, he's the one person she could go to without jeopardizing her standing in the pageant."

"Lucy went to you?" she asked Mr. McMichael, visibly stunned.

"Yes. She's been staying in my guest room. She is well, though she is shaken up. In light of what happened last night, I imagine all of the young women who expected to participate in the pageant are shaken up."

"Can I talk to her?" Charlie asked.

Mr. McMichael rested his briefcase on a chair, popped open the brass locks, and extracted a business card. "This is my address. You're welcome anytime."

"Not so fast," I said to him. "I don't think it would be fair for Lucy to stay with you, all things considered."

"Ms. Monroe, I can't say that I follow."

"You told me that Harvey Halliwell left explicit instructions for you to take over the Miss Tangorli pageant if anything should happen to him. Well, something happened. Lucy is a contestant in the pageant, and I don't care how big your estate is, she can't stay with you while you're picking up the pieces."

"I hardly think the city expects the pageant to continue."

"You said yourself, Harvey considered you a friend when a lot of people considered you a monster. This would go a long way toward showing this city who you really are."

"The fire at Halliwell Industries demolished the stage and the seating for the pageant."

"That's all true, but I happen to know at least one historical landmark with freshly landscaped yards that could accommodate the pageant on short notice."

"The Waverly House?" Mr. McMichael said. "Adelaide would never agree to that."

"Adelaide is a smart woman who would recognize the greater good in this situation," I said.

He turned his head slightly and took in Charlie's expression. She watched him warily, her face cocked off to the side, studying him as if she expected him to make a sudden move. Finally, he turned back to me. "Ms. Monroe, if you ever get tired of running the fabric shop, come see me about a job. You have a way of putting things that make me think you probably get your way quite frequently." He turned to Charlie. "I'm going to try to catch my ex-wife by surprise. Why don't you go see Lucy and help her pack her things? I won't be back to the house for several hours."

"No," Charlie said. Her face colored.

Mr. McMichael studied Charlie for a moment. He closed his briefcase and let it dangle in his right hand next to his leg. "As far as I know, Adelaide doesn't know you're the daughter we gave up for adoption. All the time you've been living in San Ladrón, she's only known you to be a member of the community. It's your decision how you handle that knowledge."

After Mr. McMichael left, Charlie pointed her finger at me. "You might think everything turned out okay but don't think you're off the hook yet."

"What are you going to do?" I asked.

"I'll think of something."

Thirty-five

One week later, I arrived at the Waverly House for what was to take the place of the Miss Tangorli pageant. Because of the murder, the embezzlement, and the fires at Halliwell Industries, it wouldn't be the pageant everyone had expected. It had been Tiffany, the head California blonde, who suggested that we make it a memorial for Harvey. She'd also suggested that, since the twenty of them had spent so much time on their dresses, there still be voting on that part of the competition. All of the contestants had been asked if they still wanted to participate in the pageant. The answer was unanimous. If San Ladrón were a big city, the idea might have been forgotten, but the community pulled together to make it happen.

As young women trickled out of the salons across the street, they stopped by Material Girl to get their dresses. Big Joe picked up Maria's gown around four. Duke wheeled himself out of The Broadside at five thirty. He wore the same tuxedo and bow tie that he'd worn to the garden party.

I stepped outside the fabric store and whistled. He waved and smiled and wheeled himself down the sidewalk toward the intersection on the corner.

"I gotta hand it to you, missy," said Tiki Tom. "You know how to get stuff done. It might not be the island way, but it works for you. Are you headed to the pageant?"

"In a bit."

Not wanting to take away from the pageant contestants, I defaulted to my usual choice of black. I slipped on a vintage sleeveless dress that I'd found at the back of Aunt Millie's closet. It was covered with tiny jet beads and weighed several pounds. It was long enough to graze my ankles. I slipped on a pair of black mules with delicate beading across the instep and a modest one-inch heel. I arrived at the party on my own. Scores of residents, pageant contestants and their family members, and local business owners and others filled the grounds. I spotted a few of the pageant contestants in the crowd. Tiffany showed off her robin's-egg-blue gown to Jun Wong. Lucy stood with two other young women, shifting from side to side, showing off how the color of the fabric in her dress changed with the light. Another cluster of young women giggled as Duke performed card tricks on a small card table that he'd rigged across the armrests of his wheelchair.

Without Harvey Halliwell, there would be no trip to China, but after what I'd said to Mr. McMichael, he'd not wanted to abandon the idea behind the pageant altogether. Each of the twenty finalists would receive a one-year full scholarship to the school of her choice. Further monies would be determined on a case-by-case basis after each of their freshman years. Harvey's money was going to make a difference in a lot of lives.

And speaking of Harvey's money, a donation had been made to the Waverly House's operating budget in exchange for the use of their property for today's memorial. Nobody mentioned it, but we all knew who controlled those accounts.

Adelaide met me by the side of the building. She greeted me with an affectionate hug.

"I don't know how to thank you," she said.

"It was a natural suggestion. Mr. McMichael would have reached the same conclusion eventually."

"I'm not talking about the Waverly House. I'm talking about my daughter."

"You know?"

"I do now. Vic and I had a long-overdue heart-to-heart last night. Details might have become public and he wanted me to find out from him."

"Have you talked to Charlie?"

"I want to respect what she's been through. I'm not going to force her to have a relationship with me if she doesn't want one." I heard the note of hope mixed with sadness as Adelaide's emotions betrayed her words.

I looked around the grounds. "Where's Sheila?"

Her smile dropped. "Sheila and I had a long heart-to-heart, too. She resigned yesterday and is moving back to Illinois to be with her family. Her father hasn't been well and the strain on her has been taking its toll."

"It must be hard for her to be so far away."

"She's been sending them money to help with their finances, but I think her presence there will do far more good than her paycheck does. And should she ever want to return to San Ladrón, there will be a job for her at the Waverly House. I promised her that."

We entered the courtyard. I looked for Mr. McMichael, finally spotting him at the back of the yard, talking to Inez Platt. She looked radiant in a sage-green shift dress. Her olive skin glowed against it. Xavier, the head landscaper, approached the two of them. He handed Mr. McMichael a flute of champagne and Inez a glass of water.

"Xavier knows Inez?" I asked.

Adelaide smiled. "They make a great couple, don't they? Two green thumbs."

Inez caught me watching her and waved. She said something to the men and came our direction.

"Poly," she greeted me. "I had no idea. None of us did."

"I'm sorry your work in the greenhouse was destroyed."

She looked at the glass in her hand, then back at me. Her big brown eyes were framed by thick lashes. Despite the scarring on her face, I could see the beauty that had won her the pageant crown all those years ago.

"I think it's time I got out from Halliwell Industries and had a life of my own. Xavier and I are going to join forces and start our own nursery."

"That's a great idea," I said. "You two know more about plant life than I know about fabric."

She put her hand on her tummy. "We're going to need the other kind of nursery, too," she said.

"You're pregnant?"

"It's early, and it's a risky pregnancy, but we've already decided we want a family."

"Congratulations!" I hugged her, and water from her glass sloshed onto both of our dresses.

"If I came to your store, could you help me pick out fabrics for a baby's room?"

"Absolutely."

Xavier called Inez's name and she returned to him. He draped his arm around her shoulder and put his hand on her tummy. She kissed him on the cheek.

"Ah, young love." Charlie handed me a flute of champagne. "Polyester, this has been one crazy week. San Ladrón will never be the same."

"San Ladrón? Or you?" I studied her face. Charlie had dealt with more than anybody else this week: the reality of Ned keeping the trust fund that had been intended for her, the secret of who her real parents were. Nobody would blame her if she pulled up the roots she'd planted and moved on so she could start over. "After all that went down, are you going to be okay?"

"Me? I'm Teflon. After today, none of this is going to stick." She sipped at her champagne and watched Adelaide.

"She never knew," I said. "Vic didn't tell her who you really were until last night. She'll respect whatever you choose to do, but think about it, Charlie. She wanted you to grow up in a loving family, not in the middle of a nasty divorce. She had no way of knowing how your life turned out."

"That makes two of us."

I shifted my attention from Adelaide to Vaughn, Maria, and Duke. Vaughn and Duke were dressed handsomely in tuxedos, and Maria fairly vibrated in the silver and gold dress that Jun and I had made her. She turned to the side and put her hand on her head and posed. I cut my eyes to her hem. It was the perfect length.

On a table next to the three of them was a white ballot box. Residents of San Ladrón paused to write their votes on index cards and feed them through the top of the box. The three official judges were off the hook this year, but the winning dress would be chosen by popular vote. Judging from the number of people who stopped to compliment Maria, I suspected the winner of the dress contest would not be one of the pageant contestants.

"Hey, Polyester," Charlie said, elbowing me in the side. "Are you and Vaughn ever going to get out of first gear?"

"I don't know. He's a shiny new BMW and I'm a beat-up VW. Maybe we don't fit."

"Maybe you don't, but there's a lot better things to worry about than money." I gave Charlie my full attention. "Listen, there's no harm in trying, right?"

"You tell me."

She pursed her lips and chuckled. "I think I'm going to go find Sheriff Clark," she said.

I raised my eyebrows. "Look at you. Talking the talk and walking the walk. Will wonders never cease?"

She swirled her flute of champagne. "How did you know that moving to San Ladrón was the right thing to do?" she asked.

"I didn't. I was scared and a little sick to my stomach. Everything I knew was about to change. It was a little like standing on the edge of a cliff and trying to decide whether to jump."

She turned to me and crossed her arms over her chest. "Nice metaphor. Most people don't survive a jump off a cliff."

I wanted to roll my eyes or make a joke, but I knew she was talking about something bigger than my metaphor. "Charlie, I don't know everything, but I know this. You can keep doing what you're doing and nothing's ever going to change. Or you can take a leap of faith and see where it takes you. It's your choice."

She stared at me for a few more seconds, as if waiting for me to push her one way or the other. I didn't. She shielded her eyes and looked out over the crowd. Big Joe had joined Maria, Duke, and Vaughn, forming a small crowd underneath the weeping willow tree. Maria said something and Big Joe threw his head back and let loose his booming laugh, which carried across the artistically landscaped grounds. The others responded in kind. Vaughn looked away from the group, saw Charlie and me, and waved. I waved back.

"Sick to your stomach, you said?" Charlie said.

"Pretty much."

"What about now that you've been here for a while?"

"I'd say it's starting to fade," I said. I raised my champagne flute. She clinked her glass against mine and we each took a sip.

"I guess anything can happen, even in a town like San Ladrón," she said.

I smiled. "That's what I've come to believe."

PROJECT: MAKE A GARMENT BAG

Giovanni's girls make garment bags for each of the twenty pageant contestants. Here's how to make a custom garment bag, which is great for travel or just for brightening up your closet. Select fabrics that make you smile! These instructions will result in a 53" garment bag, which is long enough to hold a knee-length dress.

3 yards of woven fabric in your choice of color
1 60" zipper
Yardstick or measuring tape
Chalk
1 wooden hanger
Scissors
Iron
Pins
Thread
Sewing machine
Optional: seam ripper

These instructions can be used with most fabrics. Poly suggests cotton or silk shantung. Avoid fabrics with stretch, as they will "grow" when they hang in your closet.

1. Fold fabric in half lengthwise, matching selvage edges on either side. Cut along fold.

2. Using a yardstick or measuring tape, measure 12" from center on either side. Mark with chalk.

3. Align edges of fabric (right sides together). Lay the wooden hanger with the hook jutting past the cut edge. Mark the outline of the hanger on the fabric with chalk.

4. Cut your fabric along the chalked lines.

5. Fold ½" of fabric along the side where the hanger was. Press.

6. Repeat step 5 on the second piece of fabric.

7. Mark off a 3" opening (1½" on either side of the hanger hook) with pins.

8. Place the fabric with right sides together. Pin along <u>one side</u> from the outside of the opening (marked in step 7) down 60".

9. Baste the fabrics together along the side.

10. Press the seam open.

11. Place the zipper facedown into the seam. With the machine, stitch into place along one side, across the bottom of zipper, and back up.

12. Turn the fabric over and carefully remove the basted stitches, revealing the zipper.

13. Return the fabric to the right-sides-together position. Pin the remaining edges together from the bottom of the zipper, along the bottom of the bag, and up the entire length of the opposite side, ending at the pin marked for the hanger opening.

14. Stitch together.

15. Press the seams flat.

16. Unzip the zipper and turn the garment bag right side out.

17. Put the hanger in the bag and feed the hook through the opening at the top.

18. Hang in the closet and admire!

Additional Ideas:

- Contrast the zipper to the fabric to create a whimsical combination. Harvey Halliwell might suggest shades of citrus.

- Use different colors for the front and back (yard and a half of each).

- Add a pocket to the outside of your bag to hold coordinating jewelry or accessories.

- Make plans for a glamorous getaway so you can show off your bag!

Don't miss the first book in Diane Vallere's

new Costume Shop Mysteries

A DISGUISE TO DIE FOR

Available now from Berkley Prime Crime

Turn the page for a sneak peek

"Give me the knife," demanded the cranky man in the wheelchair.

"I don't think so," I said.

"I'm not playing, Margo. Give me the knife."

"Why? I already told you I could do it. It's just going to take longer than I thought."

"That's because you can't climb the ladder in those silly boots."

"Why are you so worried about my go-go boots? You bought them for me. Besides, you're the one wearing two different shoes."

My dad—the cranky man in the wheelchair—looked down at his feet. He wore one brown wing tip and one black.

"I pay that nurse too much to end up leaving the house wearing two different shoes," he said. "And this stupid chair makes everything worse. If I can get up and down the stairs okay, then I don't need it."

"You're in that chair because you're still weak. The doctors don't want you running all over the place and having a second heart attack. And the nurse didn't mismatch your shoes on purpose. Most of the nurses don't expect to have such colorful patients."

He stuck his feet out in front of him and shook his head at the sight of the mismatched shoes. "I said brown wing tips. How hard is that?"

I was pretty sure my dad wasn't used to relying on a woman to dress him—nurses or otherwise. He'd been a widower since my mother died giving birth to me thirty-two years ago. While growing up, I'd notice the way women who came into the costume shop looked at him in his paisley ascots, tweed blazers, and dress pants. He was a catch, my father. And now that he was recovering from an unexpected heart attack, he was a cranky, stuck-in-his-ways catch that the nurses of Proper City Medical Care had the distinct pleasure of dressing, at least until I'd arrived. I wondered if the mismatched-shoe situation was payback for his attitude.

"You're going to have to let me help you. Got that?" I said, pointing an accusatory finger at his nose. He swatted it away.

"It's not right. I'm your father. I'm supposed to take care of you, not the other way around."

"I'm a grown-up now."

"You're too grown-up, if you ask me." He glared at my outfit a second time.

"What? We have this exact same outfit in the '60s section of the store." I pointed to the back corner of the shop, where a kaleidoscope mural in neon shades covered the walls.

The store in question was Disguise DeLimit, our family's costume shop. The store had been around far longer than I had, starting sometime in the '70s by a couple who had worked in the movie business in Hollywood. My dad had started as a stock boy before he was old enough to work legally, and slowly graduated first to salesperson and then manager.

Eventually, the couple decided their time running the store was over. Turns out Dad had been saving for a rainy day and bought them out, inventory and all. Shortly after he became owner he met my mother and they fell in love. They married and planned to start a family and run the shop together. Two years later, the love of his life was gone and in her place was a newborn baby: me.

"Besides, you always said the fact that my outfits are inspired by costumes in our inventory was good for business. Remember?"

He grunted an answer and rolled back to the boxes.

The outfit that ruffled his feathers was a mod, zip-front minidress colorblocked in red, white, blue, and black. It ended midthigh, which left an expanse of skin between the bottom of the hem and the top of my white patent leather boots.

The summer before I moved out of Proper, I bought a box of patterns from the '60s at a yard sale and made myself this dress. The bandleader at the local high school stopped me one day and asked where I got it. They were planning a Beatles tribute concert and thought dresses like mine would be perfect for the choir. He came to the store and placed an order, and I spent the next two weeks knocking out dresses just like it. One by one the girls came in and bought up our inventory of white patent leather boots, plastic hoop earrings, and colorful fishnet stockings. I didn't always dress like a go-go dancer, but when I got the call from Nurse Number Three that my dad was trying to inventory the costume shop against her direction, there hadn't been time to change. So here I was in the white patent leather go-go boots he'd bought me before I moved to Las Vegas seven years ago—the perfect complement for my mod minidress but not so practical for balancing on a ladder while your father glares at you—reaching for a rubber knife that someone had hung on the Western wall by the fake pistols and plastic holsters. Everybody knows you don't bring a knife to a gunfight.

I extended my reach the way I'd been taught in the ballet

class I took last year and nudged the peg until the knife fell. It dropped—the peg, not the knife—and landed by my dad's brown shoe. The knife landed by his black one. I picked up both and set them on the counter.

"Dad, I don't get why this is so important. Inventory can wait until you're better."

"We're heading into spring. Remember what that means? Outdoor birthday parties and the Sagebrush Festival. I have to know what props we already have stocked so I can start planning concepts."

"You can't expect to carry on business as usual while you're recovering. It's too much."

"That's right. I can't, but you can. You grew up here. You know as much about the costume business as I do."

He was right. While other children were playing on backyard jungle gyms, I was playing in the store. My birthday presents had come from costume suppliers and my clothes had come from our inventory. By the time I'd turned sixteen, it was natural for me to work part-time hours after high school.

After graduation, I took the occasional night course but most of my time had been inside these four walls. I'd been responsible for painting the walls around the gangster clothes black with white chalk stripes and also the psychedelic flower-power mural by our '60s section. It was my dad who encouraged me to move away—he wanted to make sure I knew there was a whole world out there before I accepted Proper City as my home base—and kicked me out on my twenty-fifth birthday. I moved to Las Vegas—which was only about forty miles from Proper but might as well have been the moon for how different it was—and experienced independence for the first time. It was far enough to feel as though I was on my own but close enough to come home for major holidays. I'd been in Vegas ever since.

"I can't stay indefinitely. You know that. I think you have to sit this season out."

"Nobody's sitting anything out. You got that, sister?" asked a black woman from the doorway. She held a small, white bichon frise under one arm. His fur was brushed out in the same manner as her natural Afro.

I rushed forward and flung my arms around her. "Ebony!"

The small dog yipped from inside the hug. I backed away and patted his puffy head. "Hello to you too, Ivory," I said.

The woman assessed me from head to toe. "Margo Tamblyn, as I live and breathe. You've grown into a fine young lady. I bet this old man wants to take the credit for that, doesn't he?" She winked at me.

"I think we all know you had a little something to do with it."

Ebony Welles was a fifty-six-year-old woman who had lived in Proper City her whole life. College had been out of her financial reach after high school, so instead she started Shindig, her own party planning business, when she graduated. She'd expanded from birthdays to all of the major holidays and a few minor ones too. She wore her hair in a brushed-out Afro and dressed in a largely '70s vibe. She bragged that she could still fit into the clothes she owned in high school, and four out of five days a week she proved it. Considering my wardrobe came from bits and pieces from the costume shop, I didn't think it was all that strange.

Ebony had become a part of my life when I was five. She'd been hired to plan an anniversary party for the local dachshund society. At a loss for inspiration, she'd headed out to clear her mind. My dad had recently redone the windows of Disguise DeLimit in a *Wizard of Oz* theme. Ebony thought it was brilliant. She reserved the six costumes he had on display and ordered flying-monkey costumes for all seventeen dogs. She asked me to help put the wings on the dachshunds and she even let me dress like a Munchkin. The pictures from the party had circulated far and wide, and I hadn't been the same since.

"How long do we have you for?" Ebony asked.

I cut my eyes to my dad before answering. "My boss gave me through the weekend."

"Where are you working?" she asked, her eyes darting to my outfit.

I tugged at the hem of my skirt. "I'm a magician's assistant. I asked a friend to fill in for me while I came here."

"I have an idea. Tell the magician you can't go back to work because we accidentally made you disappear." She slapped my dad's knee and laughed so loud I suspected they could hear her in the pet shop across the street.

Ebony and my dad sometimes acted like they didn't get along, but deep down I knew they were close friends. My dad had never gotten over the death of my mother, and judging from how often people told me I looked like her, I knew the constant reminder must have been hard for him. He'd done the best he could, even if my school clothes had mostly come from Disguise DeLimit. Some days I dressed like a flapper, others, a cowgirl. My wardrobe was more costume than couture, a fashion quirk I attributed to his influence. By the time I started shopping for myself, I found the latest trends lacking a certain spark of individuality. To this day I accessorized with props from our inventory rather than jewelry or scarves from the local department store: a holster with cap guns when I went Western, white patent leather go-go boots when I felt mod, a top hat and cane when I wore a tuxedo. Getting a job in Las Vegas had been a natural, because everybody in Vegas was in some kind of a costume.

My job history had been spotty at first: receptionist for a real estate agent, vintage clothing store clerk, concession stand clerk for a theater. The big money was as a showgirl, but the fact that I preferred to wear clothes at work kept me at a certain income level. Hey, a girl's gotta have standards.

Eventually I met a fledgling magician who wanted an assistant. I provided my own costume—a black cutaway tuxedo jacket over a red-sequined bodysuit, fishnets, and pumps—and we hit the circuit. He paid me 20 percent of the take from the door, which paid for my half of the rent and bills. On a good night, I bought steak from the grocery store. On a bad night, I ate ramen noodles.

Ebony was the closest thing I had to a mother. She taught me about makeup, clothing, and men. When I headed off to Vegas for a job, I caught her crying. She said she had something in her eye and I pretended I believed her.

"Listen up, Jerry," she said. "Margo came here because of you, so don't go getting better too fast. She and I have a lot of catching up to do." She put her arm around me and turned me away from him. "How's your love life? Anybody on the horizon?"

"The quality of men in Vegas isn't what you'd think. How about you?"

"Honey, I like my life just the way it is. Can't imagine turning my world upside down for a man."

"How'd you know I was here?" I asked.

"Elementary, my dear Watson," she said in a poorly affected English accent. "I saw the white scooter out front and took a guess. We don't have many scooter riders around here."

"She's lying!" my dad cried out. We both turned to him. He had pulled on a deerstalker hat and held a pipe in his hands. "She made no such deduction. I told her you were on your way."

Not one to let the fun pass me by, I pulled a tweed cape from a circular rack and draped it over my shoulders. "So the evidence points to a conspiracy," I said, brows furrowed. "Number one: information about my arrival was discussed behind my back. Number two: a suspicious white scooter is parked in front of the store. Number three: I smell sugar cookies, and you know they're my favorite. The mystery isn't how you knew, but what you plan to do about it."

A slow clap filled the air. All three of us turned our heads toward the door. It had been propped open since Ebony arrived, and a young blond man now filled the entrance. He wore a short-sleeved green polo shirt, madras plaid shorts, and navy blue canvas deck shoes. His glowing tan set off blue eyes and white teeth. I got the feeling he spent a lot of time on a golf course or a boat—or both.

"Cheesy, but charming," he said. "Not what I had in mind, though." He entered the store and ran his hand over a rack of colorful feather boas that hung inside the entrance. When the orange boa fell through his fingertips, he turned his attention back to us.

My dad rolled his wheelchair out from behind the counter. "Hello, Blitz," he said. "Octavius Roman says you rented out his facility space for your birthday party. You must be busy with all of the last-minute details. What brings you to Disguise DeLimit?"

"Octavius can't accommodate me. Roman Gardens had a flood in its kitchen and canceled. My birthday is this weekend and the entire plan is out the window."

"That's too bad," Ebony said. Her fingers rubbed the gold of the medallion pendant she always wore. She let go of the necklace and leaned back against the counter on one elbow, holding her other hand in front of her as if she was inspecting her manicure. "This town has come to expect an extravaganza from you. It's going to be hard to find someone to plan a full-blown party in less than a week."

The blond man scowled. "Why do you think I tracked you down here? Nobody else will even consider it."

"Who says I will?" Ebony said.

"I have money. Lots of it."

"I don't want your money," Ebony said.

"You were more than happy to take my dad's money twenty years ago. Are you going to pretend things are all that different now?"

Ebony stiffened. Ivory bared his teeth and growled at Blitz. I moved my eyes back and forth between Ebony and Blitz, gauging the number from one to ten that would best correspond with Ebony's reaction. I didn't know who this guy was, but I didn't like what he was implying about her past.

"We haven't met yet," I said. I stepped forward and held out my hand. "I'm Margo Tamblyn."

"Blitz Manners," he replied. He clamped his hand onto mine pretty hard, squishing my fingertips together. I squeezed back a second too late to block the pain, but soon enough to make it look like everything was fine.

"If I understand the situation correctly, you were planning to have a party at Roman Gardens but they're no longer available because of a flood in their kitchen. You'd like Ebony to put together a new party plan on short notice. Is that correct?" I asked. I used the voice Magic Maynard had taught me to use to divert the crowd's attention from his act. Soft and steady, and pay no attention to the man behind the curtain. Blitz took a couple of extra seconds to reply, but when he did, I nodded and stepped him away from Ebony. I picked up the pad of paper my dad had been taking inventory on and flipped to a blank page.

"How many guests?"

"Forty."

"That's a pretty big party."

"I'm known for my parties, sweetheart. Are you new around here? Better make it forty-one."

I bit back a laugh at the expense of his come-on and stayed professional. "Do you have a caterer? Music? Theme?"

"Roman Gardens was going to supply everything."

"They must still have the music and theme arranged, even if their location is out. So really, you need a location. That shouldn't be so hard—"

"I canceled everything Octavius had planned and took back my deposit. He's not getting a dime out of me. I need a new plan and I need it fast. The works."

It had been a while since I'd worked at the store, but I knew what he was asking for was borderline impossible. "I'm sorry, but I don't think that's doable."

"Sure it is. That's your business, isn't it?"

"Our business is costumes." I held a hand up and made a sweeping gesture toward the rows of clothing hanging on racks over our heads. "If you have a theme, we can suggest costumes, and you can either rent them or buy them. We do custom costumes too, but that takes time. There's a considerable price break if you rent instead of buy, but the deposit is nonrefundable. If you don't have a theme, we can show you around the store and maybe something will inspire you."

"That skit you were doing when I walked in. What was that for?"

"Skit? We weren't performing a skit." I turned around and looked at my dad. He still wore the deerstalker, but had set the pipe on the counter. "Sherlock Holmes?" I said.

"He's a mystery guy, right? That could be cool. Intellectual. Nobody's done anything like that around here. It'll be highbrow, literary. Yep, I like it. Everybody comes as their favorite detective. Bring out all the famous ones. Perry Mason, Sherlock Holmes, the works. Just remember, keep it young. I'm turning twenty-six, not eighty-six."

"I don't think you understood me. We do costumes, not party planning—"

"But I do," Ebony interjected. She stepped between Blitz and me. "Give me the night to secure the location, entertainment, and catering. Come to my shop tomorrow and we'll work out details."

"There aren't any details to work out." He pulled an envelope out from inside his jacket and tossed it on a table. "Twenty thou should get you started. I'll pay the rest when it's done."

FROM BESTSELLING AUTHOR
DIANE VALLERE

Suede to Rest

A MATERIAL WITNESS MYSTERY

When Poly Monroe was little, she loved playing in her family's textile store. But after a fatal family tragedy, Land of A Thousand Fabrics was boarded up and Poly never expected to see the inside again. Now, as inheritor of the long-shuttered shop, she's ready to restore the family business. However her two new kittens, Pins and Needles, aren't the ones causing a snag in her plans…

Not everyone wants Poly back in San Ladrón, especially a powerful local developer pressuring her to sell—and leave town fast. But even when the threats turn deadly, she's not ready to bolt. Because Poly is beginning to suspect that the murder behind the shop is tied to a mystery in her family's unsettled past that she's determined to solve…before her own life is left hanging by a thread.

INCLUDES A CRAFT PROJECT

"Smart and engaging."
—**Krista Davis,** *New York Times* **bestselling author**

dianevallere.com
facebook.com/DianeVallereAuthor
facebook.com/TheCrimeSceneBooks
penguin.com

DIANE VALLERE

A DISGUISE TO DIE FOR

A COSTUME SHOP MYSTERY

No sooner does former magician's assistant Margo
Tamblyn return home to Proper City, Nevada, to run
Disguise DeLimit, her family's costume shop, than she
gets her first big order. Wealthy nuisance Blitz Manners
needs forty costumes for a detective-themed birthday
bash. As for Blitz himself, his Sherlock Holmes is to die
for—literally—when, in the middle of the festivities,
Margo's friend and party planner Ebony Welles is caught
brandishing a carving knife over a very dead Blitz.

For Margo, clearing Ebony's name is anything but
elementary, especially after Ebony flees town. Now Margo
is left to play real-life detective in a town full of masked
motives, cloaked secrets, and veiled vendettas. But as she
soon learns, even a killer disguise can't hide a murderer in
plain sight for long.

INCLUDES RECIPES AND COSTUME IDEAS

dianevallere.com
facebook.com/DianeVallereAuthor
facebook.com/TheCrimeSceneBooks
penguin.com